Leavetaking

Standing there by the seagate in the darkness under the high, near-full moon, Sif bent down and kissed my cheek, a thing she had never done before, and passed the bone harpoon head that she wore on a string around her neck into my hand. I got my last good look at her face. She was smiling.

"You're not afraid, are you?" I asked.

She shook her head. "I know the way as far as Narby—I've made sailors at the inn tell me as much. It should not be too hard from there."

I hugged her very tight, holding the bone harpoon head until it cut my hand. I never wanted to let her go. But I did at last, when I heard her sighing, impatient to be gone. I released her and stepped back.

She bent and gathered the things I'd given her and was off—striding down the steep, narrow moonlit path toward the sea below.

I knew that I would never see her again.

—from "Rampion"

FIREBIRD
WHERE FANTASY TAKES FLIGHT™

Birth of the Firebringer	Meredith Ann Pierce
The Blue Sword	Robin McKinley
The Changeling Sea	Patricia A. McKillip
Crown Duel	Sherwood Smith
Dark Moon	Meredith Ann Pierce
Firebirds: An Anthology of Original Fantasy and Science Fiction	Sharyn November, ed.
The Green Man: Tales from the Mythic Forest	Ellen Datlow and Terri Windling, eds.
Hannah's Garden	Midori Snyder
The Hero and the Crown	Robin McKinley
The Safe-Keeper's Secret	Sharon Shinn
The Son of Summer Stars	Meredith Ann Pierce
Spindle's End	Robin McKinley
Treasure at the Heart of the Tanglewood	Meredith Ann Pierce
Waifs and Strays	Charles de Lint
Water: Tales of Elemental Spirits	Robin McKinley and Peter Dickinson

WATERS
LUMINOUS & DEEP
Shorter Fictions

By

MEREDITH
ANN
PIERCE

FIREBIRD
AN IMPRINT OF PENGUIN GROUP (USA) INC.

FIREBIRD

Published by the Penguin Group

Penguin Group (USA) Inc., 345 Hudson Street, New York, New York 10014, U.S.A.

Penguin Group (Canada), 90 Eglinton Avenue East, Suite 700, Toronto, Ontario, Canada M4P 2Y3
(a division of Pearson Penguin Canada Inc.)

Penguin Books Ltd, 80 Strand, London WC2R 0RL, England

Penguin Ireland, 25 St Stephen's Green, Dublin 2, Ireland (a division of Penguin Books Ltd)

Penguin Group (Australia), 250 Camberwell Road, Camberwell,
Victoria 3124, Australia (a division of Pearson Australia Group Pty Ltd)

Penguin Books India Pvt Ltd, 11 Community Centre, Panchsheel Park, New Delhi - 110 017, India

Penguin Group (NZ), Cnr Airborne and Rosedale Roads, Albany, Auckland 1310,
New Zealand (a division of Pearson New Zealand Ltd)

Penguin Books (South Africa) (Pty) Ltd, 24 Sturdee Avenue,
Rosebank, Johannesburg 2196, South Africa

Registered Offices: Penguin Books Ltd, 80 Strand, London WC2R 0RL, England

First published in the United States of America by Viking,
a division of Penguin Young Readers Group, 2004
Published by Firebird, an imprint of Penguin Group (USA) Inc., 2005

10 9 8 7 6 5 4 3 2 1

Introduction and story prefaces copyright © Meredith Ann Pierce, 2004

"The Fall of Ys" originally appeared in *Firebirds: An Anthology of Original Fantasy and Science Fiction*, edited by
Sharyn November (Firebird, 2003). Copyright © Meredith Ann Pierce, 2003.

"Where the Wild Geese Go" was originally published in slightly different form as the picture book *Where
the Wild Geese Go* (Dutton, 1988). Copyright © Meredith Ann Pierce, 1988.

"Icerose" originally appeared in a slightly different form in the premier issue of *Jabberwocky: The Magazine
of Speculative Writing* (Volume I, Issue 1 / Summer 1989). *Jabberwocky* was published twice a year by Chi-
mera Connections, Inc., 7701 SW 7th Place, Gainesville, FL 32607. The editors were Duane Bray and
Jeff VanderMeer. Copyright © Meredith Ann Pierce, 1989.

"Rampion" originally appeared in a slightly different form in the story anthology *Four from the Witch World*,
edited by Andre Norton. A Tor Book, published by Tom Doherty Associates, Inc., 49 West 24 Street,
New York, NY 10010. Copyright © Meredith Ann Pierce, 1989.

"Night Voyage," "Rafiddilee," "The Sea-Hag," and "The Frogskin Slippers" are original to this collection. Copyright © Meredith Ann Pierce, 2004.

THE LIBRARY OF CONGRESS HAS CATALOGED THE VIKING EDITION AS FOLLOWS:

Pierce, Meredith Ann.

Waters Luminous and Deep : Shorter Fictions / by Meredith Ann Pierce.

v. cm.

Contents: Prelude: night voyage—The fall of Ys—Where the wild geese go—Icerose—
Rafiddilee—The Sea-Hag—The frogskin slippers—Rampion.

ISBN 0-670-03687-0 (hardcover)

I. Children's stories, American. [1. Fantasy. 2. Fairy tales. 3. Short stories.] I. Title.

PZ7.P61453Wat 2004 [Fic]—dc22 2003017373

ISBN 0-14-240356-3

Printed in the United States of America

FOR SHARYN,
*without whose inspiration this collection
would never have come into being.*

Contents

INTRODUCTION 1

PRELUDE: NIGHT VOYAGE 3

THE FALL OF YS 5

WHERE THE WILD GEESE GO 18

ICEROSE 47

RAFIDDILEE 83

THE SEA-HAG 152

THE FROGSKIN SLIPPERS 179

RAMPION 219

Introduction

WHEN MY editor, Sharyn November, asked me to dig through my old manuscripts and see if I had enough short stories to make a collection, I was both flattered and intrigued. I sent her about a dozen manuscripts, and these are the ones she chose.

In reviewing her selection, what interested me the most was why she had selected these particular ones. They were all so different. Aside from their being fantasy, what else did they have in common? I wrote these tales in different places and at different times, some of them when I was very young. Several have never been published before. But what was the common theme?

And then it struck me: water. All eight feature it in some prominent way: seawater, freshwater, ice and snow. No matter what its form, water fascinates me: ever mysterious, unfathomable, alive. I hope you will enjoy reading these watery tales half as much as I did writing them. I never miss a chance to travel by water.

Night Voyage

ONE EVENING, Connor and Elspeth went down to the shore. Moonlight was combing the long, green sea with ravels of silver and winkings of fire. *We shall go voyaging,* Elspeth said. *Call the boat.*

Con began to sing a clear, cool song full of gulls crying and wood creaking, seals barking, surf breaking, and wind sighing through periwinkles caught in the seaweed's hair.

A great fish rose from the combers, smiling. The middle of his back was a wooden boat. Planks lay athwart it. *Climb aboard,* the boatfish bade them. The two children waded out and did so.

Where will you take us, Great Fish? Els asked.

Wherever your heart lies. Wherever you wish.

Connor's heart hungered for a supper of hot buttered toast. *Cast off!* he cried and told the fish where he wanted to go.

The great fish turned and swung out to sea. Holding hands, the two children sat upon a plank, while the waves around them swelled and sank. Their fish took them to the center of a broad, bright bay, where the merfolk brought them seabiscuits, hot from an oystershell oven below. They were crusty and salty and tasted of yeast.

Then Elspeth yearned for a sip of the moon. When she told the fish this, he rose up, light as a balloon, till the three of them floated high enough for one of the starmakers to hand them down a tiny basin of beaten gold in which the moon lay silver bright.

Elspeth drank half of it, and Con the rest. It tasted rich, of vanilla beans and licorice. They both began to feel sleepy then.

Lie down in me, the great fish said, *and I will carry you home to bed.*

Side by side, the two slept deep. The boat moved gently up and down, until at last they found themselves home beneath their coverlet, with dawn pouring like honey out of the sky and across the broad sea, which they could spy from the window. It lapped against the shore.

And all that was left of their night's voyaging was the taste of seabiscuits in Connor's mouth and milk-sweet moon liquor on Els's tongue, a wisp of seaweed around Con's wrist, and golden fish scales petaling Elspeth's hair.

FOR ME, the seminal moment in the ghostly Celtic myth of the fall of Ys is when King Gralon, fleeing the destruction of the city, casts his daughter into the sea to drown. In doing so, he saves himself, for his beleaguered steed, its load suddenly lightened, is then able to escape the boiling waters that have overwhelmed the kingdom and brought all to ruin.

In the several versions that I have read of this memorable Breton legend—Margaret Hodges recounts a particularly good one in *The Other World: Myths of the Celts*—Gralon is always championed as a hero, a tragic figure cursed by fate, who makes a noble sacrifice.

So I began to turn the story around in my head, asking myself what if Gralon's version hadn't been the way it was, if his alibi had failed to convince? What if supernatural forces had in fact been at work, but on the side of justice, innocence, and truth? What if it had all happened another way . . . ?

Yes, I think the souls of Ys still haunt the shores of

Brittany, and the phantom bells still toll, but they tell a tale far different from the one we have heretofore been asked to believe about what took place countless years ago and conspired to bring about the fall of Ys.

The Fall of Ys

THE CELTIC queen of Britain once had two sons, and when the time came for her to choose her successor, she set a riddle before them:

Now calm and consenting,   now cold, unrelenting—
My rhythm changes   with the moon.
When her bark rides high,   I rise and swell.
When her sphere sinks low,   I fall as well.
I buoy men up,   or drag them down:
Upon me rest,   or in me drown.
I'll seize all a man owns,   never to repay—
Yet victual his table   every day.
I smile; I storm;   I do men harm—
Or else reward,   according to my whim.
Who dares to flout   my purposes,
I'll be the ruin   of him.
So wild and deep,   no fool can tame me:
Both faithless and constant.   Riddler, name me.

Gralon, the queen's younger son, answered, "A woman's heart."

His mother frowned. "You've an odd notion of women, my son," she said. "Your brother shall reign after me. His answer was, 'The Sea.'"

Hearing this, Gralon flew into a rage and stormed from the hall, cursing the queen and all women. Loading his followers onto barks, he removed them across the Channel to Brittany, there to call himself a king. Gralon had no wife, but he had a young daughter, Myramond, upon whom he doted. At times during the crossing, the Channel grew so rough he feared to lose not only her but all his barks and followers besides. But at last, the Sea spat them out, and they made safe landfall.

"You've a woman's treacherous heart, gray Sea," shouted King Gralon, standing soaked and battered on the shore. "But storm all you will, I'll not be ruled by you or any she. I'll raise a city in your very bosom. Then shall we see who reigns in Brittany."

So Gralon built his capital upon a rocky spit of land that at low tide connected to shore, but at other times stood surrounded by waves. He named this tidal island Ys, and declared it should hold the most beautiful city ever made, full of towers and bells. He ordered a great wall raised all around to hold back the Sea's fierce, churning waves and her rushing tide. Within a year, all came to pass as the king had decreed—save for the seawall. Time and again, storms rose and breakers crumbled the wall, flooding the lower reaches of Ys. Then one morning at rising tide, a moon-prowed bark appeared, bearing a tall woman robed all in white.

"I am the highest of an order of priestesses," she said, "who dwell far on yonder misty isle just at horizon's edge, forswearing the company of men and dedicating our lives to our mistress, the Sea. We have heard of the answer you gave to your mother's riddle. Our mistress is not at all pleased that you should mistake mere mortal frailty for all her plumbless depths. But she is willing to forgive, even allow you your seawall, if you will dedicate your daughter to our service."

"Give you Myramond?" King Gralon cried. "Never! My daughter is far too young."

"In a dozen years, then," the white priestess said. "When she comes of age."

The king shook his head. "When my daughter comes of age, she must choose her own path. I'll not speak for her in this."

Then the priestess smiled, as though she had been testing him. "Very well," she said. "Our lady will be satisfied with this: Swear that when Myramond comes of age, you will *allow* her to come to us, *if* such be her wish."

"Only that?" laughed the king. "If I swear to this, my seawall will stand? Done, then!" And the white-robed priestess took her leave. Gazing after her as she sailed away, Gralon laughed again, privily, for he meant to cheat both the priestess and the Sea.

Events proceeded just as the white lady had promised.

The royal workmen completed their wall, which thereafter stood fast against even the roughest tide. King Gralon's sea-walled city of Ys prospered and grew. Years passed, and Myramond, despite her father's doting, grew into a maiden as modest as she was generous of heart, laughing and kind, simple in her tastes, steady in mien, and certain of mind.

She took little interest in worldly affairs, for hers was an otherworldly bent. She saw images in seafoam and heard whispers on the wind of mysterious realms beyond our own. Her favorite pastime was to walk the seawall, gazing across the flat, gray Sea toward horizon's edge, where the white-robed priestess's island floated, barely visible. Though her father sternly forbade her even to think of such a thing, Myramond resolved to make her home there as soon as she came of age.

She never spoke of her resolve, but her father sensed it, watching in brooding silence from the highest tower of Ys as his daughter walked the seawall below. Despite his prom-ise to the priestess and the Sea, he was determined that Myramond should never leave him. When ten years had passed and Myramond reached her fourteenth year, King Gralon began to tempt his daughter, seeking to turn her heart to worldly things. Sumptuous feasts he laid before her, heaping her table with delicacies. But of even the most savory dishes, the king's daughter ate only moderately, pre-ferring simple fare.

Undaunted, her father ordered gorgeous robes made, embroidered mantles and brooches of gold. But Myramond refused all finery, donning only the plain garb she had always worn. Concealing his frustration, the king arranged lavish entertainments of tumblers and jugglers, but his daughter only looked on politely and excused herself as early as she might, for such diversions stirred her not at all. Her heart was set on the Misty Isle.

After a year without success, King Gralon grew desperate. He knew his daughter would depart with the Sea's white priestess when she came unless he could devise some stronger snare. So, one by one, secretly, he called all the finest young men of the city to him, promising rich rewards to any who might win his daughter's heart. One by one, he sent them to her, but all in vain. The king's otherworldly daughter could not be swayed. In the end, nothing could contain the king's rage as, one by one, the young men returned to him, confessing failure.

At last, the evening before Myramond's sixteenth birthday arrived. Darkness fell. The full moon, poised overhead in the clear, dark, cloudless sky, cast a silver brilliance on the incoming tide. Myramond walked the seawall, gazing toward the far Misty Isle. Tomorrow, she knew, the priestess's moon-prowed bark would come, and she would speak her decision to leave her father and Ys. Not a breath of breeze stirred. The city's watch bells were tolling the hour. Below her, strange eddies foamed about the seawall. A wild, soft moaning reached her ears.

"Myramond! Myramond . . ." the eerie voices called.

Gazing down to where the seawall's outer steps disappeared into the waves, the king's daughter beheld the broken bodies of young men swirling through the foam. They raised their pale faces and looked at her.

"You are the dead!" gasped Myramond.

The corpses nodded. "We are the suitors whom you spurned. Your father had his servants murder us and cast our bodies to the waves."

Horrified, Myramond drew back. "Why would my father do such a thing?"

"For failing to capture your heart," they groaned. "He hoped a lover would keep you here. You spurned us to our deaths, Myramond."

"Have mercy," the king's daughter cried. "I had no notion of my father's wicked plan!"

"Fear not," the haggard spirits answered. "We come but to give warning, not to harm. Your father means to keep you in Ys by whatever means he may. You must flee the city at once, tonight."

"But on the morrow," began Myramond, "the white-robed priestess comes. . . ."

"Tomorrow will be too late!" The gray bodies slewed and washed against the seawall, muttering. "When the white-robed priestess comes, your father means to slay her as he did us. He does not mean to let you go."

"But I shall be of age," protested Myramond, "free to choose my own path. My father promised. . . ."

"Your father counts himself a king," the dead upon the waves replied, "unbound by any promises. Choose now. You are already come of age, for the midnight hour has struck. It *is* the morrow, Myramond. Flee Ys while you may!"

The king's daughter gazed hopelessly at the seething waters. "But the tide is high. Ys is an island now and shall not stand free of the waters till dawn. I have no boat; neither can I swim."

"Descend," her ghostly suitors replied. "We will make your path."

Then the spirits began rolling back the tide, bunching and shoving it in great gray folds, like some vast castoff mantle chased with silver where the moonlight gleamed. Back they pressed the Sea, and farther back, exposing the dark, mucky bottom beneath, strewn with flipping fish and ruffled weed. All the way to horizon's edge the Sea withdrew, so that the priestess's distant Misty Isle stood suddenly high and dry as Ys itself now stood.

"Make haste!" the ragged deadmen called.

Gathering her skirts, Myramond darted down the seawall steps. The Misty Isle lay seven miles away. Just beyond it, the dark Sea rose glistening. The king's daughter's feet flew across the damp and salt-rank sand. High above, in the tallest tower of Ys, prowling sleepless, King Gralon stared in astonishment as the Sea pulled back to horizon's edge and crouched there like a huge, gray cat, waiting, ready to spring. A lone figure caught his eye, cloak flying, hair streaming, silvered by the moon. Even so far, the king knew his own daughter, already halfway to the Misty Isle.

"Myramond!" he cried. Then, "My horse! My horse!"

Bolting from the tower, Gralon pounded to the stable, snatching his charger from puzzled, sleepy grooms. He spurred through the slumbering streets of Ys. Unguarded now at the midnight hour, the seagate rose before him. In half a moment, the king had thrown the bolts, shoved wide the port, and was galloping across the watery plain.

"Faithless girl," he shouted, leaning to grasp Myramond by the arm and snatch her aloft into the saddle before him.

"I am a woman now," his daughter cried, struggling furiously, "and must choose my own path!"

"Aye, you've a woman's heart: all treachery," her father roared, wheeling and galloping back the way he had come, carrying Myramond away from the Misty Isle.

With a moan, the dead that had held back the Sea released their hold. The great hill of water reared and teetered, then rushed after the king from the horizon's edge. Before it surged a foaming wash, hoof-deep at first, then knee-deep, belly-deep.... Burdened with its double load, the king's terrified mount heaved and floundered. Myramond saw terror in her father's eye as he stared behind at the towering curve of brine hurtling nearer and nearer. His gaze flicked to the shore ahead, then down at his struggling steed and the rising Sea. Lastly he stared at his own daughter as she writhed and pulled against his grip.

"Let me go," she cried. "Father, let me go!"

"The Sea take you, then, if such will save me," he shouted suddenly—and flung her savagely from him, into the churning tide.

The Sea caught at Myramond's heavy garments, dragging her down. She saw her father's charger, its burden abruptly lightened, spring on toward shore with renewed vigor just as the cold Sea closed over her. Cold forms embraced her, buoyed her, holding her fast, pulling her free of the terrible undertow. Cold, silent faces gazed at her. Innumerable cold arms raised her, lifting her upward, up toward the rippling surface above, the star-strewn night, the moonlit air—where moments later she felt strong, living hands catch hold of her and haul her choking from the foam. A dry wooden deck, firm and solid, rocked gently beneath her, only barely disturbed by the floodwaters surging all around. Soaked, gasping, shuddering, Myramond looked up into the calm gray eyes of the white-robed priestess standing above her.

"Rest easy, child," the other bade. "You are safe."

Pulling herself upright, Myramond clung to the rail of the moon-prowed bark, which stood fixed as though at anchor amid the swirling flood. Wisps of mist surrounded the craft. They began to thicken even as she regained her breath. Before her, very far away, she beheld her father's exhausted mount gaining the distant shore.

"Fool!" the tall priestess called after him, in a voice that carried even above the thunder of waters. "Did you think to rob the Sea? You did not keep your end of our agreement, and so your kingdom is forfeit. Look you to Ys!"

Myramond saw her father turn, and she, too, gazed in horror at the great wave still building, rolling toward the city, far taller now than any seawall, taller even than the highest tower of Ys.

"No!" the king's daughter cried, catching hold of the priestess's arm. "Let *me* pay the price. My father's people had no part in his broken oath. They are innocent!"

"As are you," the priestess answered. "Peace, child, and hark."

Then Myramond heard the many bells of Ys tolling, tolling riotously, and above them the ghostly voices of her suitors calling, "Awake! Rouse and arise! Your king has fled. The Sea returns. Now you, too, must flee for your lives. . . ."

Through thickening mist, as in a dream, the king's daughter saw the populace streaming from the wide-flung city gates, abandoning Ys. Women, children, and men, courtiers and commoners alike dashed for the mainland, scrambling wildly up steep, rocky banks, clambering for higher ground. Behind them, the monstrous wave broke; the bells stilled, and the ghostly voices ceased to call as the Sea swept beautiful seawalled Ys into rubble that disappeared beneath the tide. On shore, Gralon's people stood with little more than the clothes on their backs. Their king's spent mount sank dying to the sand, while its rider knelt alongside, weeping into his hands.

"Take warning, queen's son," the tall priestess cried. "Your kingdom is no more. Our lady spared you this night for your daughter's sake, but should you ever again transgress our mistress's realm, you will pay for your trespass with your life. Myramond passes now into our lady's service of her own free will. Would that you had had honor enough to let her go. It was no woman's heart you named in answering your mother's riddle, but your own: cold, faithless, and arrogant. Farewell, Gralon, king once but nevermore of Ys."

The priestess's moon-prowed bark turned toward the Misty Isle, bearing its white-robed pilot and the king's daughter with it. In time, the people of Ys built a new kingdom upon the shore. But they raised no more seawalls in defiance of the Sea, and Gralon himself never again set sail upon the waves. The ghosts of Myramond's murdered suitors guard the seacoast of Brittany still, sounding the phantom bells of Ys whenever storm or danger threatens. But the Misty Isle on horizon's edge disappeared from view and mortal reckoning for all time at the very hour of the fall of Ys.

Where the Wild Geese Go

ANN DURELL, my former editor at Dutton, once sent me five pen-and-ink drawings from an artist she had recently discovered named Jamichael Henterly. She asked me to take a look at them and see if I thought there might be "a story in there somewhere."

As nearly as I can recall, the five drawings were:

1. A girl holding a bouquet and opening a cottage gate. A woman, presumably her mother, stands waving beside the cottage.
2. A girl riding through deep snow by moonlight on the back of a stag.
3. A musk ox.
4. A girl and a puppy seated in a sled pulled by a single large, white sled dog.
5. A girl hugging a woolly sheep.

Besides the very great beauty of Jamichael's images, what struck me immediately about the five drawings was that four of them featured the same dark-haired girl, and that three of them pictured wintry settings. I thought about them briefly, rearranged their order, and wrote back to Ann almost immediately that of course there was a story in there. Here it is.

A note to the reader: A vegetable lamb is the medieval European conception of the oriental cotton plant.

Where the Wild Geese Go

TRUZJKA WAS an impossible child. She lived with her grandmother in a little cottage in the middle of a great, trackless forest. Her grandmother had no patience with Truzjka's dawdles and daydreams. There was always too much work to do and not enough time to do it.

"Truzjka," her grandmother chided while pressing the laundry one day, "you are no help. You eat the berries I send you to fetch, drop eggs, forget instructions, and cannot be trusted to persevere with the churning."

Truzjka, sitting by the open window with the butter churn between her knees, gave the dasher a halfhearted slog.

"I am trying, Grandmother," she murmured.

But what she was really doing was watching a titmouse that had alighted on the windowsill. It was picking up bread crumbs and leaving in the fine dusting of her grandmother's baking flour tiny pairs of stag's-horn tracks.

"Child," her grandmother exclaimed, taking the dasher away from her and churning furiously, "you do enough woolgathering to have an armload of fleece. Do you not realize how soon the hounds of winter will be upon us?"

Truzjka, stumbling out of her grandmother's way, tripped over the milk pail and overturned a basket of eggs on the hearth. Yolks and buttermilk slewed in the soot.

"Oh, bother!" the old woman snapped. Forgotten beneath the flatiron, the laundry was beginning to scorch.

Truzjka crept away to fetch a mop-linen.

"My dear," her grandmother scolded that night. "Can you not even manage to comb your own hair?"

"I meant to," mumbled Truzjka. Grandmother's snaggle-toothed comb bit and pulled at the tangles.

"It would be lovely indeed if your head were not a muddle. What's this?" she said suddenly, peering behind Truzjka's ear. "Tsk! Little girls who do not scrub grow feathers."

But Truzjka was not paying any attention. She was off in a daydream, watching the candlelight across the room making her shoe into a sled-shaped shadow. Grandmother kissed her good night with a sigh of despair.

If it was not one thing, it was surely another. One afternoon a rat got into the house when the old woman was not at home. She returned to find Truzjka hiding behind a stool and the rat having its way with the larder.

"Impossible child!" her grandmother snorted. "When you see a rat, kill it!" And she fetched a poker. "Come out," she said, dispatching the rat. "There is nothing to fear."

But Truzjka continued to cower. Truly, an impossible child.

Then one evening in early fall, when Truzjka lay asleep by moonlight, she dreamed the shadows of something passed over her. She dreamed she heard a great hue and a gabble above, as though all the hounds in the world ran yelping through heaven.

She awoke with a start, but peering outside, she saw only gunmetal sky and trees all silvery under the moon. Listening, she heard nothing. The air hung silent as an unstruck bell.

The next morning when Truzjka went down into the kitchen, she found no eggs in the pannikin coddling and steaming, nor nutcakes in the oven turning golden brown. The fire in the hearth was not made up. Her grandmother lay very still in bed.

"Grandmother, what is it?" cried Truzjka, rushing to her.

The old woman moaned. "Last night I saw the wild geese flying and heard them crying their sharp, sad cries. It has pricked my heart till I feel like dying—and if I cannot follow and discover where the wild geese go, surely I will die."

"No, Grandmother!" Truzjka exclaimed as the old woman struggled to rise. "You are too weak. Let *me* find where the wild geese go. When I return, I will tell you of it, and then you will not die."

"Take care," her grandmother whispered, sinking back. "The way is long. Make plans! Take a warm cloak with you, and a comb, and some journeybread. . . ."

But Truzjka heard not a word she had said. She was already out the door.

Truzjka hurried through the boundless forest. The trees all around her were bright as burning. She gazed through the branches and behind every thicket, but she saw no sign of the wild geese. At last she came to a wide, rolling meadow.

"What beautiful flowers," she told herself. "I will gather a few and take them with me."

Then she plucked for a time, this flower and that, and then a while longer as she ranged farther, gathering other and more beautiful blooms, until an old, gray bellwether grazing nearby lifted his head to inquire, "Are you gathering flowers for your grandmother's grave?"

"No!" cried Truzjka in horror, dropping her nosegay and hurrying on.

Evening came. The woods grew dark. Truzjka shivered and began to run.

All at once she came to a strange little hut made of earth and twigs. A small brown woman stood in front. Brown hair, brown eyes, brown face and hands—she wore a brown garment all covered with berries.

"Please," Truzjka panted, all in a muddle. "My grandmother is very ill. I am trying to find where the wild geese go."

"Tsk!" the little woman said. "And on top of all, you have run off from home without any plan. Your hair is as wild as a rat's nest, my dear. Come in," she added, holding open the gate. "We must sort it out."

Inside the hut was a vegetable lamb. It grew in an earthen pot by the great hearthstone. Truzjka stared at it. The lambkins at the tips of the branches were no bigger than mice. They were curled up, all of them fast asleep.

"I give them my berries," the little woman chuckled, "and they give me their fleece."

Then she handed Truzjka an old stag's-horn carding comb to unsnarl her hair, and plucked a pippin from her sleeve. It tasted delicious, like perry cider, and soon Truzjka felt wonderfully drowsy and warm.

"Now then," her hostess said, sitting down at her enormous loom and beginning to weave.

The blanket she was making was deeply blue and bordered in white geese with black wingtips, flying. Woven into the fabric, Truzjka saw a cottage in the middle of a wood, an old woman with a poker and a rat in the larder, and a little girl hiding behind a stool.

Truzjka shivered. "I don't like the rat," she whispered to herself. "I'm afraid of rats."

"Listen," she heard the berry woman say. "I will tell you how to find these geese."

She tossed the shuttle back and forth, and Truzjka tried very hard to pay attention, but the warmth of fire and the pippin's savor, the light, dreamy sighing of the lambtree beside her, and the clack of the loom lulled her so she could scarcely keep awake. The figures on the blanket seemed to wander and shift.

"Can you remember all that?" the other asked her at last.

"Yes," murmured Truzjka, though she really had no idea what her hostess had been saying, so engrossed was she in the endless crossing and crisscrossing of warp and weft.

"Sleep," the berry woman said. "Already I am weaving your way."

And Truzjka slipped at once into dark blue dreams of starlit sky and wild geese winging, the sound of the loom getting into her dreams, and the vegetable lamb snoring softly all night long its tiny, bleating snores.

When Truzjka awoke, it was broad morning. She lay wrapped in the blue lamb's-wool blanket in the midst of a wide, snowy plain. The berry woman and her little hut were gone.

Truzjka sat up with a start, utterly confounded. Where was she? She could not remember a word of what the berry woman had told her the night before. Casting about her, she found she still had the stag's-horn comb, and tucked away in one pocket lay a loaf of waybread: dense, dark cake studded with berries and nuts. She was desperately hungry.

But before she could even nibble one corner, she heard a distant baying. Turning, she beheld coming toward her a sled all turned up at one end like a shoe and pulled by an enormous dog. The sled halted as it drew alongside her. Its only passenger was a fat white puppy with eyes as black as currants.

"Ap!" the puppy shouted, wagging his tail. "Ap! Ap!"

"Are you lost, girl?" asked the puppy's mother.

Truzjka nodded.

"Ho, ho!" the sled dog cried. "The more the merrier. Take a sip from the little keg under my chin and come along with us."

Truzjka did so, climbing aboard and bundling herself down beneath the berry woman's blanket.

"Call me Gresjinka," the sled dog laughed, hauling on the traces, and off they went, hurtling over the snowdrifts at a frightening speed.

Truzjka did not mind a bit. The sip from Gresjinka's keg made her feel very merry, and the wind tangled her hair wonderfully. Gresjinka never seemed to tire. Her puppy sat on top of the blanket, scratching his ribs.

"What is it?" Truzjka asked him.

"Snow fleas," he muttered, and Truzjka saw a pair of tiny white specks go sailing off. The clear sky above grew suddenly overcast. "Brr!" the puppy growled, burrowing beneath the covers. "It's cold."

Ahead, Gresjinka lifted her muzzle. "Ap, have you been scratching?" she flung over one shoulder.

Ap pretended to be asleep. But before long he had crawled on top of the blanket again, scratching furiously. This time Truzjka saw a dozen lacy specks go flying to the winds. The sky grew darker, and the breeze picked up.

"If the wind grows stronger, I cannot keep running," Gresjinka called. "Best heed me, Ap."

But the puppy only yawned and wriggled closer to Truzjka. She put her arms about him to keep him close, but before long he had squirmed free once more and was on top of the blanket, rolling and writhing and scratching himself in a frenzy.

He gave a great shake, and Truzjka saw innumerable white specks go flying. All at once snow began to fall, and the wind rose to a howl. Gresjinka halted.

"Ap!" she cried. "You have surely been scratching."

The puppy cowered and wagged his tail.

"Impossible child," his mother snapped. "Climb down, girl. The weather has turned."

"But," protested Truzjka, stumbling to the ground, "surely you cannot mean to leave me?" She did not feel so merry now. The sled dog's dram had given her a headache. "How will I find the wild geese?"

"Persevere!" Gresjinka called, and with that, she and Ap and their little sled turned and vanished into the blur of falling snow.

Truzjka stood astonished. The snow was up to her knees, and the wind was bitter cold. She staggered a few steps, blown this way and that, until she fetched up against a tree, and there she huddled with the berry woman's blanket over her head, while the wind sang and wuthered and tried to take the lamb's wool from her.

But she held on. At long last the gale blew itself out, and the sky grew clear. The dark was the dark of evening now. She saw that she was in a forest, in a little clearing with snow heaped around her high as a wall.

She was ravenous, and her hair had become a rat's nest again. As she reached to worry one matted snarl, a great rat leaped out of the tangled mess and crouched before her on the snow. Truzjka screamed and scrambled back.

"Scream some more," the rat said nastily. "I love screaming."

Truzjka hid behind a tree.

"Now," the rat mumbled to itself, sniffing about, "have we any food? Have we any food? Yes! Yes! Delicious food."

And Truzjka saw with horror that her loaf of waybread had tumbled from her pocket and was lying on the ground.

"No!" she cried, as the rat scrabbled toward it. "If you eat that, I'll starve."

"I don't care a bit," the rat replied, preparing to pounce.

Then, before she even knew what she was doing, Truzjka laid hold of the stag's-horn comb and hurled it at the rat with all her force. It struck the creature on its twitching nose, and in a trice Truzjka had darted forward and seized the loaf.

"If you come near me, I shall kick you!" she cried, retreating and cramming her mouth with waybread—for she was very, *very* hungry and did not mean to let the rat have any. "I wish I had a poker," she shouted around the tree trunk. "Then I would *dispatch* you."

"Oh, would you?" growled the rat, rubbing its crumpled nose, its red eyes glowing. Suddenly it loomed as big as a bear, with huge snaggly teeth and a horrid smile. "Pity you have no grandmother to look after you now."

Truzjka froze, paralyzed with fright.

"Hold, rat!" a new voice sounded, and Truzjka beheld suddenly in the little clearing a stag pale as silver, with a rack of horns wider than the span of her arms.

The rat hissed, fangs bared, and sprang, but the stag drove it back, trampling it to a matted muss of cobwebs and ashes under his flatiron heels. Truzjka crouched stock-still behind the tree.

"Come out," the stag called gently. "There is nothing to fear."

Hesitantly, Truzjka emerged. "You have saved my life," she said. "How can I repay you?"

The great stag scratched his chin with one heel. "Where is the waybread the berry woman gave you?"

Truzjka looked down at her hands guiltily. There was only one nut left. Nevertheless, she held it up, and the stag bowed his head till his chin whiskers tickled her palm.

"Call me Sylvern," he said, crunching.

Truzjka sighed, casting about at the head-high snow. "What am I to do, Sylvern?" she asked. "I must hurry and find where the wild geese go, but I have lost my way."

"Gallivanting with weather hounds," the stag remarked dryly. He shook his head. "Gresjinka is a fair-weather friend, but Ap always makes it snow. Why did you not do as the berry woman bade you?"

Truzjka blushed, near tears. "I fear I did not attend to what the berry woman bade me—oh, my hair is a rat's nest! I cannot think."

"That is soon remedied," Sylvern replied, and bent his brow once more so that his horns, which were shaped like hands, reached out to her.

Then she felt as though the gentlest of fingers were combing and sorting and unknotting her hair, and braiding it into two fine, smooth braids.

"Now that is done, once for all," he said, "and you need not worry with rats anymore. Climb on my back. I will take you along your way."

Truzjka did so, and they set out through drifts so deep they breasted Sylvern's belly. The moonlight fell very cold and bright, and the northern dancers shimmered above. Sylvern's fur was marvelously soft and warm. She rested her cheek against his back.

"You are very kind to have come to my aid," she murmured.

The stag turned his head. "Do you not know me?" he asked. "Truly, do you not? I am the stag's-horn comb the berry woman gave you." He shouldered through another drift. "You had only to cast it to the ground for me to spring up to your aid."

Truzjka closed her eyes, sorry now that she had not

listened more carefully to what the berry woman had said. She and Sylvern traveled till morning. When she awoke, it was to find they had left the woods and come to a great, flat plain of ice. Ghost-white mountains rose in the distance beyond. Sylvern halted, and Truzjka slid to the ground.

"What is it, my hart?" she asked.

He shrugged great silvery shoulders in a sigh. "I am at my end," he said heavily. "It is a pity there was not more way-bread left. I could have taken you farther."

He began to grow small again.

"No, Sylvern!" cried Truzjka, throwing her arms about him. "Don't leave me."

He nuzzled her sadly. "I must."

"Stay, Sylvern," wept Truzjka. "I didn't listen. I don't know the way."

He slipped her grasp. "No matter, my heart," he whispered, his voice now dwindled to the clicking of bone. "You are on the right track."

Then he was a comb once more and nothing more. Sadly, Truzjka picked him up and set him in her hair. She felt a bitter pain deep in her breast. She was all alone. Wrapping the lamb's wool about her, she stared across the icy plain. The moon was just sinking into the far, stark white mountains. She knew that she must cross them to find where the wild geese go.

The featureless plain strayed on and on. Truzjka could not tell how long she had been walking, for the sky had clouded over and hid the sun. She was rime cold and bone weary and did not know how much longer she could go on.

Then all at once she heard a chuffing, a great puffing and a churning like nothing she had ever known. Something hove into sight, and before she could so much as sneeze, it had halted foursquare in front of her: a great ox, all white and covered with long, silky hair.

"*Huff, chuff,*" he said gruffly. "You are trespassing. Be off!"

Truzjka stared at him. "I am on my way to find the wild geese . . ." she started.

"No less," whuffed the shaggy ox, pawing the ground, "you are trampling my garden."

Looking down, baffled, Truzjka realized suddenly that the surface of the ice was traced with frost: lacy sprays and delicate fronds, fine plumes and feather-ferns. Her footprints had been scuffing them out.

The white ox stamped. His hoof left no trail. "Only I can pass here without leaving footmarks," he fumed.

Truzjka eyed his broad, dipping horns and his nose as square as a patch of leather, through which he snorted mightily.

"Please forgive me for trampling your field," she said earnestly. "Truly, I did not even see it was there. But if you drive me back, I shall only leave more tracks." She fell silent for a moment and thought very hard. "What you must do is take me across."

"Take you across?" the white ox gusted, shaking his

ponderous head and tapping first one horn, then the other against the ice. "Take you *across?*"

"Yes," she answered. "On your back. It is the only way."

He stood still awhile, blinking and blowing great quantities of steam. "Oh, very well," he rumbled at last.

With a sigh of relief, Truzjka folded her blanket and scrambled onto the ox's back. She was utterly weary. They set off at a sullen plod, the ox picking his way among the whorls of white rime and pausing occasionally to graze. Truzjka frowned. The pale, spectral mountains, very far away, seemed to come no closer.

"What is your name?" she asked in a little.

"Snuf! Snuf, the white ox," he snorted.

"Your hair is very soft, Snuf," she remarked, feeling of the shaggy locks. "Very long and fine." Indeed it was. "I know a berry woman who could weave wonderful things of this hair."

"Is it? Oh, could she?" the white ox puffed back, lifting his head. His step grew lighter. "You are uncommonly civil."

They jogged along at a fine clip then.

When they reached the ice field's edge, it was nearly night. Snuf halted and nodded toward the mountain's foot.

"Follow that trace, and do not leave it," he told her, "and you will find the ones you seek."

"Thank you, Snuf," Truzjka replied, kissing his broad, square nose. She felt well and rested now.

"Mind you do not stray from the track," the white ox said as she turned to follow the slender passage cutting between the tall stone cliffs.

The path was twisty and very steep, and sometimes so faint she could scarcely make it out. The hills shone gravely white, even as a cloud moved over the moon. She thought she heard voices calling her name.

"Come to us, Truzjka," the voices cried. "We are the ones you have sought so long."

Truzjka felt a beat of joy. Surely it was the wild geese! She ran forward along the path and rounded the bend to behold a whole slope covered with snow-white forms.

"Help us," they cried. "We are slipping. Gather us together again."

Truzjka saw they were indeed sliding away down the slippery slope. She darted forward and grabbed one goose, then another. They did not protest, lying limply in her arms as she carried them back to the safety of the path.

More geese were slipping and crying for help. Truzjka ran after them, snatching them up and filling her arms. She staggered upslope, panting, to dump them on the track. They lay unmoving in a soft, flocky pile. Truzjka shook her head, staring at them.

She realized with a start that they were not geese at all, but a great heap of docked lambs' tails, very old and fusty, which the wind had been scattering. Their lambs had long since run away to find their mothers. She heard a thrill of ghostly laughter.

"Horrid things!" exclaimed Truzjka, backing away. "I have been woolgathering. I must keep my mind upon my task if I am to find the wild geese."

She hurried on, resolved to follow Snuf's instructions. The path wound and twisted over the cold, white hills. The moon remained hidden behind its cloud. At last she grew so weary she sank down to rest.

"Truzjka," she heard voices calling. "Truzjka, here we are."

Starting up in surprise and alarm, she saw a gaggle of white geese limping toward her. Their wings were all broken. Their feathers were torn.

"Mend us!" they called to her. "It is your fault we are hurt."

Truzjka's heart welled up with pity. She could not imagine how she had harmed these geese, but she wanted to help them. They languished, sighing. She started toward them, but suddenly she remembered what Snuf had told her. One foot on the path, one foot off, Truzjka stopped, frowning. She looked more closely at the jagged white shapes.

"You are nothing but broken eggs!" she exclaimed. "No one can mend you now. And I must find the wild geese."

With a thrum of eerie murmuring, the outward forms of the false geese faded away, leaving only a tumbled basket and ruined eggshells scattered beside the path. Truzjka hastened on.

The cloud continued to hide the moon. As the way slanted downward, the path grew faint. Truzjka halted, uncertain. She could not tell which way to go.

"Truzjka!" came voices ahead of her. "You have passed our tests. You have seen through our impostors and found us at last."

Peering through the darkness, Truzjka made out pale figures ahead. Wild with relief, she sped toward them.

"Catch hold!" they cried. "We are your heart's desire."

And all at once, she paused at the edge of the ghostly track. The wind had brought a strange scent to her, like spoilt clabber. She sniffed again.

"You are only unfinished churning!" she cried, drawing back onto the middle of the path. "Someone should have made you sweet butter long ago, but there is no saving you now. Make way! You are not the wild geese."

She heard an angry shriek, like thwarted spirits, and the moon slipped from behind its cloud at last. Truzjka saw a broken butter churn and a dozen white milk pails blocking her path. She stepped carefully over them. The trace shone before her like a river of silver pennies now. She ran along it, down toward what lay beyond.

When she emerged from the haunted hills at last, the path ended. She had come to a place where the wind was wet and smacked of salt. Below her, a wild, black sea battered itself against a lean, gray shore. The tide was out.

Truzjka picked her way down over huge barnacles. They were large as goose eggs and hard as lime, all silvery rose and veined with blood purple. The moon lit them. Truzjka cast about for the wild geese.

"Where are they?" she wondered, thinking of Grandmother. "Snuf said I should find them. I must!"

She searched until she was too worn to go on, but she could discover no sign of them. The beach was deserted. It held only barnacles. Truzjka began to cry. Her tears fell onto the shells at her feet, and they opened like rose petals.

A tiny goose came struggling out. It was not a gosling. Its beak was silver; its feet were gold, its pinions milk-pale and tipped with black. Truzjka stared at it. Companions followed, emerging from their shells until she stood surrounded by a gaggle of little white geese.

Then, with a sigh like bread dough rising, they all grew to full size. They settled themselves upon their barnacles and gazed at her with their wine-black eyes.

"You are not the tide," one of them said. "Did you splash up with seawater?"

"With tears," whispered Truzjka. "Are you the wild geese I have sought so long?"

The geese all eyed her and nodded and bobbed.

"Yes. We are the barnacle geese," they said. "We hatch out of barnacles. Our shadows are ghosts. Our wings are dreams. We nest on the sea of memory."

Truzjka felt weak. She had found them at last.

"Three days I have been seeking you," she said.

"Three days?" they answered. "Three months, more like. Those who follow us lose track of time."

"Three months?" cried Truzjka. "Oh, my poor grandmother!"

"She is well enough," murmured one of them. "She has forgotten all about us in her worry over you."

"Over me?" Truzjka exclaimed. "I have been gone too long. I must go home at once."

The wild geese all looked at each other and shook their heads. "We fear that is impossible."

"Oh, bother," one of them hissed. "The tide is coming back."

The ghost-pale geese all crowded past Truzjka, hissing and jostling. She spotted something among the barnacles then, half hidden by sea wrack, something she had not seen before: a little globe, glass-smooth and clear, lit up by the moon—but she could not see inside, for it was full of mist.

"What is this?" she asked, bending down. The globe was cool to the touch.

"It is nothing," the geese answered. "It is of no consequence. Leave it and stay with us."

Truzjka put it in her pocket.

"What did you mean just now?" she said, straightening. "What makes it impossible for me to go home?"

"You do not know the way."

The wild geese all chuckled and preened their feathers, and Truzjka realized with a start that they were right. What was she to do?

"You could take me," she said suddenly. "You know the way."

The wild geese fluffed themselves and lowered. "We

would rather you stayed here," they answered. "You could become one of us and live in a barnacle."

"No," replied Truzjka, very firmly now. "I want to go home to my grandmother."

The geese muttered, consulting among themselves.

"Then you must give us something," they said at last, "for our trouble."

"What would you have?"

"Your hair," they said. "Your beautiful hair that is brown as bear's fur. Give us your hair."

They jostled about her, and Truzjka looked back at them, biting her lip. She did not want to give them her hair, which was fine and smooth now that Sylvern had combed it—but she could see no other way of getting home.

"Every passage has its price," they murmured.

She sighed and told them, "Very well."

Then *snip, snop,* as quick as sheep shears, they had all snapped shut their beaks to clip her long braids off close about her ears. Her head felt oddly cool and light. The geese divided up the strands and stuffed them into their barnacles. The tide came licking up the beach.

"Make haste," they said. "Lay out your blanket and sit in the middle."

Truzjka did so, and each goose dipped to catch a thread. Then with a clamorous yelping and a riot of flapping, bearing Truzjka along with them on the berry woman's blanket, the wild geese rose into the air.

Ghost mountains and frosted fields flashed below them. Truzjka lay back and gazed up at the moon. The sides of the blanket fanned out about her like midnight sky. Its borders grew indistinct, so that she could not always tell which were the woven geese and which the true geese flying.

Truzjka found herself growing sleepy by moonlight. She saw then that the blue lamb's wool had new figures on it, many more than she had seen in the berry woman's hut. She saw the sled of the weather hounds, Sylvern trampling the rat, Snuf grazing, the ghostly passage through the hills, and the barnacle shore. She saw a little girl turning into a goose.

Her arm itched. She scratched it, then started up in horror to realize that snow-white pinfeathers were sprouting there. She plucked them out with a cry. Her arm smarted fiercely. More feathers began to grow.

"What is happening?" she exclaimed in fright.

"You are becoming as we are," the wild geese answered. "All who follow us do."

"But I don't want to be as you are!" Truzjka cried, plucking furiously.

She felt feathers growing behind her ears and tore at them frantically. All around her, the figures on the blanket began to shiver and disappear. The wild geese were tugging out the threads. Snuf vanished, then Sylvern. Gresjinka and Ap followed. Gaps opened between the warp and weft. The blanket was unraveling.

"Help!" screamed Truzjka.

"Peace," the wild geese told her. "Don't pull at your

feathers. If your wings are not grown by the time we are done, you will fall."

"Let me go!" Truzjka shouted.

The great trackless forest sprawled below her. The gaps in the dark blue web widened. Truzjka snatched and tore at the feathers growing along her collarbone. She saw the roof of her grandmother's cottage beneath her, shining brightly by moonlight.

"There! Set me down—" she started to tell them, but just at that moment the last fraying thread parted. The wild geese beat upward all about her, calling, each bill trailing a tuft of wool, their wings clapping and buffeting like blown laundry.

Truzjka had plucked all her plumage out. Not one quill remained. For an instant, she hung above the house, her arms catching desperately at the cool blue sky. Then she tumbled through air, hurtling head over heels—down through the chimney and straight into bed, where she lay for a long moment, breathless and stunned.

Her pillow had burst with the force of her fall, and the air was full of pinfeathers and down. By the time it had all drifted lazily to the floor, she had fallen deep asleep, the cries of the wild geese still ringing faintly in her head.

Early the next morning, Truzjka smelled delicious things to eat and wandered down into the kitchen to find her grandmother frying mush.

"Goodness, child," the old woman exclaimed, starting up

as though she had seen a ghost. "You are all over soot."

"I found the wild geese," Truzjka said as her grand-mother fetched a warm, wet mop-linen and sponged her face and hands. Her skin felt sore where the feathers had been, but no new ones were growing. Truzjka gave a great sigh of relief.

"You have been very ill," the old woman was saying. "Truly, I feared I might lose you for good."

Truzjka stared at her grandmother, who strangely enough—though weary and worn-seeming—no longer looked on death's doorsill. "Grandmother, what do you mean?" she demanded, puzzled. She felt very hungry and testy and tired. "It is you who have been ill, not I."

The other seemed to pay no attention. She fetched a hearth rug and wrapped it closely about her granddaughter.

"You must take care to stay warm," she said, running her fingers through Truzjka's short, sooty curls. "You had such a fever, I had to crop your hair. . . ."

Truzjka frowned and shook her head. Grandmother was not making any sense.

"I gave my hair to the wild geese," she said. "They want-ed me to stay with them, but I made them bring me home."

The old woman began to look very alarmed.

"Oh, but Grandmother," Truzjka cried, throwing her arms about the other then, "I am so glad to be home and to find you well."

Her grandmother spooned golden fritters into a bowl.

"You must get your strength back," she said distractedly. "Here, child. Eat."

Truzjka ate the hot, crisp stuff all running with milk and butter. She was ravenous. But when she set down her second empty bowl and tried to tell her grandmother where the wild geese go, she found the memory of her journey all unraveling like the berry woman's blanket. She could not catch hold.

"Peace, child," the old woman exclaimed. "No use mooning over such things by daylight. You dreamed these geese."

Truzjka burst into tears. "I didn't! You heard them. I followed. I found them."

"There, now," her grandmother said more gently, patting her cheek. "Anything is possible, child."

Truzjka dried her tears, but she was miserable still. She could hardly remember anything that had happened to her.

"To bed with you," her grandmother said.

"But Grandmother," answered Truzjka, astonished. "Do you not want me to go fetch the eggs, or churn the butter, or tend the hearth?"

"Time enough," the old woman assured her. "You have lately been feverish. Putting you back to work too soon would coddle your brains for sure. Rest."

Truzjka wandered back to her room, but her bed was a mess of soot and feathers. The stag's-horn comb lay on the pillow where her head had rested. She felt a twinge of memory, but could not catch it. She picked up the comb and set it in her hair.

Then she donned her warmest cloak and cap and crept past her grandmother, who was sweeping the hearth. Outside, the snow was falling thick as sifted sugar. The sun was a pale disk; it was high winter now, no longer fall. Truzjka didn't feel a bit feverish, only tired, and the cloak and cap kept her warm as breakfast.

"Why can I not remember?" she wondered. "Where has the tell of my journey gone?"

Something in her pocket shifted. Reaching inside, she drew out the little globe that she had found among the barnacles. It had been cool then. Now it grew warm in her hands. The mist cleared. She could see inside.

What she saw was the vegetable lamb snoozing beside the fire, and the weather hounds gallivanting, and the white ox grazing and guarding his frost. The smack of salt came into her mouth, and the taste of waybread and perry cider. Holding the globe to her ear, she faintly heard Snuf snorting and Gresjinka baying, the lambkins snoring, and the great loom clacking. Memory stirred in her.

"Oh, berry woman," she whispered. "Where are you now?"

And looking down into the globe, Truzjka saw once more the little hut of earth and grass. The vegetable lamb was now awake, its branches bent down and the lambkins grazing on the moss that grew upon the great hearthstone. The berry woman perched at her loom.

"What is it I have brought back with me?" Truzjka asked.

The other laughed. "Don't you know? It is a pearl from the sea of memory. Keep it close and treasure it: it is worth a trove."

Truzjka frowned. "And what are you, berry woman?"

"I am the one who weaves your way," the little woman answered. "Like dreams, I am real. And as long as you keep the pearl, you will not lose me, or the remembrance of where the wild geese go."

"They coveted my hair," murmured Truzjka. "Why?"

"Oh, they line their nests with maidens' hair, and bits of lamb's wool, and the ravels of dreams. Do not worry about your hair, my dear," the nut-brown woman said, gently teasing a tuft of fleece from the back of one of her bleating lambs. "It will grow back straighter now. Sylvern has seen to that."

"Sylvern," breathed Truzjka, remembering suddenly. Her fingers tightened upon the globe. "Berry woman, give me some of your waybread. I want Sylvern back."

"Certainly, my dear," the little woman said, fetching a loaf out of the sleeve of her garment and handing it up through the glass.

Truzjka held it to her nose and smelled its rich, dark scent.

"Call him up whenever you like," the other added. "Only pity your poor grandmother, who just now got you back. Wait till spring before you go traveling again."

Truzjka smiled and stowed the waybread. She nodded.

"Look deep," the berry woman said. "What do you see?"

The image of her hut faded. She faded, and Truzjka bent closer, gazing into the pearl. It felt smooth and weighty in her hands.

Faint and far, she heard a wild clamor, like hounds, which pricked her to the heart. She smelled sea wrack and tasted buttermilk. She saw moonlight, and snow falling, and ghost-white geese with burnt wingtips flying.

They turned black as hearth soot, crossing the moon.

"ICEROSE" IS one of two inspiration stories I ever wrote. (The other one was my first novel, *The Darkangel.*) I remember waking early one Saturday morning in a fever of creative energy, the story burning inside me. I can recall literally pacing for an hour or more, just jotting down phrases and words, then sitting down on the couch and scribbling the whole thing down in one go. I must have been about seventeen years old.

Later I did some cutting, a little revising, but not much. The story before you is pretty much the way it came out: full-blown on the first try. What I remember most about its creation was how viscerally real the sensations seemed: the cracking of the ice, the frigid breath of cold. I can still hear the rattling of the dragon's scales.

*I*cerose

EVENING WAS cold and stale as the wine. Gunther gazed at the dregs in the bottom of the cup. He started to finish it, then thought better, and tossed it out into the snow. He pulled the fur-lined hood up over his head and glanced around him at the blue-gray drifts. The trees stood dark beside him, barren branches fettered with ice. The sky above tossed with clouds, and the wind ran past him into the woods.

"By the rose," he murmured, "it's cold," and threw another piece of kindling onto the fire.

He should have come better prepared. He had thought a single flask of wine would suffice, but he had not known how cold it would be. He looked at the slender shoulder pouch of food and wondered how long it would last him. Still, he had a good sword of dwarf-made steel, very strong. He had his magician's pentacle hanging from the chain about his neck, and his book of runes, and the little deer-bone flute to keep him company.

More importantly, he had the chest. It was not large— perhaps one handspan by another by two. It fit nicely in the crook of his arm. It was very old, the wood stained dark with age, the brass lock grown green as lichen. He laid a hand on it, tried the lock again to be sure it was secure, fingered the key that hung alongside the pentagram on the chain about his neck. The wine was making his eyelids heavy. He turned back to the fire and dozed.

Demian-Guendolyn glanced down the trail. The woods glided past her as she ran, shortsword thumping against her thigh. She paused where the snow had drifted over his tracks, but hurried on as she saw where they emerged. She tugged at the straps of the pack riding her shoulders, rubbing sore places there. She had been traveling since midmorning. Night was settling down, softly as a raven over its chicks. Watching, she plunged into thought once more.

"Gunther, you nitwit," she muttered. "Rash, young, starry-eyed fool . . ."

Strange. If truth be told, he was the elder by a good half year, but she always thought of him as young. It must be his dreaming.

"Aha! I shall slay you, Icewitch," he had shouted as a child, rushing their snow figures and hacking vehemently with a wooden sword. Evenings beside the hearth, he had talked of nothing but the icerose, which the Winter Sorcelress had stolen from her sister, Maker-of-Summer, years upon years ago, when their ancestors had been young.

"Once I am grown, I'll go in quest of it. I'll find it. I know I could, and conquer the Icewitch! Then I'll melt the rime from the enchanted flower so it can become the sun-rose once again, and summer be restored to the land. . . ."

Demian-Guendolyn had smiled then, little knowing. She was not smiling now. She used to know him better, in their very youth. They had grown up together, he shy and impractical, she beating the bullies off. Gunther had shown her wonders she never would have discovered on her own: that salamanders tread through fire unscathed, that a howlet's scream will curdle milk, that speckled wood sprites hide beneath the buckled bark of trees.

But last year they had both entered their sixteenth sum-mer and been apprenticed, she to the miller and he to the mage, and the friendship had drifted. She should not have let it. She felt a smile quirking her lips. Then again, perhaps it had not drifted so very far. Had she not set out after him immediately, without the slightest hesitation, in the same hour she had been told that he was gone? A laugh escaped her, and the woods swallowed it hungrily. Perhaps it was she who was the more rash of the two.

"Dreamer," she whispered fondly, panting. "Dunce."

The woods ticked, rustled, creaked. Time sifted like sleet through the stillness of the trees. Evening deepened. A sound then, suddenly. Gunther started from his doze, rose up stiffly, sword in hand. He stood tensed, listening—but once again, the only sound was that of ice, snapping with the cold. Then:

"Gunther, is that you?" her voice called, very soft.

"Demian?" he cried, astonished.

"Oh, it *is* you. I've caught you at last." She emerged from the gray dimness to stand in the low firelight.

"What are you doing here?" he demanded, sword clattering back into its sheath.

"What are *you*?" she returned, grinning, moving past him to the fire. He sighed and sat down.

"How did you find me?"

She laughed.

"You left a trail a blind troll could follow."

Unshouldering her pack, she seated herself across from him.

"Why did you follow me?" he asked, leaning forward to build up the fire.

She sobered suddenly. "I've come to persuade you not to go."

He looked at her and said nothing.

"Why *did* you come?" she insisted, chafing her hands. "Was this your thought, or the mage's?"

"Mine! Solely mine."

But his eyes shifted, evading hers. Demian-Guendolyn's lips compressed.

"The mage planted the thought, didn't he?" No answer. She waited. He held his tongue. Finally, "It's madness!" she burst out, exasperated. "How long have you been planning this?"

He sighed. "Let me tell you of it," he said, sitting back. She eyed him warily. "Some time ago," he began, "the mage said something to me that made me think. It was early one morn, perhaps two weeks past. I had just ruined another conjuring."

Demian-Guendolyn's eyes narrowed. Gunther fumbled nervously with the collar of his cloak.

"I was never much good at anything I tried, you know. First I thought I might be a smith, but I had not the stoutness of build for it. Then I thought perhaps a potter, but the clay seemed to have intentions of its own. I never came up with what I'd set out to do. Then I thought a wood-carver, but my fingers lacked the dexterity. I tried weaving, but the warp . . ."

His fingers twitched, as though remembering some past nick or bruise.

"I know all this," she said testily. She held her hands out over the popping, fizzing flames. Her skin felt flushed. Still, she was not quite able to repress a smile. She remembered, yes. Encouraged, Gunther went on.

"Then I thought, if only I could be a magician, I could be someone. Someone of note. Someone respected. But you see, on this morn, the mage took my arm and pulled me aside, saying, 'Gunther, you know you will never make a magician. You know that.'"

Demian's eyes widened. Listening, watching him across the fire, she caught the astonished hurt of his tone as he recalled what his master had said, the utter bafflement in his eye. Her fists clenched.

"That blackguard!" she fumed. "I'll box his ears."

Gunther smiled painfully, cleared his throat.

"I told the mage no," he continued. "No, I didn't know that. Why would I never make a magician? And he answered, 'My lad, what I said just now I did not mean unkindly. I merely meant that your nature seems poorly suited to magicking.' I said, then for what did he think me suited? And he replied rather sadly, 'I truly do not know.' "

Demian took her sweating hands back from the fire. Gunther sat slumped, eyes downcast, his mouth tight.

"We said nothing for a while," he went on. "Then I asked, did he want to hold me to my seven years' apprenticeship? And he said no, he did not think that wise. So I asked, did he wish me to leave? Again, he said no.

"He said, 'Gunther, you are a puzzling young man. You were past fifteen when finally you were apprenticed to me. I asked you then why you were so late, and you replied, "Master, because I did not know what I was seeking." I think you must be seeking still.' "

Gunther shrugged awkwardly.

"Then he patted my shoulder. 'But pray feel no remorse for having tried magic and found it not within your grasp. One can but try varied things in hopes of discovering that which suits one best.'

"My master paused then, stroking his beard. At last he said to me, 'Perhaps you are a quester. Perhaps you seek something you cannot find here. But please, do not go until you have found for yourself a goal—or at least a path. Stay as long as you like.' "

Gunther shifted in the amber firelight, chafing his arms. Still he avoided Demian's eyes.

"So I considered my mage's words. After half a month, I decided the thing I most wanted to do, the noblest goal to which I could aspire—the finest thing I was capable of seeking—was to free our land from the Icewitch's grasp."

Demian drew breath to speak, but he hurried on before she could get the words out.

"When I told the mage of my decision, at first he begged me not to go. We argued, but at length, I convinced him. . . ."

"Of your own pigheadedness, if nothing—"

Gunther held up his hand and plowed on. "Convince him I did. And when at last I had done so, he gave me my release, blessed me, gifted me with a charm for luck, and let me go."

Demian folded her arms. "That man needs to be stabbed several times with different knives," she muttered, livid. "I don't know which of you is worse. The utter absurdity: seeking the Icewitch. Gunther!" she said sharply, nodding at his hip. "Do you think you can slay her with that?"

He glanced down at his sword. "No."

Demian-Guendolyn threw up her hands. "Then I don't understand, Gunther. To what end, this quest? You'll fail."

He cocked his head. "Perhaps not."

Demian snorted. "Do you even know where you're going?"

"I know the way as far as the icebound lake. There lives

a sorceller who has seen the witch. He can help."

Exasperated, Demian shook her head. "How can you even think you'll succeed? Others have gone, either knowing the way or not knowing. They've all failed."

Gunther smiled. "The mage has given me a weapon none have ever had before."

"What weapon?" she cried. "Your mage is mad! The witch gave him madness as well as a humped back when she touched him. I think he's sending you for revenge—and he's sending you to your death!"

Gunther bristled. "You don't understand the mage at all."

"I understand a fool!" She wanted to take him by the shoulders and shake him. "Gunther . . ."

Already she knew it was too late. His brow had furrowed. She would never dissuade him now. He set a little oaken chest upon his knee.

"Look," he said softly and lifted a brass key from the chain about his neck.

The key's bit tripped the tumblers of the lock, and the shackle fell open. Gunther raised the lid. A fluid, golden dust lay glowing in the hold, rolling gently, like a sea of gilded talc. Demian-Guendolyn stared. She had never seen such a thing before. In all her life, among all the mage's worthless, moldering trinkets, she had never so much as glimpsed something real—something of genuine power. She gazed at the shifting, powdery waves.

"What is it?" she whispered, leaning near.

Gunther's smile broadened. "Sundust. Dust-dram from the Golden Lands where the Icewitch's winter cannot reach. It was for smuggling this that the Icewitch touched the mage. She thought she had destroyed it all, but he managed to hide a little, keep it hoarded away for fifty seasons. This is what I'll use to slay the Icewitch. With this and a drop of living blood, I'll revive the icerose."

His breath had quickened, eyes grown bright. She felt the quester's fervor radiating from him like heat. His words loped on, like an eager horse.

"I can do it, Demian; I know I can. This is the one chance in my life to do something worthwhile, something noble."

She gazed at him sadly. "You're not going to listen to reason?"

He shook his head, closing the dark chest and locking the shining dust-dram away. The firelight dwindled. The woods ticked. Night deepened. Demian-Guendolyn sighed.

"I feared as much." She hauled the pack closer and unlaced its flap, began rummaging. "I brought provisions—the ones you took won't last two days—wine, journeybread, pemmican. . . ."

With an exclamation of surprise and delight, he came to kneel alongside the pack, sorting through it with her, mumbling thanks. She turned to him, taking hold of his hand.

"Gunther," she told him, "I'm going with you."

He stopped, pivoting to look at her, as though about to protest. Then all at once he seemed to realize how futile that would be. He squeezed her hand, smiling like the mad fool he was, and she had to laugh. Who was madder, the fool or the fool who followed him? She closed the pack. Gunther rose to bring more kindling as the embers flickered toward death. They drowsed beside the fire a while, and later slept.

Icewitch. She stood before them crowned in silver, throat aflash with jewels. Her pale robe shimmered softly. Her teeth were bared in a mocking smile.

"Turn back, you silly children. Why should you wish to venture my forest of perpetual snow? Turn back, and you will be safe. Turn back and you will be warm in your houses, content with your little lives. Turn away from this fool's quest."

Demian groaned, shuddering, shaking her head. Trapped by the Icewitch's spell, she could not move. The tall white figure before her smiled.

"What chance have the two of you against me: a miller's girl, a baker of bread, and a half magician who can barely stumble through his runes? I am a sorcelress. I locked this land in ice. I could—"

She checked.

"But soft. I admire your courage, if not your folly. Let me not turn you away so unsatisfied. Would you like to see the icerose?"

The white queen beckoned.

"Here, child. Here it is. You may even touch it. Would you like to? Touch it."

The sorcelress held the frost-covered bloom before

them. Demian-Guendolyn glimpsed the palest blush of pink beneath the frost. It lived, but lay dormant beneath a coating of ice. Her limbs stirred. She felt irresistibly drawn to the flower. Unable to help herself, Demian reached for it.

Without warning, the witch's frigid talons closed about her wrist. She felt the rose's brittle petals shatter as they were crushed against her palm, cutting her flesh. Her hand welled blood. Frantically, she tugged at her weapon, but the sword hung frozen in its sheath.

"Gunther," she gasped. "Gunther!"

Gunther started up and reached for his sword. He peered through the dim amber light.

"What? What is it?" he called.

Demian-Guendolyn sat up, shivering. The dream swam away like gray fishes into smoke.

"Icewitch," she muttered, confused.

"Hush!" said Gunther. "Only a dream."

She shuddered. It had seemed more real than dreams, more real than any nightmare she had ever known. She pulled at her cloak. "I'm cold."

"I'll freshen the fire." He tossed more kindling on. The flames made the snow dance hot, coppery orange. A little black salamander ran out of the fire and away into the nothing-darkness of the woods. She trembled still.

"I thought I saw the Icewitch."

He nodded. "Oh."

"I don't think I can sleep," she said softly.

He reached for his scabbard, half laughing. "Neither can I."

The earth was the wing of a gray goose, and the sky was its darkling shadow. Gunther put up his sword, lifted his deer-bone flute. Breathing across the broad blowhole, he danced his fingertips across the line of tiny openings. The sound whispered at first, soughed, then became a run of clear, strong notes that filled the emptiness all around. Demian listened as Gunther played, grateful for his presence and his music that kept the stillness from her ears.

∞ II ∞

"How much farther to the lake?" she asked, a bit breathless. They had been traveling all morning, pressing hard through drifted snow.

"Not much farther," panted Gunther, just ahead of her. "It can't be."

Demian-Guendolyn grunted dubiously. "You're sure this sorceller lives there?"

He nodded over one shoulder, breath steaming like a dragon's. She adjusted the pack again, rubbing the chafed places. The snow was bright in the dazzle of a hidden sun, the thinner clouds of morning already thickening toward noon. Icicles clinked softly with their passing. No other wind stirred. She and Gunther trudged on through the endless trees.

"Would you like to hear a story?" he asked as they sank down beside a drift.

She handed him a cold loaf of bread and took one herself.

"I'll tell you the tale of the Icewitch," he added, not waiting for a reply. "It'll help to pass the time."

Demian sighed, too weary to protest. He never tired of the tale. In fact, she realized uneasily, it might have been she who had first told it to him, long ago in their childhood. How many times since then had he told it back to her? She recited the words silently to herself as Gunther began.

"There was a time before the perennial winter. It was seasons upon seasons past, when the wind was warm as kitchen air, the heavens unclouded, the sun visible. At night, the sky was black as an ermine's eye, and it glittered with fiery jewels called stars. There was no snow, no ice. Rivers freely flowed, swans sailing their waters like graceful boats. The trees were green with leaves. Flowers grew everywhere. All because Maker-of-Summer had given the sunrose to bloom in our midst."

Gunther set his loaf down barely touched. Demian gnawed at her own with a will. It was mealy with ice crystals, tasteless as snow.

"The sunrose had been a gift to Calin, our people's first king," Gunther continued, "from the queen of the Golden Lands far across the sea. Some call her a goddess and some a witch, but what is beyond doubt is that she fell in love with Calin. He had set sail in search of new trade and new shores and come at last to the Golden Lands. And there he dwelt a year in the summer court before duty called him home again.

"At his leave-taking, Maker-of-Summer, all in tears,

pressed a rose from her garden into his hand, saying, 'Take this, my love, and guard it well, for so long as you hold this fast in your keeping, your people will never know want. Your kingdom shall be as my kingdom, ever fertile, ever warm. Remember me, I pray you, and the Golden Lands.'

"Thus it was that when Calin returned from across the sea and founded his kingdom here, the sunrose kept the season of plenty ever upon the land in remembrance of Maker-of-Summer and the very great favor she had bestowed."

Gunther tensed, his words growing more vehement. He gestured expansively as he spoke, sketching the scenes before him in the air.

"But with the coming of the Icewitch, all things changed:

"Maker-of-Summer had a younger sister, who had no kingdom of her own. She gazed with jealousy upon the good fortune of Calin's kingdom, which her sister had blessed. She resolved to wrest it from him and fashion from it a land as cold as her wintry heart, colorless as her bloodless skin, a land where nothing vibrant or beautiful might grow, where rain fell not in droplets warm as tears, but in lacy crystals of ice.

"Disguising herself as a mere mortal, a small sorcelress, she took service as a diviner in the king's own house. Calin was old now, and growing careless in his age. His memory of the Summer Lands was becoming dim. Feigning humility, using all her cunning and guile, the Icewitch gained the king's confidence, for she was as beautiful as Maker-of-

Summer, though her heart was gelid, congealed in ice.

"At last she was able to snatch the rose from the king's own grasp with the aid of a dragon she had conjured out of her coldest sigh. Not the king himself nor all his heroes could best her then. Bright bloom in hand, she breathed upon it, imprisoning it in a perpetual frost. Her triumphant laugh echoed through all the king's halls: 'Despair, for my sister's enchantment is broken! I am the only mistress here.'"

Gunther's half-eaten loaf toppled unnoticed from his knee. Without a word, Demian retrieved it, brushed the snow from it, held it for him. Lost in his tale, Gunther continued, oblivious.

"The Icewitch's laugh sent a cutting chill through the land. The air grew cold. Clouds obscured the sun. As the first snows began to fall, flowers withered, crops failed, and the trees cast away their dying leaves. Folk sickened. Kine died in the fields. Fish grew sluggish in the freezing lakes. Squirrels retreated to their dens, and the swans flew away to the Golden Lands.

"Any who rose in defiance of the ice-hearted sorcelress, she destroyed. Those who sought to flee, she struck down. Only those huddling like mice in their houses did she spare. 'Calin is no more,' she told them. 'I am your queen now. Honor me.' And the people obeyed her, for she left them no choice."

Gunther subsided, tone quieting now as his tale drew to a close.

"The witch made her lair in a tanglewood of briars within a barren of ice, and there she has remained for seventeen times a hundred years. She keeps the icerose in a crystal case watched over by her dragon. He guards the flower jealously, for his mistress has made it the crux of all her power. Should ever it be captured and freed from the frost, her sorcel will be at end."

Gunther fell silent. Demian handed him back the last of his loaf. He looked down at it, puzzled. The wind sighed, and Demian with it.

"Best move on," she told him.

They had rested too long. Her legs were stiff. Gunther got to his feet as she shouldered the pack. For a while, the only sound was that of their feet breaking the ice crust as they tramped on.

After a bit, Demian asked him, "How will the dust-dram kill the Icewitch, Gunther?"

"It's . . . a rather complicated alchemical process," he replied. Gunther thought baking bread a complicated process. She nodded patiently.

"I know it must be, but try to explain it."

Gunther glanced off, thinking.

"Very well," he said reluctantly. "The mage explained it to me so: The Icewitch is the daughter of a necromancer and a spirit he conjured out of the wind. . . ."

"I thought she was the sister of Maker-of-Summer."

"She is," Gunther answered distractedly. "Maker-of-Summer is the daughter of the sun and that same wind sprite. Her blood is pure light, so the dust-dram wouldn't harm her a bit. Her sister, though, has silvery blood, a fluid sort of ice."

His tone steadied, gaining confidence.

"The dust-dram is powdered gold from the heart of the sun. When gold and silver meet, they fuse, forming electrum. That's the alchemy. And when ice and sun meet, they engender a morning mist. That's magical, not alchemical. . . ."

His words trailed off. He cast about, searching for his lost thread, found it.

"All we have to do is cast the dust-dram into the witch's eyes," he said triumphantly. "Her earthly form will dissipate directly into an electrum vapor. We just have to be careful not to breathe in too much of it, because it's a fairly potent—"

"I don't understand," Demian told him flatly.

She had not really expected to be able to grasp it, but she was disappointed just the same. Gunther paced along beside her in silence for a few strides. His hopeful grin had turned sheepish.

"Well, neither do I, exactly," he admitted finally. "But the mage assured me that it works."

Evening caught them still in the woods among the silent drifts. Demian-Guendolyn set down the pack, and Gunther started the fire. They sat, bone weary after a meal of dry bread and cold wine, staring drearily into the fire while Gunther played his flute.

"Gunther," she asked him, "what happens should we fail?"

He stopped playing. "I guess she'll kill us."

She remembered her dream from the night before and shivered. "You don't think she'd torture us, do you?"

He shrugged, looking cold and discouraged. "I hope not."

Toeing a fallen branch back into the flames, Demian pulled her cloak tighter. "You don't suppose she'd turn us into creatures, or crook our backs like the mage's?"

For a moment, his smooth young face grew hard. "We mustn't fail."

She gazed at the snowdrifts, the icicles, the barren trees and dared to say it: "And if we succeed?"

"Ah." His expression softened once more into the smile she knew. "Then, when I mingle the dust-dram with my blood and touch it to the stolen rose, the bloomfrost will fade. It will be alive again, everlasting, the sunrose once more. As we bear it homeward, it will bring summer to every place we pass."

She sighed, still toeing at the fire. "I wish . . . I could know what summer's like. I wish I could see it, just for a moment, to know if it's worth the risk."

Gunther had put the deer-bone flute down. They sat a moment in silence.

"You can," he told her.

She looked up in surprise. "How?"

"I'll show you."

"How?"

He did not answer, only groped for the key hanging beside the pentacle on the chain around his neck and worked the lock of the little chest. The tumblers clicked. The lid creaked. The golden stuff inside shimmered, undulating gently. Taking a pinch of the dram, then a finger of feathery snow, he knelt before her.

"Don't blink."

First the snow, then the dust he touched gently to her eyes. Demian flinched back, startled. The dust burned pepper warm, the snow a bracing, mintlike cool. She would have blinked, but before she could even breathe, the world dissolved in an electrum shimmer.

The trees around her blossomed, greened. White swans winged through cobalt air. The snowless landscape lay dappled with scarlet and yellow flowers. The warm wind against her cheek made her heady, like long draughts of hot, spiced wine. Directly overhead, the sun was an amber jewel flashing at the bottom of a blue glass bowl. *Summer.*

"Oh," she said, very softly, when she could speak—but the snow in her eyes was already melting, washing away the dust. Gray clouds smothered the sun. The land rippled gray. The swans became ravens, arcing like ebony daggers against an ermine sky. How long had it lasted? Two seconds? Three? She shook her head and realized that her cheeks were streaked with tears, now freezing in the winter air. She let them, too stunned still to brush them away. Gunther was speaking.

"Worth the risk, Demian, to have it, summer, always?"

She turned toward him. "By the rose," she whispered fiercely, "we mustn't fail."

The following morning, they came upon the frozen lake, a vast china bowl brimming with ice, stretching into the far distance. They halted at its edge, gazing across the smooth, clear surface to where it met the rim of earth and the mirror of the sky.

"Well," said Gunther, blinking in the glare. "I hope the sorceller can show us where to cross, and in what direction."

They walked along the shore.

The wolf materialized out of the snow as softly as a mirage. He looked immeasurably old, lean as death, his thick pelt the same pale silver as the sky, his head proud, eyes dark and deep. He stood watching them silently. Dropping the pack, Demian-Guendolyn reached for her sword, but held it only half drawn as Gunther waved her back. Taking his rune book in hand, the magician's erstwhile apprentice stepped forward. The young man spoke. The wolf replied.

"We wish to cross the lake," Gunther said. "A sorceller bides here who can direct us. Can you tell us where to find him?"

"Only one reason exists to journey beyond the lake," the wolf answered, his voice like the low, soft soughing of wind. Demian's sword clattered as she started. "You seek the Icewitch." The wolf eyed them steadily. "Do you come to do her homage or to do her harm?"

Gunther glanced at Demian-Guendolyn. She returned the gaze uncertainly. Should they lie? Before she could speak, Gunther had turned boldly back to their questioner.

"We have come for the icerose."

The wolf nodded. "Ah. Questers. I see." He smiled sadly. His teeth were white and sharp. "Children, I have seen scores of you come. None ever return. There is no defeating the Icewitch. When will you ever learn?"

"Can you guide us to the sorceller?" Demian-Guendolyn managed.

"To what purpose?" the wolf asked. "He cannot help you. Only the swans know the way to the icerose. And they are gone long since, across the sea to the Golden Lands."

Demian and Gunther looked at the white wolf a long moment without speaking. Demian felt her jaw set. Two and a half days of trudging was worth better than this! There must be a way.

"How do you know he can't help us?" demanded Gunther.

The white wolf sighed. "Because I am he."

Silence.

After a few heartbeats, he continued. "I met the Icewitch years ago. I was one of the mages that paid her homage. She allowed spellworkers such as I to exist near her lake, the enchanted waters of which were essential to our magics. But one season, my luck ran all to ruin. I had no treasure with which to pay her.

"Well I knew of her vengeance against those who could

not meet her ever-increasing demands for coin, jewels, magical trinkets. I decided to try to escape—fool that I was! She sent her dragon after me. I was almost to the sea when he caught me. Instead of a quick and merciful death, he dragged me back to his mistress, who turned me into my present form.

"Now I roam the frozen surface of this lake—companionless, unsheltered, with only what little food I can catch in my teeth—for I am as shackled to this lake as though I wore a chain about my neck. I may venture no more than a few paces inland past its shore, or I will perish. Quite an agonizing death I imagine it would be. One thing of which to be sure, children, the Icewitch has no mercy."

"But you cannot direct us to her?" pressed Demian-Guendolyn.

"No, alas. The only one who could have helped you is the swan, but she is icebound as the lake."

"Icebound?" said Gunther suddenly. "Can you take us to her?"

The wolf cocked his head. "To what end?"

Gunther hesitated, glanced at her again.

"We have sundust from the Golden Lands," he whispered at last.

"Sooth?" the wolf exclaimed.

His drooping frame started upright suddenly. Now he stood with his head up, ears pricked, all four legs braced, as one who has just heard a long-awaited trumpet call. Gunther nodded. The other's dark eyes gleamed.

"That changes everything. Come."

Without a backward glance, he loped away along the shore.

The swan sat still as a porcelain statue, the arch of her neck perfect as the handle of a crystal cup. She rested poised, her breast cleaving the frozen water, forever setting forth and forever held. Her eyes stared outward, empty as brass. The wolf crouched before her, watching intently as Gunther knelt in the snow. Demian-Guendolyn stood back, puzzled, then smiled suddenly as understanding dawned.

Taking the key, Gunther worked the lock of the chest and turned back the lid. The dust glistened like water. With the pin fastening the throat of his mantle, Gunther pricked his thumb. Then, mixing a drop of blood into the dust on each forefinger, he touched them to the swan's eyes.

They melted into golden pools, and the cold platinum feathers turned to living pearl. A sigh ran through her pinions, and a cry escaped her bill.

"By the rose," she said. "Seventeen times a hundred years have I been waiting."

She ruffled her feathers and settled herself, nodded courteously first at Demian and then the wolf. Lastly, she turned her perfect head to Gunther.

"Well, young man," she said matter-of-factly. "I take it you seek the icerose."

"Yes," called the swan, gliding low on the lake wind. "I was caught by the witch's ice the evening before I had meant to depart. My fellows had all flown, but my wing was strained, and I thought to let it mend another night. Little did I suspect how long a mending that would be!"

The wolf walked beside them across the flat plain of the lake, and the swan skimmed ahead. Gunther held the oaken box closely under his arm as they went. The three on foot spoke little, listening to the swan, who circled them overhead, telling them tales of the time before.

They spent a night on the ice, shivering from lack of a fire, for they had brought no kindling. Even had they, Demian realized, the flames would have quickly doused themselves by melting through the lake's frozen surface. So they huddled together, the wolf, two humans, and the swan.

In the dawn light of the following morning, they spied the opposite bank far in the distance, so far away that the snow looked like sky. The swan said:

"Behold, questers. There lies your long-sought shore. The Icewitch and her captured rose lie thither, within a thornwood lost in a desert of snow. I leave you the wolf to guide you the rest of the way. I am off across the sea to the Golden Lands. Later, perhaps, but at least I come. Fare well!"

And she circled away to the west.

The land they eventually reached was indeed a desert of snow, without growth or marker of any kind. Drifts lay before them like the backs of sleeping snow geese. The barren wasteland stretched all the way to the horizon's brink. Demian could imagine it going on forever. She caught no glimpse of any thornwood. As they struggled up onto the shore, the wolf, too, bade them farewell.

"Children, I must leave you now as well, for yours is the quest, not mine. Yonder lie the barrens of which the swan spoke. Somewhere beyond, the thornwood waits. May you find the one you seek—but allow me, before you go, to speak one word of warning. She is a witch true enough, but do not call her 'Icewitch.' Do so and she will immediately know you false. She cannot endure the term spoken in her presence. Instead, her followers all call her 'Sorcelress of the Snows' or 'Fairest Queen.' "

Gunther bowed ceremonially in thanks, and Demian managed a grateful nod. Already the wolf's dark eyes were straying back over his shoulder in the direction they had just come.

"I must away," he panted. "My appetite calls. May hope of summer keep you safe and grant you luck."

He turned and was gone, running easily across the ice. Gunther and Demian-Guendolyn watched until his pale figure disappeared into the shimmer of whiteness that obscured the horizon in that direction. They turned themselves away at last, starting out across the hills of snow. It proved an exhausting trek. Dusk found them only a scant mile from the wood, but they were too weary even to make that last short leg. They slept another night in the snow.

The next morning, they reached the wood, which stood

like a thorny blemish amid the pristine drifts. They entered it, hacking with swords through heavy thickets of icicles and briars, abandoning the pack after only half a mile because it proved too bulky. The thorns clutched their clothing and caught at their heels. They struggled on.

"How are we going to find her?" panted Demian-Guendolyn. "We could wander here till we drop. . . ."

Gunther shook his head helplessly, drawing breath for some reply.

Then they heard the dragon's roar.

❧ III ❧

She stood very tall, very slender, like a slim horn flask hollowed to hold but a single flower. Her robe was of fine silk, edged in erminetail and sewn with sea pearls. A silver dirk hung at her hip. Her skin was bleached and cool as porcelain, her nails chips of ivory, her wrists circled with delicate bangles of ice. Her face might have been called beautiful by some, had not her eyes been pale and blue as snow in shadow, her cheeks blushless, her bloodless lips curved in a mocking smile.

Beside her crouched the dragon, the size of a haywain. Its skin was translucent, its tail an arrowhead of frost. The claws of its forefeet bit the snow. The scales were clear as crystal glass, tinkling softly when it stirred. It watched them, its nostrils flaring rhythmically. Its breath was cold steam. Only the eyes were fire.

"Well," said the witch, her voice like winter wind. "What business have two young travelers with the Snow Sorcelress?"

Gunther spoke first, stepping forward, head carefully bowed. Holding the little chest before him, he knelt in the snow.

"We have come to pay homage to our Lady of the Snows," he said.

"How delightful," replied the sorcelress.

"We come with gifts to lay at your feet, O queen," he added, feigning reverence.

"Charming," she murmured.

The dragon breathed.

"You look worn. You must have traveled far."

Demian-Guendolyn edged forward to kneel alongside Gunther. "Six days and five nights was the length of our pilgrimage to your sacred wood," she told the snow at the sorcelress's feet. High above, one colorless brow arched.

"That is far indeed," the enchantress pronounced. "But surely you have not come all this way merely to honor me?"

"It is so, O sorcelress," replied Gunther to her knees.

Expectant stillness.

"But perhaps there was something else?"

"Oh no, your majesty," said Demian-Guendolyn to the dagger at her hip.

A musing pause.

"You did not come for some other purpose?"

"Certainly not, O queen," Gunther assured the jewels at her throat.

Silence. Demian began to tremble.

"You had nothing else in mind?"

The dragon stirred restively, lashing its tail.

"No," the two of them breathed as one to the shadows of her eyes.

"But of course you did," he sorcelress said, almost kindly, stilling the dragon with a caress. "It's perfectly natural. You came to see my rose, didn't you? They all do, all you pilgrims. I've no objection to showing you. Here. Look."

She turned and, with the greatest care, raised the cut-glass casing on the stand beside her. The icerose, a flawless crystal flower, lay upon a slab of ice. Its petals were delicately sculptured, the thorns symmetrically positioned along its stem. The pointed leaves gleamed as of beaten silver.

Yet Demian-Guendolyn could just make out the hint of color glowing beneath the patina of frost. It only lay dormant, she knew, not dead. It lived, and with it, their snow-locked land's only hope of summer. The sorcelress smiled.

"Lovely, isn't it? But enough." The case hovered down again, enclosing the flower. "Let me see what you have brought me."

Demian felt her heart skip. Almost too eagerly, Gunther seized the key upon his chain.

"No, no," the white queen bade him. "Come closer."

Demian saw Gunther ducking his head, biting back a

smile. What incredible luck! They had never expected to come within paces of her, let alone arm's reach. Eyes shining, Demian rose along with Gunther. Reining their eagerness, the two of them approached and knelt once more, so close this time that either of them might have touched her had they but extended a hand. Solemnly, Gunther turned the key in the lock and raised the oaken chest unopened to the tall sorcelress.

Leaning forward, she smiled, allowed one ivory hand to rest lightly on the clasp. The light in her eye was cordial, condescending and self-satisfied. A cold vapor respired from her skin. Demian could feel wafts of it chilling her to the bone. Smiling, the witch fingered the hasp. Her fingers tightened, as though to open it. Then in the next instant, she sent the chest crashing to the ground.

"Fools, did you think me deceived?" she shouted. "Did you think for one instant to cozen me?"

Gunther sprang up, his sword of dwarf-made steel in hand, but the witch had already seized Demian-Guendolyn by the collar of her cloak and dragged her up beside her. The crystal bracelets tinkled warningly above the silver dagger. Panting, half-strangled, Demian stood staring in horror at the chest. It lay overturned at their feet.

The sundust ran over the edge and spilled across the icy ground. It pooled into a mirror of golden mercury, then in the next heartbeat hardened, froze. The sorcelress pulled one perfect pearl from her gown and tossed it onto the gold.

The mirror shattered in a shower of fragments. The white queen's laughter filled the wood.

"Toss your sword into the air," she commanded Gunther.

When he hesitated, she tightened her grip on Demian's collar till the girl felt her knees weaken. Clawing at the throat of her cloak, she fought for air. *Don't do it*, she wanted to cry, but she could get no words out. *Gunther, save yourself!* She felt herself sagging in her captor's grasp. The bangles tinkled.

"Do as I say, or she dies."

With an anguished look, Gunther obeyed. His sword flashed up, turning slowly in empty space. The queen murmured a word to the dragon. It lunged and blew a great purling cloud of white breath. One tendril caught the spinning sword, and its ashes sifted down like dirty snow. Roughly, the witch shoved Demian-Guendolyn onto hands and knees beside her.

"Stay where you are, girl," she snarled. "I'll deal with your companion first."

Demian rubbed her bruised throat and gasped for breath. Gunther stood watching the ashes still, his face stricken.

"Would you like that to happen to you?" the sorceress inquired. "My dragon is a useful creature. I conjured him up when first I planned to steal the rose, seventeen times a hundred seasons past. Ichor makes his windy blood, and winter gels his flesh. Venom fills his poisoned tail, and fatal ethers form the vapors of his breath. Perhaps I shall feed you to him."

The dragon stirred, scales rattling like tiles. Its mistress shook her head.

"But no. That would be too easy, too swift. I must be delicate. Fare for my dragon would be no fit end for such a brave adventurer as you."

Demian flinched along with Gunther as the ice queen's contemptuous smile slipped suddenly into a grimace.

"O you vile, irksome little questers. I warned you. The very first night, I sent you a dream. . . ."

Why listen? thought the girl in the snow. It was already over. Still, she refused to regret. It had been a noble endeavor, well worth the risk. If only they had succeeded, they could have brought the bounty of summer again to the land. *Summer.*

Something was glinting. Some light, soft and fleeting, caught her eye and dazzled it. Some object shone. Demian turned her head. The mirror fragment lay beside her in the snow. It was the size of an acorn, golden as sun, turning the silvery light of winter back to her gaze in an electrum twinkle.

Demian's hand felt hot. The jewel glistening enticingly. She reached for it, slowly. The sorcelress was still speaking. Gunther stood helpless. The dragon rustled. Demian took the fragment into her palm and held it hard, willed it to melt. The cold gem grew tepid.

"Perhaps I shall turn you into a wolf like the magician

who tried to escape me. Doubtless he showed you the way. I'll devise his punishment later. But what for you—torture? Perhaps merely run you mad and let you go. Or hump your back like that boy half a century past who dared to defy me—did you get the sundust from him? Or perhaps, perhaps I shall freeze you into immobility, ever so slowly, over a season or two. . . ."

Gunther stood as if paralyzed, face haggard, eyes dazed with fear. Demian knew her own face looked no better. She was so frightened she almost could not move herself. This was no blustering village lout. Their tormentor smiled.

"This is really so hard. I receive visitors so seldom anymore, I hardly know what to do with you. . . ."

"Sorcelress," whispered Demian. Urgency filled her. Her voice trembled.

"Be still," snapped the queen, not even glancing at her.

Demian squirmed. The dust was growing blood-warm in her hands. The enchantress kept her gaze fixed on Gunther, toying with him still. Enjoying her power.

"Yes. Freezing you would be gratifying," she continued amiably. "To watch you chill over the months, the ice creeping up your limbs. . . ."

"Sorcelress," repeated Demian, more forcefully.

Without looking, the queen reached to give her a hard, impatient shake. "I bade you be still. Don't be overanxious. Your turn will come."

Still her head did not turn.

"If I freeze you, boy . . ." she said to Gunther. His jaw

clenched. He swallowed hard as though to speak, but the other's taunting voice drowned out his words. "How long do you think it will be before you are begging me for death?"

Demian bit her lip. The dram was beginning to scald her palm. In another moment, it would be too hot to hold. She thought frantically. The dust cupped in her hands swirled goldenly. The queen talked on. The dragon yawned. The sundust glowed.

"Icewitch," she hissed suddenly, then shouted it. "Icewitch!"

The witch stopped speaking.

"Why, you impertinent—" she cried, whirling, her eyes wide with rage. "Never call me that!"

Her hand closed on the haft of her knife. The blade flashed up. Demian-Guendolyn threw the sungold into the winter pools of her eyes.

The witch screamed, a long, piercing cry. The dagger slipped, falling hilt first to earth. Knifelike nails clutched Demian's shoulder. The dragon sprang up with a roar. Unsheathing her sword, Demian swept her gold-drenched hand across the blade. She struggled to rise, but the witch's grasp dragged her down. The dragon rushed at her, the cloud of its poisoned breath surrounding her.

Don't breathe, she thought.

Too late. The monster's roaring filled her ears. Then Gunther hauled her back, out of the swirling vapors. She heard the dragon's jaws snap empty air, heard Gunther shout some mage's curse, felt him seize the gold-washed blade

from her nerveless hand, heard it break on crystal scales—
all in the instant before darkness enveloped her like a heavy,
smothering cloak.

She was rising through shadows, feeling the dark mists fall
behind her, felt them clear. She surfaced. The sky stretched
gray above her. Her shoulder throbbed fiercely from the
Icewitch's talons. *Icewitch*, she thought dazedly. *Gunther*.

"Gunther?" she croaked, struggling to rise against the
pounding in her temples. Her throat felt scathed. Breath
rasped in her lungs. Gunther leaned closer.

"Lie down. You're hurt."

"I'm well enough," she gasped. "Truly."

She shook her head to clear it. He caught her gently by
the shoulders. She sagged against him, glad of the support.

"You breathed the dragon's breath," he insisted firmly.
"You should rest."

"The Icewitch?" Whispering proved less painful.

"Dissipated. Dead."

"The dragon?"

"Dead, too. The dram from your fingers killed it, not the
sword."

She looked at her hand. Gold and scarlet swam sluggishly in her palm. She had cut her fingers on the sword
blade, she realized. Her mind felt numb and slow. Gold and
scarlet. Dust-dram and blood. Dust-dram and bloomfrost.
Icerose.

"Icerose," she muttered. "Icerose."

"There," he replied, turning her with the greatest care. The pale flower lay in the snow beside them, crystal case shattered, icerose bedded on the glittering fragments.

"Why haven't you revived it?" she burst out, feeling the burning in her lungs as she drew deep breath. Her words came out a rusty shriek.

"I wanted you to."

She turned to him, astonished. "This was *your* quest."

He smiled sadly. "I failed. You threw the dust-dram into her eyes. It was your sword killed the dragon, not mine." He gazed at the flower with a desperate longing, but after a few moments, shook his head. "The rose is yours, Demian. Take it."

She looked at him, then touched his cheek, whispering, "Not without you."

Palm to palm, they knelt in the snow, letting the blood and dust-dram on their fingers mingle. Demian nodded. Gunther smiled. Slowly and together, the two of them reached out their hands to touch the perfect crystal stem.

$\mathcal{R}$afiddilee

I WROTE "Rafiddilee" when I was fourteen years old, and when I finished, I knew I was a writer. Here it is, only slightly revised. The title, by the way, as well as the main character's name, is pronounced rah-FIDDLE-ee. The story came to me in my high school German class. I'd been reading a lot of fairy tales—the originals, not the modernized versions. The Grimms and Hans Christian Andersen and Oscar Wilde can be unsparing: pretty, well, grim. Life isn't all about happy endings, even if you are a queen. The best intentions do not always suffice. Getting things right on the first try is a lot less costly than mopping up afterward. Take heed, all. This is a cautionary tale.

Rafiddilee

∾ I ∾

ONCE THERE lived, many years ago, a young queen with eyes the color of evening sky. A dark, clear blue, they were cool and still as a deep, deep well. Sometimes courtiers could see her thoughts stirring restlessly below the surface, like fishes in their very depths. But they rarely surfaced, for the queen spoke little of her inmost heart, having learned early in life the wisdom of keeping her own counsel.

The queen was only fourteen and missed her parents dearly. They had both succumbed to plague the previous year, so her great-uncle, the archduke, ruled for her as regent. A widower without children of his own, he was a wise old soul, both practical and experienced in the ways of political necessity. The young queen was on the best of terms with him, because he was very fond of her, as was she of him. And from him she got most everything she wanted that was prudent for her to have.

The castle in which the young queen lived had many courtyard gardens, and the queen's own secluded garden was located to the northeast, just below her apartments. It had at its center a stone bench beside a well, where the young queen would often come to sit and ponder, gazing deeply into the smooth, dark waters. This was her own most privy garden, where none of her courtiers, not even her great-uncle, were allowed to enter.

The queen's castle perched high on a hill at the heart of her realm. Hers was a small but prosperous kingdom, quite mountainous and surrounded by other, larger states. To the west of the castle, the hill plunged down sheerly into gently rolling farmland. To the east, it sloped away into a dense forest sparsely peopled by solitary woodsmen.

One such man lived at the very center of the wood. He was a trapper. Each day he set his traps along the animal trails that threaded between the trees, baiting the traps with poisoned delicacies. Each afternoon, he made his rounds again, checking and resetting the traps and gathering deadly toadstools, roots, and berries for his poisons.

He lived alone except for a little dwarf he called Rafiddilee. The word was not even a name really, just a bit of nonsense from an old children's rhyme:

> *Rafiddilee rum, rafiddilee ree,*
> *So crook'd and glum. What cumbers me?*

Rafiddilee was an odd little man, with one humped shoulder and a bit of a limp, though he was very agile just the same. He was not old, but his face was wizened, with one drooping eyelid and his brows set in an expression of perpetual surprise.

His mouth was lopsided, too, as was his smile, but for all that, his crooked little face was quite adorable, his eyes so bright and quick. Even though he was mute, he could play the fife like none other, making it trill like birdsong or plash like water. The old man kept him to look after the house while he was away, and to help him mix poisons in the evenings.

One evening, very late, a troupe of players traversing the woods became lost. They were making their way from castle to castle and town to town, performing at feasts and fairs. Having missed their road, they stumbled by chance upon the old man's cabin. The night was dark and cold, and when they begged shelter for the night, the old man grudgingly gave it. For a price, he included some food.

Rafiddilee was very curious about the players. He had never seen another living soul before besides the old man— and his own mother, who had sold him to the woodsman when he had been barely able to walk. Being unable to speak, he could not engage them in conversation, so he set about doing whatever lay within his power to entertain them. Soon, despite the cramped quarters and paltry rations, everyone in the troupe was delighted with Rafiddilee's agile leaps, his expressive face, and his sweet piping.

In the morning, the troupemaster offered to buy him for twenty copper pence and a good, strong hunting knife. The huntsman pretended to be uninterested until the offer rose to six silver coins and a small keg of spirits thrown in with the knife. Then he laughed heartily and said that for such a price, he could buy himself a wench to tend his house, and one with a tongue in her head. Good riddance to the speechless little dwarf; the players could have him and welcome.

So saying, he shook the other's hand and turned Rafiddilee over to his new master without a backward glance. At first, Rafiddilee was downhearted and lonesome for the old woodsman, who had been the only family Rafiddilee had ever known, but soon he found he liked the performers of the troupe much better, for they were kinder and rarely cuffed or swore at him.

The troupe traveled from place to place all over the queen's small, mountainous kingdom and neighboring nations besides, performing for townsfolk as well as nobles. Usually the show began with the minstrels singing merry songs to loosen the crowd, followed by magicians and acrobats. Often they performed one or more short skits and dances, too. Jugglers and fire-eaters took their turns. Meanwhile, Rafiddilee would sit with his knees folded, perched inside a basket hung from the rafters, watching the performance from above and playing his fife.

At last, the basket would be lowered. Out he would leap, doing handsprings and cartwheels before the surprised onlookers. At the very end, just as the troupemaster had instructed, he would present a nosegay to one of the ladies in the audience. The crowd was always delighted and would throw coins, sometimes even jewelry, to the performers as they bowed to the applause. The troupemaster boasted that

Raffidilee had increased their revenues by a fifth or more and was worth a coffer of silver coin. The huntsman had been a fool to part with him.

Rafiddilee had been with the players for a year and a half when they were engaged by the queen's great-uncle to perform for her majesty's sixteenth birthday. The troupemaster was beside himself with glee, for this was sure to be a most lucrative engagement and, as many of the most influential nobles in the kingdom and even a few foreign dignitaries would be in attendance, a performance that was sure to bring them further work. He and his company arrived the morning of the appointed day and were directed to the great dining hall. While the others were setting up and practicing their acts, Rafiddilee meandered off to see what he could see.

He was so small that, in the bustle of preparations, he could pass almost anywhere unnoticed. He peeked into the tapestry-weavers' room, where gorgeous wall hangings were created on vast handlooms; the music room, where many exotic-looking instruments of wood and brass were kept; the records room, full to overflowing with inkpots and quills, codices and scrolls; the armory, racked with weapons of every sort. Before slipping out of the castle altogether, he sneaked into the steaming kitchen and stole a pastry full of raspberry jam.

Outside, he visited the smithy and the stable, and finally wandered into the queen's privy courtyard. She was sitting on her stone bench, gazing pensively down into the well, looking not at all like a happy girl about to turn sixteen—

or a young noblewoman with everything in the world one could wish for. Wearing a gown of the most wonderful dark blue velvet edged in erminetail, she was gazing so intently that she did not even notice as Rafiddilee slipped into the courtyard. He thought she must be the most beautiful lady he had ever seen.

Gingerly, he tiptoed over to where she was sitting, taking great care to move silently so as not to disturb her. Slowly, he reached out one hand to stroke the lovely evening blue material of her gown. Feeling the slight tug his fingertips made passing over the velvet, she sat up with a start.

"Heavens," she exclaimed. "Who might you be?"

Rafiddilee leapt back, afraid she might be angry. But when he saw her smile, he knew that she was not. Since he could not reply with words, he took from his head his little green felt hat with its jaunty pheasant's feather, and made a low and courtly bow just as the troupemaster had taught him. Then he turned a cartwheel for her, so she clapped in surprise. He went through his whole routine of handsprings and flips. He walked on his hands and stood on his head. For the finish, he danced a lively little jig, accompanying himself on his pipe.

The queen was truly pleased, and when he was finished, she helped him up onto the stone bench beside her and talked to him for the better part of an hour. Having not the power of speech himself, Rafiddilee was an accomplished listener. The young queen poured out her heart to him, things she had never dared to say to anyone else, of her hopes for her future and her own maiden dreams. Rafiddilee nodded and smiled and quirked his brows, never disputing or uttering a word of criticism. She would have talked longer, had not the bells for morning prayers sounded at last.

"Little man, I'm afraid I must go," she said with a sigh. "My great-uncle will be expecting me. A queen must never be late for prayers, especially on her birthday. Thank you so much for a lovely morning."

Then she kissed him on the top of his tousled head and hurried away through the gate to the royal chapel that abutted the main courtyard.

That evening was the queen's birthday banquet. Rafiddilee had to be hoisted up in his basket well before the banquet began, for none of the audience must know he was there until the very end of the entertainment, lest that spoil the surprise. So, in the gray darkness of the torches' haze, Rafiddilee sat for three dull hours without a bite to eat or a sup to drink in the basket above the feasting court.

The basket was positioned just in front of the queen's chair so that he might be lowered squarely before her. Rafiddilee watched in eager anticipation while the troubadors and jugglers and magicians impressed their royal hostess with their music and sleight of hand. At last his turn came. He felt the basket descending. Almost before he felt it touch the ground, he had thrown off the lid and leapt out, so eager was he to perform once more for the queen.

When she saw him, she cried out in delight, "Great-uncle,

that is the odd little man of whom I spoke. Isn't he clever?"

Her great-uncle watched Rafiddilee's inspired capering, which was drawing such gasps and cheers from the courtiers, and nodded to the queen with a smile. "That he is, grandniece. I wonder if his master would be willing to sell him. He might make an excellent fool."

At the end, Rafiddilee took his nosegay from the basket and scampered up the steps to the daïs on which the queen and her regent sat viewing the festivities. There he fell on one knee before the seat of honor and offered its occupant the bouquet. The queen reached down to accept it, smiling warmly at the crooked little dwarf. When she took the nosegay into her hands, her smile turned to an astonished laugh as out of the flowers flew a dove with a beautiful blood-drop marking upon its breast.

It was called a heartsblood and was quite expensive and rare. The troupemaster had scoured the markets for one the moment he had received the regent's summons to perform, knowing what a special occasion this was to be. He had kept it alive in a wicker cage all these weeks, feeding it the choicest morsels and crumbs but never daring to let it fly free until the moment Rafiddilee released it from the flowers.

Now it beat about the great hall, swooping this way and that while the courtiers uttered gasps and sighs at its loveliness, and the young queen both laughed and wept to see such a beautiful creature trapped within the merry hall. Its soft, mournful cries tugged at her heart most peculiarly until, finding a wrinkle where one of the tapestries hung not quite flat against the unglazed windows, the snowy thing slipped into the night and was gone.

Then Rafiddilee bowed once more to the queen. With warm words of praise, she handed him back the largest and most perfectly formed of the white blooms she held pressed to her breast. The troupemaster puffed his chest with pride. The beaming players bowed half a dozen times and then withdrew. Eventually, the queen's guests rose and came forward to kiss her hand and express their thanks and wish her well.

After the queen and most of her court had at last retired, servants entered the room and began clearing the dishes and stripping the linens and carrying the tables away. The queen's great-uncle spoke with the troupemaster. First he paid him handsomely for his company's fine performance, which had so enthralled the court and entranced its young queen. Then he got down to the business of negotiating the purchase of Rafiddilee—but try as he might, he could not convince the troupemaster to sell.

"No, Sire. I'm terribly sorry. I couldn't part with the dwarf. He's much too great an asset to my livelihood."

Though not particularly fond of Raffidilee, the troupemaster recognized his worth. Besides, if the queen of this picayune little country with its modest treasury fancied the dwarf and was willing to pay, think how much more he might be able to wrest from some larger and more lavish court desirous of a fool. Truth to tell, the troupemaster had never considered this possibility before, but now that the queen's regent had engendered the idea, he was determined to turn Rafiddilee to the greatest advantage he could.

"How unfortunate," the queen's great-uncle said sadly. "Her majesty was so taken with him."

"I'm afraid I hear the same nearly every day, Sire." The troupemaster sighed. "Everywhere we go, it seems, someone wishes to acquire him. I have to lock him up at night, for his own safety, to prevent thieves from making off with my little friend."

The queen's regent said nothing to this. It saddened him to hear that Rafiddilee's master felt he must keep his star performer caged like a bear.

"Well, my lord, I'm sorry I cannot oblige you," the troupemaster finished smoothly. "Thank you again, most kindly, for your custom. Good even."

"Good even," the archduke said and left the banquet hall for his own chambers. On the way, he stopped by the queen's apartments to leave word with her maidservant of the troupemaster's refusal to part with Rafiddilee. When the queen heard of it, she sighed a great sigh and gazed out the window after the vanished dove.

"What a pity," she said gloomily. "I had liked him so very much."

The next morning, as the troupe was preparing to leave, they discovered that Rafiddilee was missing. When the juggler in charge of locking Rafiddilee into the large wicker trunk that contained his bedding had not been able to find him after the banquet, the man had mistakenly thought the dwarf to be with the troupemaster still and gone off to amuse himself with a kitchen wench. Following his conversation with the archduke, the troupemaster, not seeing Rafiddilee, had naturally assumed him to be already under lock and key. It was not until daybreak that anyone realized him to be gone.

The troupemaster, normally the mildest of men, cuffed the juggler about dreadfully for his error and uttered the most fearful curses. Then he rousted the rest of the troupe from their beds and organized a search. The players searched all morning. They searched everywhere—in the tailors' workshop, in the oil painter's studio, in the cartographer's drafting room, even down in the deepest wine cellar—but they could find not hint nor hair of him.

At length, when the sun stood high in the noon sky, the queen's great-uncle spoke once more with the disconsolate troupemaster. Because the troupe was already late for its next engagement, the regent suggested that the troupe go on and he would direct the castle servants to continue the search. Should they come across Rafiddilee, they would send him to the players.

The troupemaster was not at all confident of the arch- duke and secretly suspected him of holding his property captive until he and his band were gone. But though the queen's was a tiny realm as nations go, when all was said and done, the queen's great-uncle was a lord, far more powerful than he, a mere man of business and a commoner. In the end, he had no choice but to agree. He told the archduke the city where the troupe was headed, which was across the border in a neighboring land, and they left within the hour.

And Rafiddilee? Had he indeed been seized by the queen's unscrupulous regent and held a prisoner? Nothing of the sort. The archduke was a most practical man, and he had stooped to a fair number of subterfuges over the years, for the good of the realm, though never so low as purloining a dwarf. True, he was concerned over his grandniece's rather pensive nature and quite willing to do anything he honorably might to lighten her heart, but deceiving the troupemaster over the whereabouts of Rafiddilee did not, in his opinion, merit the effort.

No, the little man's disappearance was all his own doing. Crawling beneath a table in search of morsels after the banquet the previous evening—for he had had nothing to eat since noon; the troupemaster had neglected to feed him again—he had overheard his master and the queen's great-uncle talking. How his heart had soared when he learned the queen wanted to buy him!

She had seemed to him so sad and earnest and kind, he was sure she would never lock him in a wicker box and perhaps, if he were lucky and pleased her well, never even speak a rough word to him. He was certain she would see him fed every day, at least twice. When he heard the troupemaster refusing the queen's regent's offer, he immediately made up his mind to hide himself so that he might stay.

First, he snatched a half-eaten chicken from a tray and stuffed his pocket with cakes and tarts. Then he stole out to the queen's privy courtyard. There he lowered the well's bucket halfway to the water below, secured it, and shimmied down the rope, to climb in. The well's bucket was not so different from the basket in which he had sat many a time, so there he perched the night and all the next morning. First he ate every cake and tart until he felt almost sick, but also deliciously full.

After that, nothing much remained to do but wait. He was quite used to sitting very still, suspended from a rope, so he was not in the least afraid. He had no desire to sleep. By noon, however, he was beginning to grow hungry again, so he unwrapped the chicken from the pudding bag in which he had stowed it, and set to work devouring it joint by joint and dropping the clean white bones over the side.

After morning prayers, the queen went out to her privy garden to think. She was gloomy and pensive again, despite her wonderful birthday feast of the night before, because of her great-uncle's message that the troupemaster had refused to sell Rafiddilee. She had not yet heard that the little man was missing.

After a few moments, she heard a splash. She looked up, puzzled, listening, but as she heard no more, decided the sound must have been made by a loose bit of mortar falling into the well. But presently, she heard another splash and then, not long after, another. Frowning, she leaned over and gazed into the well. Rafiddilee looked up at her and smiled.

Licking his fingers, he dropped the last ivory chicken bone into the dark waters below.

"Rafiddilee!" cried the queen, hurrying to the other side of the well and using all her strength to crank up the bucket. She was a strong girl, and the mechanism was ratcheted. "You silly thing!" she panted as soon as she got the bucket near enough to the well's lip to catch hold of it and draw it over. "Why are you not with your master? Surely your troupe must have left the castle by now."

She gave him her hand to help him climb out of the bucket.

"Were you waiting for me?"

He nodded, beaming. The queen put her hands on her hips, trying hard to look stern.

"But surely your folk missed you and searched for you? You must have heard them calling."

The little dwarf had indeed heard the members of his troupe calling his name, but he had paid not the slightest heed. He had known that if he were patient and silent and simply waited long enough, the troupe would go away again and the queen would eventually find him. He was quite proud that his plan had worked so well, for now he felt sure that the queen, for all that she was pretending to be angry with him, would let him stay.

The queen lifted him down from the edge of the well and onto the stone bench where she could talk to him. He smiled his biggest, most endearingly crooked smile at her, and bowed. But the queen did not seem as happy to see him as he had hoped. On the contrary, she seemed quite troubled.

"Why were you in the well, Rafiddilee?" she asked.

Rafiddilee shrugged in his elfin way, leapt off the bench, and turned a cartwheel on the stone cobbles.

"You were hiding from the troupemaster, weren't you?" she continued.

Rafiddilee shook his head and turned another cartwheel.

"But you were," insisted the queen. "Don't tell me you weren't."

Why was she so persistent? What did it matter? The troupemaster was gone now, and he, Rafiddilee, was here and might amuse the queen all she wanted. He did a handspring for her, but the queen did not seem to want to be amused.

"Rafiddilee," she pronounced sternly, "you have run away." Her tone sounded not at all pleased. "Was it because I wanted to buy you, and the troupemaster would not sell?"

Rafiddilee smiled and nodded and danced his little jig. The queen sighed and looked near tears.

"Come here," she said softly.

He scampered over to her. She knelt down so that she might look him squarely in the eye.

"Rafiddilee," she said, "running away was wrong."

The little man stopped dancing and did not smile anymore.

"The troupemaster paid six pieces of silver for you," she told him gravely, "a good hunting knife and a flask of spirits besides. My great-uncle told me. Because of this, you belong to him. You cannot leave him until he sells you or lets you go. Each of us has his place, like it or no. Mine is here, within this keep, and yours is with your master. You cannot stay here. You must go back to the troupe."

Rafiddilee fell back a step, stricken. He stared at the young queen, quite stunned. He felt as though she had just taken a great pin and pierced him through. He had thought the lady wanted him. He had believed she would let him stay with her. He had imagined she would be amused at his cleverness in hiding in her well—but no. Now that she had found him, she intended to thrust him away again.

The queen rose to her feet. Rafiddilee looked up. Tears slid out of each eye and rolled down his wizened cheeks. Seeing them, the young queen felt close to tears herself. She bit her lip, knowing full well what must be done, what course of action her regent would insist upon. She turned, intending to start toward the gate to summon the gardener. She meant to ask him the send word to her great-uncle that Rafiddilee was found—but the little man threw his arms about her knees to stay her, for he could not speak.

The young queen gazed down at the crooked little figure that embraced her. Tears did well in her eyes this time, for Rafiddilee had buried his face in the folds of her skirts and would not look at her anymore. Pierced to the heart, the young queen shook her head. Truly, in this instance, necessity was too cruel. She knelt down again.

"Dear Rafiddilee," she said softly, "how can I let you go?

I shall tell my great-uncle to pay the troupemaster many times over what he paid for you. Right or wrong, you belong with me, and here is where you shall stay."

Rafiddilee looked up then, joy sweeping over his wry little face. He jumped and danced and clapped his hands. Then he reached inside the collar of his shirt and pulled out a bit of twine that looped loosely about his neck. On it hung a silver ring that had been tossed to him by a lady at one of the castles where the troupe had once performed, to the high hilarity of her companions.

It was the only thing of any value that he had ever owned, and he had kept it hidden next to his heart these many months so that the troupemaster would not take it from him. Breaking the twine, he handed it to his new mistress, who accepted it graciously. Smiling, the young queen put it on her finger, then taking Rafiddilee by the hand, left the courtyard garden to find her great-uncle herself and tell him what he must do.

A fortnight after the queen's sixteenth birthday, the troupemaster received a missive from her regent, accompanied by two hundred pieces of silver, five large casks of the finest spirits, and half a dozen jewel-encrusted daggers. The troupemaster was rendered pale with astonishment. He had never expected to hear from the archduke again.

Because he had already bought another dwarf—not so able as Rafiddilee, to be sure, but most crowds were not particular—the troupemaster spent the queen's silver on a new wardrobe for himself of splendid silk and velvet doublets, with matching hose and boots. The fine spirits he hoarded jealously for his own use, not allowing anyone else in the troupe to touch a drop, and he sold the daggers for more than enough to keep him comfortably for the remainder of his life.

The royal missive, with its impressive seals and calligraphy, he brought out from time to time to flourish before a crowd. Since he knew nearly no one in his audience would be able to read, he claimed the letter to be an official commendation from the Pope, which did wonders to increase the troupe's revenues. The other dwarf worked out tolerably well. To the end of his days, the troupemaster never ceased to denounce the queen's regent the archduke for a liar and a cheat.

❦ II ❦

From that day onward, Rafiddilee was the queen's fool. He was her constant companion. Wherever she went, there Rafiddilee was to be found. He was one of only a handful of people whom she allowed into her garden—the other two being her favorite maidservant and the old gardener, both of whom she had known since childhood. There in the courtyard-garden, beside the well, Rafiddilee would entertain his mistress and her maid for hours with his fife.

Whenever the queen was downcast or melancholy, she would call for her fool, and soon she would be smiling and cheerful again. He was also the delight of the court. The nobles and dignitaries laughed at his merry antics. The maids-in-waiting loved him, for he always had a flower or a trick for them. The huntsmen and falconers applauded his capers. The cooks and laundresses adored him, as did the needlewomen and the armorers. The pages and kitchen boys all thought him great fun.

He was very quick in so many matters: how to stack playing cards into great complicated castles taller than himself, or twist pine straw into a basket, or fashion flower stems into elaborate garlands. His hands were so clever he could unknot even the most badly tangled thread.

Yet other things seemed completely beyond his grasp. When the queen sat reading her prayer books or storybooks or histories, he gazed at the woodblocks and colorful illuminations, and, when she allowed him, turned pictures sideways and upside down, but he could not seem to understand that they were figures of people and animals, manor houses and ships.

The queen tried to teach him to read at first, and also to write, thinking that by doing so he might overcome his muteness, but to no avail. When she read to him, even short and simple stories, he fell asleep, lulled by the sound of her voice. When she gave him a quill and parchment and tried to teach him to spell his name, he smiled willingly at her and managed only to smear ink all over himself, till the queen fell down with laughing and Rafiddilee had to be sent to the scullery to be scrubbed clean.

The court physician pronounced that his condition was

not likely to change: his wit appeared to function aptly enough in some areas and to be sadly lacking in others. So the queen let him be. He remained as he had always been, a curious and unpredictable combination of canny and simple, savant and fool.

He had been at court just over a year—the young queen was not yet eighteen—when the marchioness Ermengarde visited. Ermengarde was the queen's cousin, some years her senior, and her only living relative besides her great-uncle, the archduke. She had been raised on foreign soil, for her mother, the queen's late aunt, had married abroad for the good of the realm and left her homeland many years ago, never to return.

The marchioness brought her own household with her to her cousin's court: her private cook, her pages, her personal dressmakers, her horses' grooms, her little silk-haired dog, and her old nursemaid. When she arrived by coach with her many attendants, the queen's whole court turned out for the occasion. Because of the lady's royal connections, were her young cousin to die childless, Ermengarde stood next in the line of succession to the throne.

The queen had not seen the lady since she herself had been a young child, when both her parents had still been alive. She did not remember her cousin well at all, but welcomed her as warmly as if she had known her always. The marchioness curtsied low to the queen, but her young cousin kindly bade her dispense with such stately formality.

Ermengarde then presented the queen with the costly gift of a gorgeously bejeweled snuffbox, with which the queen was delighted, although she did not take snuff.

Next, the queen introduced her great-uncle. He was the queen's kin on her mother's side, and thus no relation to the marchioness, but she called him dearest uncle just the same. The regent smiled diplomatically and kissed the marchioness's hand, but privately, he was not smiling. He had encountered the marchioness on more than one occasion years ago in her own realm, when matters of state had sent him there at the king's request, and only now that he had become regent did she seem to consider him worthy of her notice.

Nor had she shown any interest in her young cousin until her parents' untimely death, which had put Ermengarde so unexpectedly near the throne of a small but prosperous realm. There had followed a steady stream of letters then, first of condolence, and then of the chatty, artfully witty sort designed to dazzle a young and impressionable girl. Those missives had culminated at last in the queen's extending an invitation to her cousin to visit and the marchioness's instantaneous acceptance.

To the archduke's way of thinking, the lady Ermengarde presumed rather overmuch upon her naïve young cousin's good graces. Her sumptuous gown and crowded retinue seemed immodestly lavish, her flowery manner of speaking affected, her effusive affection feigned. In short, the queen's great-uncle did not trust the marchioness and suspected her visit to be motivated less by goodwill than a desire to advance her own position. But he smiled outwardly and welcomed her with a few crisp, well-chosen words.

Next, the marchioness offered her little panting, featheryhaired dog for the queen to pet and fuss over. He barked and wiggled and growled and wagged his tail all at once. The archduke stood ready to stab the little monster to death should it make bold to nip the royal hand that caressed it. But by chance, it did not. Smiling, unaware of her danger, the queen beckoned to Rafiddilee, who had been peeking around her skirts at the lady Ermengarde. The archduke noted that, though usually delighted to meet strangers, Rafiddilee now sidled forward uneasily. The marchioness bared her teeth in the semblance of a smile and bent forward to peer at him.

"My, my," she gushed, "what a darling little thing. I must have one just like him. His shoulder is humped, is it not? Has he a club foot? Wherever did you find him, cousin dear?"

The queen laughed gaily, not realizing these words were anything but kindly meant, and bade her fool bow to the marchioness. But Rafiddilee also sensed the fetid air of ambition that wafted from the lady like a spoiled perfume. He stood wide-eyed, motionless, staring at the marchioness's big teeth and knobby chin. Then at the queen's second, slightly puzzled behest, he twisted up his little face, shook his head violently, and ran away to hide in the library.

His mistress was quite astonished, for her young heart was too unsullied and trusting yet to detect, as her greatuncle and Rafiddilee did, the falsity of the other's nature.

She was so delighted at having her only cousin now beside her, and at the marchioness's extravagant gift—in which she intended to keep pins, not snuff—which appeared to her so generous, and at Ermengarde's gleeful little dog, which seemed on the verge of expiring in the other's grasp from sheer excitement, that she had no inkling why Rafiddilee should have run away.

"I'm so sorry, cousin," she stammered, mortified. "I don't know what has come over my fool. He is usually so forward and merry. Perhaps it's only that he is unused to dogs."

Ermengarde laughed and took the younger lady's hand confidentially. "Dearest cousin, never fear. What could a silly little dwarf know?" The dog growled and twisted against her stays. "I'm sure before long, he and Tidbit will be the best of friends."

But the marchioness judged very astutely what Rafiddilee must know and marked him out at once as her enemy. She had indeed come to court with an evil design in mind. The last of her tireless attempts to marry into the royal family of her own land had recently fallen through, and, thwarted in this bid to make more of herself than she was, she had turned her thoughts to other possibilities.

Knowing that she was the young queen's only paternal relative, and that should anything happen to the queen, she, Ermengarde, would have the throne, she determined to see what could be done to move matters along in that direction. First, however, she must establish herself at court.

So by day, she pretended to be the queen's closest friend,

showering her with gifts and advice and seeking to become her confidante. She attempted to recruit through false kindness and flattery the goodwill of the queen's trusted handmaid, a girl no older or wiser than the queen herself, and did everything in her power to undermine the royal affection for Rafiddilee. She called her cousin's fool a childish toy which any young woman as prudent as her majesty must surely be intending to renounce soon enough. Her attempts in this regard did not get far, and Rafiddilee remained very dear to his mistress's heart.

Ermengarde soon found, though, that by spending as much time as possible in her cousin's company, dog in hand, she could keep Rafiddilee away. The little fool loathed and feared both her and her creature every bit as much as they did him, so when the marchioness was with the queen, the queen's fool was seldom anywhere to be found. This pleased the queen's cousin no end. To the court at large, she seemed a fine, noble lady, a bit old perhaps to be yet unwed, but with a saucy wit and a lively step for dancing. She made such a show of religious fervor at morning prayers that many assumed her chastity to be devotionally inspired.

It was only at night that her true nature revealed itself. Then she would sit, late of an evening, closeted in her tower apartments out of the public eye, carping with her old nursemaid about what had transpired during the day, how well this or that subterfuge had worked to deceive the queen or gain the loyalty of this or that influential noble. The only nobleman with whom she had no success at all was the queen's great-uncle, who remained to her ever cool, courtly, and reserved. She felt his wariness and resented it deeply.

On several occasions, the archduke tried to speak with his grandniece of his misgivings, suggesting that perhaps the lady Ermengarde had stayed overlong, or spent too extravagantly on gifts to the queen's advisors, or sought to occupy too much of her cousin's scarce and valuable time. This he had to do with the greatest tact and care, so thoroughly had the marchioness succeeded in worming her way into her royal hostess's maiden heart.

But the queen would not listen to him, for she could not believe the lady Ermengarde to be any but the sweetest, kindest noblewoman alive.

"Great-uncle," she would laugh, "how you talk. You are so suspicious! I'm sure you would believe every spider in my window frame to be plotting against me."

At last the old regent could but hold his tongue and conceal his opposition to the marchioness's continued stay at court and ever deepening influence. Clearly talk was of no use. His young ward simply would not listen. Deeds must now speak. With luck, the marchioness would tip her hand in time. Meanwhile, he resolved to keep an even closer eye upon the lady to ensure that she brought no harm to the queen. And what better spy than Rafiddilee? He could hide anywhere, and no one would suspect him.

Before long, at the archduke's bidding, Rafiddilee was climbing the winding tower stairs every night to crouch in the shadows outside the marchioness's chambers, listening to her hobnobbing with her old nursemaid while they stitched embroidery by candlelight. For six long months he kept up his weary vigil, but though he overheard much catty gossip and remarks both ugly and unkind regarding various members of the court, he learned nothing specific enough to incriminate the marchioness.

Then early one dusk when ruddy storm clouds brewed heavy in the eastern sky, Rafiddilee saw the nursemaid slip in through the postern gate from the direction of the woods. She skirted the stable yard and crossed the kitchen garden, clutching something in her apron. Scurrying to the tower, she darted inside. Rafiddilee waited a few moments, then made to follow, but the nursemaid had bolted the stairwell door behind her. This she had never done before, and Rafiddilee backed away, frowning.

Presently he saw a light in the tower window high above. The shadows of the marchioness and her old nurse played against the wall. They were standing, the pair of them, face-to-face. Both appeared to be peering down at something held between them, engaged in an animated discussion that Rafiddilee, being so far below, could not hear. He realized at once that he must get up to the marchioness's window to see what she was about.

Now that the stairwell was denied him, the only way up was the flowering briar that climbed the tower's eastern side. It was not so thorny near the ground, but as the viny limbs grew slimmer and greener, they grew more prickly as well. Rafiddilee began to climb. Up, up along the twisting, biting tendrils, their barbs scratching at his face and hands and catching at his clothes.

Higher and higher he went. The wind was beginning to blow, the fiery storm clouds sweeping in from the east. The thorny brambles raked at him and held him back. He thrust his way upward. On and on he climbed, until finally he reached the lofty window of the marchioness's room. It had begun to rain, great spattering drops that stung like falling stones and wet him to the skin. He crouched there, high above the courtyard cobbles, just below the level of the sill, clinging to the slippery, rain-soaked briar.

As he peered into the room, he could see the marchioness and her nurse standing beside a table by candlelight. None of the marchioness's other servants seemed to be about. The apartments appeared deserted save for the two women beside the table. All sorts of herbs, toadstools, and berries lay before them, also a mortar and pestle, a mincing knife and various bowls, as well as a great candle with a wick as thick as Rafiddilee's little finger.

With a start, the queen's fool recognized the toadstools and some of the berries as those he had once helped the old woodsman gather to prepare his poisoned bait. His heart hammered. His head spun. Rain ran into his eyes. Blinking, gripping the painful brambles hard, he edged closer, craning, trying for a better view.

Ermengarde and her nursemaid were smiling and muttering to one another as they ground the herbs to powder and crushed the juice from the blood-red berries. When they had finished pulverizing the tougher ingredients, they scraped them all together into a little iron pan, added honey and a generous splash of cordial, then crumbled the brown, white-flecked mushroom caps on top.

Carefully, they poked at the sludgy mess with the tip of the mincing knife, stirring it over the great flame of the candle until it bubbled sullenly, like phlegm in a dying man's throat. Removing the tiny pan from the fire, at last, they poured off into a glass vial a deep purple liquid, thick as stew broth. The old nursemaid set the vial down on the table with a sigh of satisfaction.

"Now, my dear," she told her mistress, "we must let it settle."

Ermengarde smiled a wicked smile. "How long will it take for the dross to separate?"

"Perhaps an hour," the old woman said. "I'll prepare you for the banquet while we wait." She turned and crossed the room to the clothespress where the marchioness's gowns were kept, but Ermengarde lingered, gazing down into the vial.

"What rises to the top will be clear?" she asked. "And tasteless?"

The other nodded, not turning, sorting through her mistress's clothes. "Odorless as well. The little ninny will never suspect a thing."

Ermengarde's smile widened. "And her great-uncle?"

The nurse selected a gaudy gown of ginger-colored silk stuff beneath a moss-colored surcoat. "I'll see to him as well, dearest, never fret. The throne of this backward little realm's as good as yours. Now come along. The poison won't rise any faster from your staring at it."

Carrying the two garments, she disappeared into the other room.

"What would I do without you, nurse?" Ermengarde murmured fondly, running one finger around the rim of the vial. Then she followed the other into the adjacent chamber, where Rafiddilee could hear them discussing how many combs the marchioness wanted the old nurse to use in the dressing of her hair.

The moment they were both out of sight, quick as thought, Rafiddilee clambered up over the windowsill and dropped into the room. He knew he must get rid of the poison at once, for clearly it was meant for the queen—and perhaps her regent, besides. Throwing the whole vial onto the coals would surely suffice. He tiptoed hurriedly across the room.

But just as he was reaching for the poisoned vial, the marchioness's little silky-haired dog ran out from under the bedskirt and began barking and snarling at him in a frenzy. Rafiddilee lunged as hard as he might, but the vial had been placed too far back on the table for him to be able to reach. The dog seized his trouser leg and, sinking its sharp little teeth into his calf, jerked him back from the table, shaking its head from side to side so violently that Rafiddilee would have screamed, had he been able.

He staggered, flailing for balance, fearing that at any moment the dog might succeed in slinging him to the ground and be at his throat. Stooping, he caught up one of the marchioness's many discarded shoes and struck at the creature's nose. It lost its grip. Then, yapping and growling, it feinted at him again and again as he tried once more to reach the table and the vial. Hearing the commotion, the nursemaid came to see what the trouble was. Catching sight of Rafiddilee, she cried out.

"Devil take it! It's the queen's dwarf. My lady, come quick!"

Ermengarde ran into the room clad only in her shift, her red hair unbound. She cuffed Rafiddilee away from the table's edge while her nursemaid captured the scrabbling dog.

"Been spying, have you?" she snarled at Rafiddilee. "Well, dwarf, you have spied your last."

So saying, she swooped and caught him, pinning both arms to his side and holding him tight with her long, lean fingers. Kicking her was out of the question. His legs were too short.

"What shall we do with him, my lady?" said the nursemaid, clutching the dog. "Give him a taste of our mixture?"

The marchioness shook her head. "There'll be scarcely enough as it is. We must save every drop for the after-dinner wine."

"Smother the little wretch?" the nurse suggested, feeding the wriggling lapdog a bit of cake.

Ermengarde considered. "Too much bother," she said at last. "Best just drop him out the window."

Hefting Rafiddilee into the air as easily as a sack of potatoes, she rose. Desperately, Rafiddilee struggled and kicked, but the marchioness simply held him at arm's length and marched resolutely to the open window. Rafiddilee thrashed and writhed. Cursing, the marchioness nearly lost her hold, recovered it, and heaved him up over the sill. Thrusting him out into the pelting rain, she smiled at him and released her grasp.

Down Rafiddilee dropped, straight down through darkness toward the cobbles below. The wet stones rushed up to meet him so the little man nearly fainted with fright. But suddenly, with a mighty jerk, he was no longer falling. It felt as if something stronger than Ermengarde had reached out and snatched him by the shirt. It was the thorny briar, its spines entangled in the fabric. The rain continued pelting all around as there Rafiddilee dangled, caught midway between the tower window and the pavement below.

At the banquet that evening, the marchioness was talking gaily with the queen. As the main courses were served, the lady Ermengarde told such witty jests that at times the queen was nearly helpless with laughter. Her great-uncle, however, was not laughing. He had waited for Rafiddilee in his chambers before dinner, but the little dwarf had never arrived. The archduke was worried as to what might have befallen him, yet when he noted her fool's absence to the young queen, she seemed unconcerned.

"He's probably in the kitchen, stealing a pastry," she said airily. "You know Rafiddilee!"

The lady Ermengarde was tugging at her elbow, urging her away from conversation with her great-uncle. The marchioness was in a fine mood, her jokes very wicked and merry. As the evening progressed, the queen's regent became more and more apprehensive. Despite his antipathy for Ermengarde, Rafiddilee had never been absent from one of the queen's official dinners before. More worrisome still, the queen scarcely seemed to notice, so engrossed was she in her cousin's banter.

At last came the after-dinner wine. The marchioness's nursemaid carried the goblets on a tray herself from the kitchen. The tray was to be offered to the queen first, of course, and the foremost goblet contained the majority of the poison she and her mistress had lately concocted. Head bowed, the nurse walked, smiling to herself, for the other cups contained poison as well, but considerably less, a few drops only—not so much as to kill, but enough to make it seem as though death had been intended.

In this way Ermengarde and her nurse had plotted to divert suspicion from the queen's cousin by making it seem as though she, too, had been marked for death. The nurse smiled, mounting the daïs steps, thinking of the rich rewards her mistress would bestow upon her for aiding in this murderous endeavor. She reached the queen's table, dropped a curtsy, and offered their hostess first choice of the wine. Just as the young queen was reaching for the foremost cup, Rafiddilee—wet to the skin and covered with scratches, his shirt badly rent—rushed from behind the tapestry and threw himself at the nursemaid's knees. The old maid went down with a yelp, dropping her tray. All the goblets overturned.

"Rafiddilee!" the queen exclaimed in dismay.

She was about to rebuke him further when she noticed how torn and tattered were his clothes and the deep, blood-red gouges raking his face and forearms. The queen's great-uncle had half risen from his chair, but before anyone else could move or speak, the marchioness's little silken-haired dog ducked out from underneath the table and dashed over to lap up the spilled wine.

"No, Tidbit!" cried Ermengarde. Now this little dog was one of the few things in the world the wicked marchioness could find it in her stony heart to love, and before she could think, she was crying, "Nurse, keep him away—"

But the little dog had already lapped from the queen's own cup—and it had taken no more than a half dozen laps before it fell over in agony. The marchioness began to wail.

"Why did you not shut him up in our apartments as I bade you? He was not to be at table this night!"

"Fool," shrieked the nursemaid. "We are undone!"

For the queen's great-uncle was already summoning the guards. "How could you have known the wine was poisoned," he said to Ermengarde, standing between her and the queen, "unless you had poisoned it yourself?"

Rafiddilee picked himself up and limped over to the little dog, but it was quite past help. Its yelping was terrible, and its death throes fearful to watch.

"That would have been your cousin the queen, had you had your way, you vile, false-hearted betrayer," the archduke said to Ermengarde as the guards surrounded her and marched both her and her craven nursemaid off to the dungeon. "Had not our brave Rafiddilee discovered your treachery, this would surely have been her majesty's fate."

So saying, he joined Rafiddilee at the side of the dying dog and dispatched the wretched thing with his own dagger, to put an end to its suffering. The queen stood shaken, as did the entire court.

"Great-uncle," she cried, "is this what you have been trying to warn me of all this while, that strangers may come to court not to honor me but to advance their own dark purposes? Would that I had listened! What a maid I have been to have trusted my cousin's flattery instead of your wise counsel and that of my dear Rafiddilee."

She held out her arms to the little man.

"Rafiddilee," she exclaimed, "my fine fool, you have been far wiser than I. Where did you listen and what did you see that told you of my cousin's plot? Where have you been, that you are so torn? Come to me, Rafiddilee, my beloved eyes and ears!"

∽ III ∽

Half a year passed, and the queen was just eighteen. All during this time, besides being the queen's fool, Rafiddilee was also her tireless intelligencer. He brought her news of everything that was happening in the court. Though he could not speak, of course, such was his skill at pantomime that he could convey to his mistress nearly anything he needed her to know. If the queen herself were unable to interpret his gestures, chances were her favorite maidservant could. The queen learned to listen to him above all other counselors. Many were the times his information saved her from a faux pas. His official title became Master Rafiddilee, Queen's Fool and Her Majesty's Eyes and Ears.

The queen was now far more cautious in her dealings with others, courtiers and strangers alike, as well befitted a prudent head of state. She had learned to mistrust all flattery and hearken to the wise counsel of her closest friends: her great-uncle and regent, the archduke; Rafiddilee, her fool; and her loyal maidservant, who had been by her side since childhood.

That she might more easily forget the late falsity of her cousin, which so troubled her still, her great-uncle arranged for her to spend the spring and summer in gay amusements out of doors, such as fêtes and masques, boating excursions, pageants, theatricals, hunting, and hawking. These the sober young queen took to with great delight, for though she had received dancing lessons all her life and well knew how to play the lute and virginal, she had never had instruction in sport before now.

Her great-uncle purchased for her a white palfrey mare that was both willing and easy-gaited. He saw to it that her favorite maid had the use of a pretty dapple gray, equally gentle, and for Rafiddilee, he obtained a wonderful little nut-brown pony, long-legged enough to keep up with the courtiers' larger mounts, and had him trained to lie down at a certain tugging on the reins so that the queen's fool could both mount and dismount unaided.

The archduke also retained any number of aides and instructors on his grandniece's behalf—archers and huntsmen, coursers and dogmen of every kind. To one in particular the young queen took a fancy. He was one of the huntsmen, assistant to the queen's chief falconer. His master's duty was to handle the queen's hawks and instruct her in their use. But the queen grew so fond of his personable young assistant that she began always to inquire of him whether his assistant would be accompanying them on an outing.

This the queen's great-uncle noted with some dismay. The young man in question was hale and well mannered, comely to look at, handled his hawks well, and never put himself forward in the queen's presence. It was always she who spoke to him, asking his view on some point of falconry or requesting a demonstration. The queen's maid was openly infatuated with the man, sighing after him with great shining eyes.

He was a good deal freer in his conversation with the maid, as was fitting, but took no liberties. The queen's attention was far more subtle than her maid's, but the archduke observed that she, too, seemed to watch the young man's every move with admiration. Soon, it seemed, all the court was beginning to take note of the young queen's fondness for her junior falconer. This, her regent knew, would never do.

When he questioned her at midsummer, as delicately as

he might, as to her seeming attachment for the young man, she dismissed his concerns with a laugh, saying she asked for the young falconer only because her maid was so fond of him. This the archduke pretended to accept, although he was not at all sure it was entirely the case. He complimented his grandniece on her care for her dear maid's happiness and discussed the necessity of a sovereign's avoiding even the appearance of impropriety.

She wholeheartedly agreed, and he was secretly relieved to see that matters had not advanced too far in the wrong direction. Three weeks later, the archduke found the young man a post as chief falconer at his own estate, far from court. The queen accepted his resignation with dignity and grace, but her sadness could not be entirely concealed.

Her handmaid, on the other hand, was nearly beside herself with distress, so much so that her mistress felt constrained, although reluctantly, to allow the girl to follow the young falconer to the archduke's estate and join the sewing women there, which position the queen's regent graciously provided for her. The two were married within a few months' time, and the queen's sorrow was put off by the court as her missing the company of her devoted maidservant.

Her regent, of course, knew better, but all was for the best. A hard thing, perhaps, but necessary for the good of the kingdom and his grandniece's good as well. Better, perhaps, if she could not admit to herself much less to him the ultimate cause of her sorrow. Or, perhaps she did not even know herself whence her sorrow came. High time she were wed.

He remained close at her side thereafter, striving to lift her gloom in whatever way he could, and hired her two new maids-in-waiting, each of whom had a sunny disposition. But the queen took little note of them. She remained gloomy and distant. Rafiddilee proved her greatest solace, ever beside her, ever ready with a caper or a cartwheel, a lively tune on his little pipe or a jig. Gradually, it seemed, the queen's melancholy lifted. By Christmas, she was seen to be smiling again and even, now and again, making a gentle jest.

On the night of the queen's nineteenth birthday, her regent arranged for her diversion a grand celebration, with a banquet and players, and sumptuous fare. The queen received wonderful gifts from all her courtiers and foreign dignitaries as well. In return, the archduke saw to it that she gave them a feast to remember. The entertainment was magnificent, and Rafiddilee's antics were the life of them all. Her spirits seemed higher than at any time since her beloved maidservant had left court to marry the young falconer.

After the banquet, as the queen prepared for bed, her great-uncle came to see her. She sat at her vanity in her night cloak, while one of her two new maidservants took down and combed out her long black hair and the other applied balms and perfumed unguents to her face and hands. They seemed a merry enough pair, very cheerful and energetic, but the queen's uncle noted in some sorrow that their mistress did not seem to confide in either of them as she had done with her previous maid.

"Dear niece," said her great-uncle, "tonight you are nineteen years of age. In just another year, you will be twenty. On your twentieth birthday, you will become the ruler of this land, and my duties as your regent will be at end."

She smiled at him, a little wearily perhaps, for the evening had been a long and demanding one. For the last year or so, he had been allowing her to assume more and more of the burden of diplomacy he had formerly shouldered. All in all she was doing quite well. A bit too sober at times—but better that than the reverse. And she was tolerably fond of him, which he considered a great mercy, for he wanted only her own and the kingdom's good.

"Now a ruling queen should be married," the archduke continued, "so that she may have children to ensure the line of succession."

"You think, Uncle," murmured the queen, "that I should be thinking of taking a husband?" The one maid who had finished combing and plaiting her mistress's hair, was now massaging a sweet-scented oil into the royal temples. The other girl was trimming her mistress's nails.

"Just so, grandniece," the archduke replied. "Perhaps sometime in the next year, you should consider choosing some eligible prince or nobleman to be your consort. If you are able to make a decision in good time, arrangements could be made for you to wed him at your birthday coronation."

"Have a triple ceremony?" she inquired, opening her eyes. "To celebrate my coming of age, crowning, and marriage all in a day?"

She considered a moment, smiling ever so slightly. The

queen's regent was delighted that the idea so immediately appealed to her. Indeed he had been right in his thinking that it was quite time to see the succession assured. His grandniece smiled at him.

"Uncle, it sounds enchanting!"

"And practical," he replied. A kingdom so small as this could not afford to dispense with practicality. "So doing, we might spare the expense of three feasts and put them all into a single grand occasion."

The queen gave her assent, and so for the next month spent the greater part of her time writing personal invitations to all the dukes, margraves, earls, barons, and other eligible lords of countries far and near. She ordered an entire wing of the castle furnished to accommodate them, with scores of extra servants hired to attend them. She had her horse dealers comb the countryside for the finest mounts available, that her stable should not appear wanting in the eyes of the visiting nobles.

Next, she bade her gardeners clip and trim the gardens as never before, putting in countless new flowers and shrubs. Her masons repaired and renovated every inch of the castle, while tapestry weavers created scores of new and vividly colored hangings. Lastly, she commanded her dressmakers to set to work at making her beautiful new clothing to wear before her distinguished guests.

In a few months' time, the nobles began to arrive from everywhere under the sun. She welcomed each one of them personally in a private audience. Each had a gift to bestow upon her and tales to tell of his kingdom and travels. Masques and revels were planned, that the queen might become even better acquainted with her suitors, to every one of whom she gave a fine, graceful horse, so that even if he went home unchosen, he would not depart empty-handed.

And Rafiddilee? Where was the queen's fool during all this bustle? He was everywhere. He was in the kitchen where the cooks were creating culinary works of art for the pleasure of the guesting nobles. He was in the armory, where special swords and lances were being created for the contests and tournaments. He was making a nuisance of himself in the spinners' and weavers' chambers, tangling himself in their skeins of thread until they shooed him out, a few strands still clinging to him. And he was with the queen every morning as she told him all about each new arrival. Truly he was everywhere.

And such a time had never been seen at the queen's court before. There were feasts and banquets, promenades and dances, tournaments and competitions, hunts and hawkings, leisurely rides down the river in barges, and picnic rambles over the hills on horseback. The fair young queen, even more the center of attention than ever before, seemed almost gay. Clearly she was well distracted from her grief.

The court had never had a grander time. More and more nobles were arriving every day—and some leaving as well, for these had seen rightly enough that the queen's eye did not fall upon them any more than it did upon others. They were not her heart's choice, and so they took their horses and their leave and returned to their own lands, full of tales of the marvelous months they had spent at the young queen's court.

But strangely, with the flower of all the noble youths in the region around her, the queen could not find any she liked more than a brother or a friend. Privily, her thoughts strayed over and over to the young falconer with whom she had, not a year past, been so taken and ashamed to admit as much to her great-uncle or even to herself. But he was married himself now, and she knew she must put him entirely from her thoughts.

How she envied her former maid, now happily made a wife, having been free to choose the man she wished, while the young queen herself might only have a marquis or a count—and soon—whether she truly fancied him or not. But not just yet. Her special gift—a beautiful prancing, arch-necked sorrel roan destrier—which she wished to give to the nobleman she eventually chose, remained ungiven.

Then one day he came. He was a young prince of one of the grand states that bordered to westward the queen's far more modest one. He was the youngest of the three sons of that land's king, not more than a handful of years older than the queen herself, and seemed to share her quiet, serious temperament. Gazing upon the prince, for the first time since she had lost her falconer, the young queen felt her heart stir.

Truly his face and figure were something to behold. His hair was as fair red-gold as the rising sun. His eyes were the misty blue of a morning sky. His nose was straight and high-bridged, his jaw firm, his teeth white and evenly place/

His figure was athletic and trim, and he stood a good height, but not too tall. His laugh was sincere, his words well chosen, and his wit keen and clear. Almost from the moment she saw him riding into the courtyard on his chestnut with a white-starred forehead, she thought that he must take the sun with him wherever he went.

After her private audience with him later that afternoon, she was sure of it. He spoke her language fluently, with only the barest trace of accent. And he was the first to ask her to tell him of herself, as well as replying courteously and completely to her questions of him. For his gift, he gave her a simple but elegantly crafted brooch of polished silver surrounding a beautiful night-blue stone. It was exactly the color of her deep blue eyes.

"How were you able to match it so exactly," she exclaimed in delight as she pinned it to her breast, "without ever having seen me before?"

"My father's ambassador told me, my lady," replied the prince, "that your eyes were as dark a color as the evening sky. So I called my jeweler to my chamber window one evening and pointed to the west, where the sun had lately sunk away. I told him, 'Make me a silver pin fit for a queen, with a stone as blue as that.' And he did. I am most gratified if it has pleased you."

"Now for my gift to you," the queen replied. She rose and walked with him across the royal audience hall to the balcony overlooking the stable yard. To the stabler, she called, "Bring the sorrel roan!"

Then the archduke smiled, for he knew. The young man was well chosen, high born and well bred, and provided a valuable alliance to a powerful neighbor—yet not so near the throne of that realm as to make for divided loyalties or bring his and the queen's eventual heirs too much to the attention of that foreign king. The queen's regent smiled both with affection for his grandniece and relief for his country's welfare, satisfied that within the year he would relinquish his duties as regent with both the young queen and her kingdom well settled.

So save for the queen's intended, the prince, all the visiting young noblemen at court went away, riding or sailing back to their own realms. Most were not greatly disappointed at not having captured the queen's eye, each had had a few months of the most excellent entertainment and board, and now a new horse besides. The queen thanked them all graciously and invited all to return upon her coming birthday to attend her coronation and wedding.

As for Rafiddilee, he had not understood so much as a whit of why so suddenly all the young men had converged upon the castle, or why so many feasts and competitions had been given, or why the cooks had made such a steady stream of exceptionally tasty delicacies. Of course, he had enjoyed the fun and merrymaking while it had lasted, even though the queen had oftentimes been so busy she had barely had time for him. To his reassurance, they had, more often than not, managed to take their usual morning hour in the garden together.

Nor did he understand why so suddenly all the young men had disappeared, except for the young foreign prince with the red-gold hair. Not that Rafiddilee disliked him—not at all. He was ever ready with a kind word and in all ways most considerate of the queen's fool. It was only that he seemed determined to linger long after the others had all gone home.

Well, now at least, so Rafiddilee reasoned, things would begin to get back to normal. As soon as this last young man could be encouraged to depart, he thought, things would return entirely to their regular regimen. Except that the prince showed no indication of going anywhere. Indeed, the queen had him moved to much more sumptuous apartments much closer to her own.

Within a few weeks, Rafiddilee saw that things were far from reverting to their former course. Indeed, the whole castle seemed to be entering a new and infinitely more concentrated state of frenzy. The tailors and dressmakers were working harder than ever. Bolts and bolts of white silk and spool after spool of gold thread were cut and stitched. The tapestry weavers were all crafting new patterns, while the metalworkers were designing a great set of silverware fashioned all of yellow and white gold. And the jewelers were hard at work on two lovely, bejeweled crowns and a beautiful silver ring.

But these were not the changes he noticed most. What troubled him greatly was that even though all but one of her many guests were now gone away, the queen had less time for him than ever. She spent all her days, so it seemed, in the company of the prince. She still smiled at Rafiddilee kindly, of course, and gave him a soft word and a nod when she saw him, but she rarely spent time in her privy garden with him anymore. She still laughed along with all the court at his antics at dinner, but somehow it had all changed. He did not much feel like being amusing anymore.

Then one morning, he was running to the gate of the queen's private courtyard, hoping she might be there that morning, as she was more and more seldom these days. He had caught a heartsblood dove on the kitchen roof and was eager to show it to her, remembering how she had laughed and wept to see the one fly out of the nosegay he had presented to her on the evening of their very first meeting nearly four years before.

He was hoping with all his heart that she might be there, for these were the only times now when he might be with her alone, and the dove was restless, ready to fly. Reaching the courtyard gate, he stopped in his tracks. The dove flew away as he opened his hands. There before him in the courtyard garden, upon the stone bench beside the well, sat the queen and the foreign prince, hand in hand, speaking earnestly to one another and gazing deep into one another's eyes.

Save for the old gardener and her former maidservant, his mistress had never let another besides himself enter her garden refuge. It had been their private place where he could be as silly as he pleased, and dance and play his fife for her alone. Now the prince was there, and this spot was no longer solely Rafiddilee's and the queen's.

Seeing this, Rafiddilee knew that the queen no longer held a special corner in her heart for him alone. What had been that spot was now the prince's place. So he ran away to the stables and hid in the hayloft above the stalls. He hid there all day and halfway into the night. Nobody looked for him. He heard no searchers calling his name, for the queen had been too busy with her trousseau and her wedding plans to notice his absence and send for him.

Nobody else in the castle had time to care much about his whereabouts. The queen was dining privily with the prince that evening, so there was no grand feast or entertainment to be missed. A little after midnight, Rafiddilee climbed down from the loft and crept back to the queen's apartments, where, four years ago, he had been given a little chamber hardly bigger than a linen cupboard, and a child's trundle bed in which to sleep.

He had resolved to let no sign of his grief show, thinking that perhaps in time, the queen might tire of the company of the prince and think once more of her loyal little fool. So the months passed, and Rafiddilee kept his grief locked tight inside so that no one, save perhaps the queen's great-uncle, guessed how deep his heartache ran. One morning, as the appointed day drew near, the archduke came to the queen.

"My dear," he said to her, "I have a difficult matter to put before you. As the day of your coronation and wedding approaches, far be it from me to do anything to diminish your happiness, but the matter must be dealt with, and swiftly."

The queen turned from her writing desk, where she was reviewing petitions, a task to which, before this year, her great-uncle had always attended.

"What is it, Uncle?" she asked him earnestly.

The old lord was glad to see that her coming marriage had not, as it did some maids, made his grandniece flighty. He was confident that she would assume her future duties as sovereign with all the seriousness and attention that they merited.

"It is the matter of your fool," he said simply.

"Rafiddilee?" she asked him, puzzled. Then, half rising in alarm, "What is the matter? Is he ill?"

"No, no. Nothing of the sort," her regent assured her. "Sit down, my dear, I pray you. But the matter is serious, no less."

The queen reseated herself and gave him her full attention. She had been so busy these last weeks—no, months—that she had scarcely had time to think of the dear little man. She looked forward to the aftermath of the grand celebration to come that she might once more have leisure to enjoy his company. Her great-uncle's suggestion that Rafiddilee might somehow be in difficulty pressed on her heart. The old man sighed.

"Your intended's father has written me a letter," he began, drawing the missive from the inside of his doublet to show to her. "Do not be alarmed. He remains delighted at his youngest son's contract to wed you, and wishes the pair of you many years of great happiness together, and many fine strong children, and so on. But he does have one major concern."

"What is that?"

The archduke thumbed through the pages, searching for the passage, found it, and began to summarize.

"He is concerned for the health of your future children. His first consort bore a child that was misshapen. It died at birth, and she not long after. This was a decade or more before your intended was ever born, by the way," he added, glancing up. "He and his elder brothers are the issue of the king's later marriage. I am sure the prince knows nothing of this."

The queen looked at her regent. "The poor king. I mourn his loss," she said. "But what has this to do with Rafiddilee?"

"Patience, I pray. I am coming to that. His first wife kept a dwarf among her serving women. She accompanied her mistress everywhere and attended at the birth. The king blamed her for his child's misfortune and his wife's subsequent death. He had the dwarf maid put to death for high treason, saying it was her nearness to his consort that had caused the harm."

"But that is folly," protested the queen indignantly.

"No less," her regent reminded her gently, handing her the letter, "he is a powerful king. Folly or no, his words should be weighed with care."

The queen set the missive down unread. "Does he mean," she demanded, "to have me put away my fool?"

"He fears for the health of his future grandchildren," the archduke answered with a sigh. "His wishes are misguided, I know, but he is adamant. He and I have exchanged several letters on the subject. What you have before you is merely his latest. He will not yield. He insists that you send Rafiddilee away."

"Never!" The queen was on her feet now and near tears. "I love my fool dearly. I will never send him from me."

"Of course," her great-uncle said soothingly, "nor am I suggesting that you do. Now listen: Your intended's father is old, nearly as old as I, and not in the best of health. He will not live forever. I advise only that you put Rafiddilee out of your privy chambers for a while, a few months, a year. Perhaps the king will soften, or become preoccupied by other matters. Illness may take him, God willing, or more likely, you will be brought to bed of a healthy child, and the old man's fears can be set to rest. Then, if you so wish, you can bring Rafiddilee back into your apartments. Till then, he is welcome to stay with me."

The queen paced back and forth, quite agitated. Much as she did not wish to, she understood the wisdom of her regent's words. Painful decisions were part and parcel of growing up and assuming the mantle of responsibility her great-uncle had heretofore shouldered.

"He would remain at court, you mean," she said carefully, "and retain his title and his place?"

The archduke nodded. "He would remain your official fool, and entertain at all your banquets and royal functions, as before. He might still attend you in your audience hall when you receive court visitors. Only not so near as to cause your future father-in-law discomfiture. For the time being, he must no more sit beside you at banquets, or attend you alone in your garden, or sleep in your chamber, as those places must belong to your husband now."

Slowly, the queen nodded. "Very well. I will do as you advise in order to spare my father-in-law's feelings. But not forever. I have no wish to give up my fool."

Her old regent rose, relieved, embraced her, and kissed her brow. "Already you are becoming a wise and careful queen."

"I thank you for your prudent council, Great-Uncle," she answered. "I will prevail upon my husband-to-be to approach his father on this matter at the earliest opportunity." But she felt troubled still. "I pray you," she bade him, "say nothing of this to Rafiddilee. I would be the one to tell him this regrettable news."

The archduke nodded and took his leave, though privately he wondered when it would be between now and the ceremony that his grandniece would be able to find the time to attend to this among all her many other duties. Rafiddilee, of course, knew nothing at all of this conversation. The archduke had made quite sure before ever he had approached the queen that her fool was far away, down by the fishpond, finding turtles for the cook.

By the time Rafiddilee returned to the queen's apartments, she had already gone to the sewing room for the final fitting of her white silk gown, and then after that, to the music master's to discuss the morrow's fanfares and other flourishes, after that to inspect the decking of the banquet hall, then to chapel, then to a light supper with her intended, who was looking nearly as excited and harried as she. Then after that, on to other things, so that by the time she returned to her apartments and looked in on Rafiddilee, he was already asleep in his trundle in the little linen cupboard outside her chamber door.

The following morning, the queen called him into her privy chamber. He came at once, for she had not done so for many months. When he arrived, the queen stood attired in a magnificent gown all of white silk with gold stitching. She greeted him with a warm smile and presented him with a new suit of clothes of the same white silk cloth, golden-stitched. There was even a cap with an ostrich plume. Rafiddilee had never owned anything even half so fine, and his heart leapt for joy, for he thought perhaps the queen still kept a place in her heart for him after all.

He turned cartwheels and did handsprings. He tumbled this way and that. He played his fife and danced, so delighted was he that the queen still loved him. Both the queen's new maids were laughing and clapping their hands. The queen, too, was laughing, but also weeping, as she did sometimes when she was happiest. She was trying to get him to stand still long enough to tell him something, but his joy was so great, he could not contain himself.

The two maids were tugging at the queen's arms and telling her she must sit down and let them dress her hair now for the coronation, or there would be no time. As the queen at last let them draw her away, Rafiddilee ran after her and caught her by the hand, which he kissed just on top of the silver ring he had given her four years ago today, for the queen had just turned twenty years old, he knew that much, and there was to be no end of celebration for it.

He skipped out of the queen's apartments in his finery, the white plume on his new cap bobbing, and ran down to the audience hall where all the folk were gathering. Later in the morning, there was a long dull ceremony with prelates in pointed hats droning on and on, and children in golden robes singing hosannahs. The queen entered the hall, draped in a long purple robe, ermine-trimmed, and walked the length of the aisle to the daïs, where sat the throne.

Only there were two thrones now, one high-backed and ceremonious, the other slightly smaller and to one side. The queen ascended the steps and turned to face the well-wishers crowding the hall. The prelate in the tallest, shiniest hat placed a crown upon her head, and then held out another on a purple pillow. The queen took this slightly less elaborate crown and placed it on the brow of the foreign prince who had come to kneel before her.

He was wearing a new suit, too, Rafiddilee noticed. The prince's was also of white silk golden-stitched, and very like Rafiddilee's own, though much stiffer and more richly orna- mented. The little man quite liked his own suit of clothes better, since they let him move so much more freely, and took this as another sign of the queen's preferring him to the young prince and perhaps beginning to tire of him at last. He noted with glee that the prince wore no cap. After today, the queen's fool hoped, perhaps the foreign prince would finally go home.

The prince rose and took the queen's hand in his. The two of them seated themselves upon the twin thrones, the queen upon the grander one, smiling and carrying the crown upon her head as though it weighed nothing at all. Many fanfares and flourishes ensued, followed by a great hullabaloo of cheering from the crowd. Onlookers approached and knelt before them for a long, long time. At last, arm in arm, the queen and the prince rose and departed. Rafiddilee was swept out of the hall in the rush that came after. Everybody seemed to be heading for the supper hall. Rafiddilee was glad for that, for he was very hungry after the long morning's boredom.

Then in the afternoon, there was another great bustle. Pages and servants ran back and forth from the church to the castle carrying all sorts of lovely things. Rafiddilee wandered in the direction everyone was hurrying and found the church quickly filling with lords and ladies of the court bedecked in all their finery. Splendid tapestries of white and gold hung everywhere, while a long, narrow carpet of the same rich material ran down the central aisle.

Rafiddilee's eyes grew wide at the sight of it all. He stood at the doorway, bedazzled, afraid to go in. There the queen's regent found him and presented him with a little silken pillow on which lay a beautiful silver ring set with a stone as blue as the queen's eyes. He told Rafiddilee that soon there was to be another grand ceremony, in the church this time, and what Rafiddilee must do was to stand at the altar with the pillow and the ring and hand the ring to the prince-consort when he should have need of it.

Rafiddilee was not quite sure whom the archduke might mean by "prince-consort," but thought perhaps he might be referring to the foreign prince who had been visiting the queen's court for so very long, refusing to leave. Perhaps this ring was a gift to him from the queen. A parting gift. It was certainly magnificent enough, if a little small for the young man's hand. Perhaps he would have to wear it on a thong about his neck, as Rafiddilee had done with the lady's ring he had received before he had given it to the queen.

And so it was with great good cheer that Rafiddilee, dressed in his new suit of clothes, his cap tucked under his arm, took the silken pillow and the ring and scurried up the aisle to the altar, where the three prelates stood, two in white robes and one in crimson. Presently the foreign prince came down the aisle, garbed in white and gold and wearing the crown the queen had placed upon his head that morning. Surely he looked as handsome as any man who had ever lived.

Then a fanfare sounded. The musicians began to play a lovely tune on harps and flutes. The queen and her great-uncle and her new maids came down the aisle, the queen still wearing her gorgeous gown of white and gold. She wore no purple robe now, so the gown was fully visible, only a long veil floating down from her crown. The veil was white lace and delicately beaded with seed pearls. Obscuring her face from view, it lay like a dusting of snow upon her unbound black hair.

Rafiddilee had never seen the young queen look so radiant. Her great-uncle escorted her to the altar, then moved to stand beside Rafiddilee. The queen's maids stood on the other side. Smiling, the queen herself took the hand of the foreign prince, and the pair of them turned to face three prelates, who droned on in turn, one after another, strange words in solemn tones. The great church was silent.

Then the red prelate spoke to the foreign prince, who turned, beckoning. Rafiddilee felt the archduke urging him forward and realized this must be the moment when he was to hand over the ring. He held up the pillow to the prince, who smiled at him warmly. Taking the ring from the pillow, the young man took the queen's hand. It was only then that Rafiddilee saw in dismay that the queen's hand was bare.

Where was the silver band he had given her, that she had worn on her ring finger all these years? Gone. What had become of it? Had she lost it? And now the foreign prince was slipping the bejeweled ring not onto his own finger, but onto the queen's. The whole church broke into rapturous sighs as the prince lifted the queen's veil and the two of them kissed. A blare of music then, and the pair swept out of the church arm in arm amid a stinging shower of rice.

Rafiddilee stood stunned. He did not know what to

make of any of this. Where was his own ring that the queen had always worn? Clearly he must find out, he must ask her, in pantomime, and at once. But where had she gone? Everyone was leaving the hall. The archduke was bidding him come along, come along, my good fellow, they must not be late to the feast. So there was to be another feast! Rafiddilee's heart lifted. Hurriedly, he donned his cap. Was this to be the foreign prince's farewell feast? Surely the queen would be there.

And she was, of course, sitting beside the foreign prince with her veil thrown back, laughing and chatting, as merry as Rafiddilee had ever seen her. She and the foreign prince held hands and spoke much to one another throughout the evening, the blue stone of the queen's new ring blazing in the torchlight.

The feast lasted into the evening, with toast after toast drunk to the royal pair. The dishes were sumptuous, the music sublime. Countless players and dancers, jugglers and acrobats entertained with marvelous skill. And of course, Rafiddilee was the finest of them all. His antics had never been so delightful, his manner so charming, his playing so enchanting. The whole hall laughed and cheered until tears came.

And yet, it seemed, he could never quite capture the queen's attention. She appeared always to be gazing at the comely young man beside her. He spoke to her, and jested, and laughed, and she did just the same. It seemed the pair of them could never completely turn away from one another or give their full attention to others in the hall. Rafiddilee was baffled, but undaunted. He would ask the queen tonight, in her chambers, after the feast.

At last the feast ended. The queen and the prince made their good nights and left the hall together. Servants began clearing the hall as all the courtiers and guests went off to bed with smiles on their faces, sighing and weeping and laughing all at once. Rafiddilee hurried as best he could through the great throng, back toward the queen's chambers.

But when he neared the queen's door, he found it garlanded with flowers and shut tight, flanked by an honor guard. His few possessions were set out in bundles in the hallway, along with his little trundle bed, which two of the archduke's serving men were just lifting and carrying away. One of the queen's new maids slipped through the door carrying Rafiddilee's cap and boots.

"He's not to be let in, mind. Not on any pretext," she told the captain of the honor guard. "That's by order of the archduke with her majesty's blessing."

She laid Rafiddilee's clothes beside the other bundles, then turned, dusting her hands.

"You're to fetch me when you see him," she told the man as she slipped back through the door. "I'll do as needs to be done."

He had heard the cook once saying the same thing to one of the kitchen maids regarding a scullion she intended to dismiss. Rafiddilee stood stunned. He could not believe his ears. His chest tightened until he could scarcely breathe. The floor seemed to tip beneath his feet. A roaring filled his ears, and the air all around grew cold as a catacomb. The guttering torchlight dimmed and receded till shadows seemed to fill every corner, every space.

One of the distant guardsmen looked up and peered in his direction. The queen's fool turned and ran away down the hall. He fled out into the night and groped his way, gasping, across the cobbled yards and courts to the queen's own privy courtyard garden. He sank down in the darkness under the stars, leaning back against the rough stones of the well, gazing up at the queen's chamber window above, hoping for a glimpse of her.

Rafiddilee laid his cap on the well's edge and thought of the great dark forest in which he had begun his life and the surly woodsman with whom he had lived, always ready with a curse and a cuff. He thought of the traveling players, and the troupemaster who had locked him in a trunk every night. He thought of the young queen, who had laughed and clapped her hands in delight at his leaps and somersaults, who had kissed his cheek and made him her fool, and called him her beloved eyes and ears.

He caught no glimpse of the queen, for a white-and-gold tapestry hung across the window, obscuring all. But what he did hear was the murmur of voices, one of which, by its slight accent, was unmistakably that of the foreign prince. The other, lighthearted and nervous, was the queen's. So Rafiddilee knew beyond a doubt who it was who had taken his place in his mistress's heart. Presently, he heard the queen's maids bidding the royal pair good rest. Then the light went out, and the window grew dark.

Rafiddilee pulled himself up onto the lip of the well. The bucket had been hoisted and set to one side. The queen's fool sat a moment gazing down into the cool, deep water far below. The shadowed surface was smooth, like a mirror's face. He discerned dimly a faint, pale gleam: the white suit of clothes the queen had only this morning given him. His own visage was obscured by shadow. He could make out nothing of his own wizened cheeks and crooked mouth, his drooping eyelid and both brows perpetually lifted as though in surprise. It might almost have been the prince's visage gazing back at him.

He felt as though if only he could see more clearly and understand, he might learn why the queen had decided to put him from her and love the prince instead. But he could not get his mind around it. It ran away from him like spilled ink, like a bird fluttering.

The pain in his heart made his fingers numb. Peering, craning, he did not even feel the well's edge slip his grasp. The long fall was mercifully swift. The castle slept. No one heard the splash. And in the morning, one of the queen's maids came running into the queen's chambers where she and her new husband sat at breakfast. The girl was shouting.

"Your majesty! O my lady, come quick. The gardener says—your little dwarf. Rafiddilee has fallen into the well. He's dead!"

The young queen leapt to her feet with a cry and dashed down the stairs with her chambermaids and the prince-consort at her heels. Outside in the garden, her uncle and some of the guard and many of the courtiers stood, peering over the well's edge and milling about in dismay, for they had heard the maid shouting all the way across the courtyard, down the hallways and up three flights of stairs.

"Out, out, all of you!" cried the queen. "This is my privy garden."

Presently only herself and her husband, her great-uncle, the two maids-in-waiting, and the gardener remained. The prince-consort shook his head.

"But what was he doing here so late at night? The well's edge is so high. How could he have fallen?"

Sadly, the gardener shook his head. "My lord, I doubt he fell." He held in his hands Rafiddilee's white-plumed hat. "I found this on the well's edge."

"How many times did he dance for my lady there upon the well's edge, capering and cartwheeling, so sure-footed," murmured one of the maids.

The prince-consort stared at the pair of them, shocked. "But who could wish ill to such a cheerful little man?" he asked. "The whole castle loved him. He had no enemies."

"No true friends, either, so it seems," the archduke answered solemnly, with genuine regret.

The other maid spoke up. "One of the guards said he saw Rafiddilee in the hallway last night, just after we took his bedding out—but the little man ran off and the guard didn't think to go after him. He only just mentioned it, my lady. I was coming to tell you when. . . ."

She glanced at her companion, who had brought their mistress the news.

The young queen began to weep then, and neither her great-uncle nor her husband could comfort her. At last, one of the maids-in-waiting asked, very gently, "My lady, shall I bid someone come and take him out?"

"What?" said the queen, quite distracted and beside herself. "Oh, no. No. No one is to disturb him. Pray bid the masons wall it up. Wall up the well."

Then she turned and walked away, deeper into her garden, where she stood quite alone, leaving the rest of them standing at a loss beside the well.

∽ IV ∽

A handful of years ran by. The young queen and her consort lived together contentedly enough, save that the queen was never after so merry as she had been when Rafiddilee had been her fool. She refused to engage another fool, though the court would have greatly enjoyed one. And she could abide no tumblers or jugglers at courtly entertainments, nor could she bear to hear the sweet trilling of a fife. She was much alone in her privy garden, into which she would allow no one at all to enter now. Often she would sit by the walled-up well, gazing at the plain, silver ring she now wore on a silken thread about her neck.

"Rafiddilee," she would often say to herself, "my fine, crooked little man. My friend, my fool, my eyes and ears. You had everything to live for. Why? Rafiddilee, why?"

The well held no answers for her. Since it had been walled into a tomb, no echo sounded from its depths. The queen went about the business of her court and of her marriage dutifully enough, but there seemed always a measured melancholy that no merriment might lift.

The queen bore her husband a single living child, a daughter, straight and strong and as fair as her father, who adored her, for he was a kind and loving man. The queen's great-uncle took ill of a fever one fall and died before winter. That spring, her husband's father went to war with a neighboring state and both his elder, unmarried sons were killed. The prince-consort was then required, with great regret, to return to his father's kingdom, for he had now become, quite suddenly and unexpectedly, its ruler's only surviving heir.

The queen's young daughter missed her father mightily, as did the queen. She and her far-off husband exchanged fond and loving letters, but he, too, died the following year, of a pestilence that swept in from the west. So fiercely did the pestilence rage that the queen ordered the borders closed, hoping to save her people thus, and she did. But not her husband, absent in a foreign court. Now his father, the king of that land, had no heir at all but the queen's and his youngest son's only daughter, who was had just turned five years old.

Six months into the queen's mourning, he wrote his daughter-in-law a letter demanding that his grandchild be sent to him at once to be raised in his own court, since his own kingdom, which she would inherit upon his death, was so much larger and more important than the paltry little nation of her birth, the land her mother ruled. The queen retired to her privy garden. She sat there beside the walled-up well, robed in the somber attire required by her late husband's passing and the coming loss of her only child. The old king's letter lay unfolded on her lap.

"What am I to do?" she said to herself. She had no counselors now, no confidantes. "What would my great-uncle have had me do? Well I know what he would have said: 'Your land is a small one, and so you must listen to the dictates of those more powerful. Why risk war? Send him the girl. She will be well tended.' "

The queen's hand tightened on the letter's edge until the parchment crumpled. "But not by me!" she protested softly, to herself, to no one. "She would not be tended by me. I am her mother. She has already lost her dear father, far younger than I lost mine. Why must she now lose me? And I her?"

The queen sighed, heavily, painfully. She found her mourning dress almost unbearably heavy.

"How lonely I am," she murmured, almost in surprise. "All my friends, everyone I once held close has left me now, save for my daughter. And now, she, too, is to go. Oh, I cannot do it! I cannot. It would crush her heart, and mine. What am I to do? Tell me, Rafiddilee. My heart is breaking. I wish I were dead."

Her own words, being so impassioned, surprised her, and just as she said them, an answer came to her, so suddenly that she sat up straight.

"Rafiddilee, my little man," she whispered, "you thought that you had lost me, that I no longer loved you and was sending you away. That is why you died."

The queen laid down the letter from the neighboring kingdom and reached out to touch the sealed well.

She thought of how, as a very child, she had known her parents' unfailing devotion. Later, she had enjoyed the trusted friendship of her chambermaid. Until his death, she had ever had her great-uncle's wisdom to guide her, and after her marriage, the euphoria of her daughter's birth and her quiet, thoughtful husband's stalwart loyalty.

And yet, nonetheless, she had walled up her heart to follow her head in all matters but one: allowing Rafiddilee to remain at court in spite of her great uncle's qualms of conscience and her own better judgment. It had been the single happiest decision of her life. Her practical, efficient, dispassionate great-uncle had weighed as little all matters of the heart. Regardless of his noblest aim, he had not succeeded in teaching her everything a sovereign should know.

"O Rafiddilee, I never meant to break your heart," she whispered. "My great-uncle loved me. Well I know how much he did. My childhood friend did as well, my beloved first maid who left me to wed the young falconer. My dear husband loved me, and my daughter loves me, too. But I think you loved me best of all. How careless I have been— of all your love. I should have guarded it far more ably than I did. Than I must now do."

With sudden decision, she lifted the foreign king's letter and folded it up again, neatly and precisely, into a little square.

"I will write my late husband's father and thank him for his concern for my daughter's welfare. I will invite him to send her whatever tutors and instructors he may so desire for her betterment. But I will not give her up to him. She is too tender far for that. I must keep her by me while I can and guard what love remains to me. Let him bark all he will of war. He is too old for that, I judge, with far too much to lose, and the pair of us both know it."

She gazed resolutely about her, at the inner walls of the castle all around, from which, upon receiving news of her husband's death, she had had all colorful tapestries and gay hangings removed.

"What a dreary place I have allowed my palace to become. This is no merry home for a child to grow in, or for my courtiers, or for myself. It is half a year since my husband's death. I should wear half mourning now. I must send for tumblers and jugglers again, musicians and players. I think a dancing master, and huntsmen, and a handler of hawks."

She paused a moment, considering, then let her heart decide.

"I will send for my great-uncle's falconer." She thought of her dear maid, dead of the racking cough two summers past. "Since his wife died, so I am told, he has been quite beside himself. A change of air will do him good. How deeply I regret that when word of my friend's death reached me, I mourned alone and allowed my secretary to pen her husband such a formal letter of condolence, that did not say at all what I meant to say. I will say it now, when he returns to court."

Despite herself, her heart lifted.

"How I look forward to seeing him again. I am young enough yet for coursing and falconry, feasting and merry-making. I have been too cautious, too easily led. From this day onward, I must be bold. Life is brief. It can all end tomorrow—or today. I must do whatever lies within my power to savor each moment, every soul and thing that I hold dear. I have given myself over entirely to prudence and reason at the cost of joy. I will do so no longer, and I will teach my daughter to weigh her tenderest sentiments every bit as much as ever her conscience or her head. She will be a cannier person for it, and a better queen."

She stood beside the well that was Rafiddilee's tomb, both laughing and weeping at once. Bending down, she kissed the well's cool, rough stones.

"My eyes and ears? O Rafiddilee, you were more than that. You were my heart as well, and I never knew. It is I who have been the fool."

Rafiddilee rum, rafiddilee ree,
So crook'd and glum. What cumbers me?
Two ears to hear, and eyes to see—
My mind is clear as clear can be.
All's well to tell, I fear, and yet
I pine in sorrow and regret.
Endure tomorrow; when it ends
Another day bereft of friends:
Another month, another year
To count the loss of what was dear.
Aloof, alone—alack, alas!—
In stone, eternity would pass.
Sing fiddilee rum, rafiddilee ree,
Lest gloom become the tomb of me.

The Sea-Hag

I HAVE an unusual sense of humor—which is to say, I don't get most jokes and don't consider myself very funny. I think it has to do with intellect. Life being a comedy for those who think, a tragedy for those who feel, one has to be smart in order to be a comedian. I, unfortunately, spend far too much time emoting to take the world anything but deadly seriously.

Oddly enough, despite my gloomy, Eeyoreish personality, I am, at the end of the day, an optimist. After all, if there weren't even the slightest hope of jailbreaking out of the various messes one makes of one's existence, what would be the point of going on?

So, while I am by no stretch of the imagination a humorist, "The Sea-Hag" is my attempt at literary wit. Such as it is.

The Sea-Hag

THERE WAS once a young man who was his father's mortification and his mother's despair. He seemed to have no talent whatsoever. Not a bit lacking in wit, he nevertheless could not keep his mind on any task that was set to him. His father, a miller, diligently attempted to teach him the trade, but after half a year of his son's grinding orders too coarse or too fine, delivering the wrong sacks to the wrong customers, charging too much, or worse yet, forgetting to take any payment at all, the poor man was forced to forbid his son ever again to set foot within the mill lest the family be bankrupted.

"But Father," his son assured him, genuinely distressed, "I only did as I thought you would wish."

"You're a simpleton," the miller replied.

"Give him to me," the miller's wife said tartly. "I'll teach him."

The young man's mother was a weaver, but sadly, her son fared no better at the loom than he had in his father's mill. He could not string a warp to save his life, nor keep from tangling the threads. If his mother told him to start her a brown linen mantle with a basket weave, she invariably found him attempting a blue woolen blanket with a diagonal stripe. Apparently, even throwing the shuttle efficiently was beyond his capability. At last, in a passion of frustration, his long-suffering dam turned him out of her weaving room on threat—should he ever come near her looms again—of turning him out of the house altogether.

"But Mother," her son protested, truly baffled, "I only did as I thought you would wish."

"You're some sort of changeling," his mother exclaimed. "You look like your father and me, but there's something wrong with you. Why can't you work?"

The young man hung his head. "I couldn't say," he sighed.

Other sorts of labor were tried, but alas, with no better result.

"What's to be done with the lout?" his father asked gloomily after supper one evening. "He eats like a horse and does nothing to earn his keep. The farmer bends my ear with tales of lost cattle and trampled crops. The taverner says he can't keep ale straight from mead. The money changer won't even speak to me anymore."

"Do you think the baker'd reconsider?" the young man's mother ventured.

Her husband groaned.

"Tailor?"

The miller shook his head.

"Blacksmith—"

"No."

The pair sat a moment in baleful silence.

"Sign him up for the army?"

The miller ceased massaging his temples. "There's a thought."

"Mother, Father, hold a moment," their son interjected hopefully. He had been sitting at table in full hearing of their conversation. He held up a battered tin fife he had found half trampled at the fair. "I can be a musician. Just listen."

He blew a few lusty notes. His father clapped his hands over his ears.

"Stop it," his mother shrieked, more shrilly than the fife. "You're splitting my head with that thing. You're no musician. Give me that."

She snatched the whistle from him and threw it in the fire.

"What ails you, son?" his father demanded.

"You perfect dolt," his mother chimed in. "Why can't you do an honest day's toil?"

Their son stared at the puddle of tin rapidly forming on the hearthstones. "I don't know," he said helplessly. "It just isn't in me."

"How about starving to death?" his father snarled. "Is that in you? Do you think we're made out of food? How do you expect to keep yourself if you can't earn a living?"

The young man shrugged disconsolately, which only served to increase his father's headache.

"It's the army for you, my boy," the miller said, rising. "If that doesn't put you in order, nothing will."

"No, Father. Wait!" the young man pleaded, but his father would not be moved. "Mother!" he cried, but she, too, was at her wit's end.

"Perhaps when you've done your stint in the king's service, you'll be willing to apply yourself elsewhere," she said crisply.

"Pack your things, boy," his father pronounced. "We'll walk to Dooming first thing in the morning to enlist you."

So the young man wept and packed his things—and ran away from home in the middle of the night. As determined as his parents were to fashion him into something more to their liking, he was even more determined that he would *not* become a soldier. Though he had as yet not the slightest inkling of his true vocation, he knew for a certainty that soldiery was not the thing.

So he hiked along in the opposite direction from Dooming, stealing a loaf from a windowsill now and again when his hunger got the better of him. The farther he walked, the lower the hills became and the tangier grew the air until, after several days, he came to the sea. The young man had never before seen the sea, and he found it wonderful, dove-gray and foaming, with a salty nip to the breeze that blew from it. Far in the distance, he could see white sails from some vessel just at the limit of his vision.

"Now there's a thing," the young man said to himself. "To ride the waves to horizon's edge and farther still! Perhaps I'll go to sea."

So he continued following the road as it turned and ran along the cliffs above the shore. In half a day, he reached Blissport, a town much larger than the modest hamlet near which he had lived all his life until now. This was a harbor town, with scores of boats bobbing at the wharves and much larger masted ships lying at anchor out in the bay. One of these caught his eye particularly, for it was gracefully made and smartly trimmed, with the most beautiful figurehead upon the prow in the shape of a lovely, bare-breasted mermaid with a fish's tail and long, green hair blown back by the wind.

"Tell me, sir," the young man asked a passerby, "what is that vessel?"

The fellow halted and peered in the direction his questioner pointed.

"That?" he snorted. "That's *The Sea-Hag*. Best steer clear of her, boy. She's a pirate ship."

The fellow moved on and left the young man scratching his chin, considering. Two things perplexed him. The first was what, exactly, pirates do, and the second was how so splendid a boat, with so beguiling a figurehead, had come by such a vile name. As he had no pressing business and no other purpose to distract him, he set off at once to find out, making inquiries of merchants and seamen and others he encountered along the quay. Oddly enough, no one seemed eager to talk about *The Sea-Hag*.

The day wore on. At last, very hungry and weary, the young man took shelter in an ale shop, hoping to beg a pint of stout, as he had no money. By way of striking up a conversation with the taverner, he inquired after *The Sea-Hag*.

"You want to know about that ship?" the taverner said gruffly. "Ask her captain yonder, for there he sits in his cups."

And so it was. Sitting alone at a table in one corner, the young man saw a man about his father's age, but infinitely more hard-bitten and weathered. The man had a dark black beard and three gold teeth. A ring of silver pierced one ear. A pistol and a sword hung from his belt. One leg was a wooden peg.

As the young man watched, the captain of *The Sea-Hag* drained his cup and shoved it to one side, against a handful of empty ones. He began looking about blearily for another. Seeing the taverner now otherwise occupied, the young man quickly snatched an unattended pint from the bar and made bold to cross the room and set it before the pirate captain. The man eyed him suspiciously.

"There now, what do you want?" he muttered.

"To make you a gift of this fine ale, Captain," the young man answered, "and to ask you for something in return."

The captain sniffed the mug and took a cautious sip. "It's mead, you lunk," he said curtly, then took another swill, "but sweet enough. Say on. What would you have?"

The captain indicated the chair across from him, and the young man sat down.

"I want to know about your ship," he said.

"You want to sign aboard?" the other inquired.

"I want to know how she came by her name."

The captain's eyes narrowed. "That you might learn only if you sailed with me a good long while," he answered. "Why are you asking? Do you want a job?"

The young man shook his head. "Nay, sir. That's just it. It's a job I'm trying to avoid at all costs. I've tried work, but I just don't seem to be good at anything."

"Hm." The captain scratched his bushy beard. "Have you considered piracy? It's the furthest thing from work there is."

The young man's ears perked up.

"I, too, was once a raw young swain such as yourself," the pirate captain continued. "From up near Dooming, isn't it? Aye, I recognize the accent. I wasn't much good at anything, either, and spent far too much time wondering why that might be—until I ran away to sea, and *The Sea-Hag* answered all my prayers."

Seemingly from nowhere, the captain placed a gold coin on the table. The young man leaned nearer, his eyes wide.

"Take this over to the barkeep, now," the captain instructed. "To pay my tab and buy me another pint of ale. Mark you that it must be *ale*, boy. It's ale I want. And something for yourself. Whatever you like. You look dusty dry."

The young man happily complied, bringing pints for both himself and the captain. The two talked on, or rather, the captain talked, describing the delights of piracy and the merits of plunder for spilling vast quantities of gold into a man's lap without needing to do a moment's labor in return for it. And the young man listened, drinking up the captain's words as deeply as the spirits his companion pressed upon him until, two hours later, after his fifth cup, the young man's eyes rolled back in his head, and he slid gently from his chair onto the floor.

Seeing this, the pirate captain drained his own cup and what remained of the young man's, fished him out by one ankle from under the table, slung him snoring over one shoulder and, peg leg or no, carried him easily out of the tavern, down to his rowboat at the docks, and out to *The Sea-Hag*, which was lying at anchor in the bay, awaiting only its captain's return to set sail. By the time the young man awoke to find himself a conscript with no means of returning home, they were far out to sea.

"This is worse than the army!" the young man gasped, staggering to one rail and puking over the side.

But it wasn't. As soon as the seasickness and his hangover passed and he was able to keep a bit of food down, he gained his sea legs and began to discover that there actually existed certain similarities between the idyllic life the pirate captain had described and the one the young man now began to lead. Pirates were far from idle, true—there was much to learn of swabbing decks and trimming sails—but they were also lazy, and spent fully as much time devising ways to avoid work as they did actually performing it.

As time went on, the young man found he loved the tang of the sea air and the toss of the waves. His shipmates were companionable enough, all useless fellows like himself.

There was plenty of grog to go around, and the ship's cook was better than decent. The plundering—though there was not nearly as much of that as the captain had, in the ale-house, led him to believe—was a merry enough enterprise, and moderately profitable.

Best of all, *The Sea-Hag's* captain took a shine to him, and though he never spoke a word of the origin of their vessel's name, he did begin teaching the young man such singular skills as mapmaking and navigation. His young protégé, being only lacking in good sense, not brains, picked it all up in a trice and was soon plotting and charting and dead reckoning with a will.

Not many months had passed before the young man was calling himself ship's navigator and swaggering about the decks as though he owned them. His shipmates, being affable, feckless brutes, put up with all this in a high good humor, which only encouraged him. Alas.

After nearly two years at sea, the day finally came when the pirate captain went belowdecks with the first, second, and third mates to polish off a keg of plundered brandy, carouse, and consult their treasure maps—leaving their young, inexperienced ship's navigator alone at the helm. It was a mighty mistake, but most of the rest of the crew were too drunk to stand, so it was not as though the captain had a wealth of alternatives.

"Sail boldly, boy," the captain slurred, clapping the eager young fellow on the back for luck. "Do as I'd do. Make me proud." So saying, he went below.

All went well for an hour or two until, of a sudden, *The Sea-Hag* found herself among dangerous reefs. The young man was not at all sure what was to be done, but far too willful to admit his quandary. Various groggy shipmates pleaded with him to trim the sails and plot a new course, or at least let older, more experienced hands take the wheel, but the young man shook his head.

"The captain left me in charge, so I know best. Steady as she goes."

"Have it your own way, then," his uneasy mates replied, throwing up their hands in despair. Before the third hour was up, the young man had run *The Sea-Hag* soundly aground and breached her hull besides. The pirate captain was furious.

"You reckless nincompoop," he cried, storming back on deck. "What have you done to my ship?"

The mortified young man blushed and crossed his arms, still too stubborn to admit his error. "I sailed her boldly, Captain, as I thought you'd wish."

"Sailed her onto the rocks, you bilge rat," roared the captain. "Is that what you thought I'd wish?"

The young man hemmed and hawed.

"Well, how was I to know," he burst out at last, "what you or any other living soul might want?"

"Use your noggin, you lunatic," the captain exclaimed. "Are you yourself not a living soul? Extrapolate!"

The young man cast about him at his sundry shipmates—uplanders and lowlanders, Finns, Turks, Cathaymen and Moors, all milling about on deck now in assorted stages of inebriation, hangover, and stupor. Old and young, fat and lean. Several of them were actually women pretending to be men.

"But we're all different!" he argued. "None of us wants the same thing—and you of all folk should know that."

The moment the words were out of his mouth, he realized he had taken a grave misstep.

"Don't presume to tell me my business, boy," the captain growled drunkenly. "All men are the same. If you haven't learned that, you've learned nothing. I've done with you. Fetch the plank!"

Though his shipmates muttered unhappily, they clearly feared their captain's ire more than they were willing to risk their own skins in a mutiny to save their friend. A plank was located and lashed clumsily to the rail. The captain staggered over to inspect it, kicked several of the deckhands with his peg leg, and ordered them to do it over. At this point, realizing into what a narrow strait his own pigheadedness had sailed him, the young man fell to his knees and begged for a chance to redeem himself. At last, the captain relented.

"Very well," he mused. "You'll man the brig while we make repairs. If by the time *The Sea-Hag*'s fit to sail, you can't tell me the one thing in this world that all men desire, the sea can have you."

Though far from overjoyed by his captain's decision, the young man had no choice. His fellows, on the other hand, were most relieved at their companion's momentary reprieve and bundled him off belowdecks with the greatest good wishes and dispatch, well assured that the witty lad would soon call a satisfactory answer to mind.

Their confidence, however, was sadly misplaced. There in the dark, cramped, nearly airless brig, their clueless friend spent the next three days clapped in irons, undernourished, desperately racking his brains to remember every wight he had ever known and what each had longed for.

Some, he recalled, had valued riches above all else, others vanity or love. Many, he knew, had desired wisdom, some adventure, some fame. Pleasure had motivated any number of the people he had known. Others lusted after power. A few in his acquaintance appeared to welcome only misery, seeking woe above all other things. But for the very life of him, the young man could not imagine a single desire common to them all.

Repairs to the hull of *The Sea-Hag* were completed by the evening of the third day, and the wretched prisoner passed a sleepless night, well aware that on the following morning he must proffer his answer to his captain or walk the plank. Just as the ship's bell was dolefully tolling the midnight hour, he heard softly whispering from the porthole behind him the gentlest, most melodious, most beautiful voice he had ever known.

"Do not despair," it said. "I understand your plight. If on the morrow none of your answers please your pirate master, clap your hands to your mouth and call the name of this vessel three times. I will come to your aid."

The young man jumped up and lumbered to the dark

brig's tiny porthole as rapidly as his chains would allow. As he reached the port, he heard a splash and just glimpsed something pale and indistinguishable disappearing beneath the moonlit waves. He stood a long while at the porthole, transfixed, hoping for another glimpse, but he saw nothing more.

At last, he retired to the brig's tiny berth, where the second half of the night passed as sleepless as the first—save that the young man's thoughts were now consumed not with contemplations of a watery grave, but with a burning curiosity over who or what his mysterious helpmeet might be. Surely she must be as lovely as her voice!

The following morning, the young man's cheerful shipmates came to fetch him. His chains were industriously struck away. The cook fed him something a bit more nourishing than the bread and water he had heretofore received. Then he was brought up on deck to stand before the pirate captain, full sober now, but in no better temper than he had been in when they had parted three days before.

"Well," he said, "my feckless apprentice—have you an answer for me? Can you tell me what it is that all men want?"

The young man was too proud not to try his own answers first. "Riches, vanity, love?" he asked.

"What about monks?" the captain snorted.

Undeterred, the young man tried again.

"Wisdom, adventure, fame?"

The other snarled deep in his throat—or it might have been a scornful laugh. "I never met a spendthrift who wanted to be wise, nor an accountant who sought adventure or fame. Is that all you can manage?"

The young man swallowed hard.

"Pleasure, power . . . uh, misery?"

The pirate bared his three gold teeth. "Surely each of those is a thing *some* of us want," he sneered, "but none of them is what *all* of us want. I thought you cannier than this, knave. You disappoint me. Fetch the plank!"

This the third mate dutifully trotted off to do, but before his fellows, the first and second mates, could so much as lay a finger on the young man, he had clapped his hands to his mouth and shouted, "Sea-hag! Sea-hag! Sea-hag—save me!"

Immediately, the waters to the ship's starboard side began to boil. Flotsam and jetsam roiled to the surface. Schools of flying fish leapt into the air and flitted away. Sharks circled warily. Luminous jellyfish swirled by, poisoned tentacles streaming. And in the midst of all bobbed the most hideous creature any of the pirates had ever seen.

"It's some sort of squid," one of them exclaimed.

"A sea cow!"

"A stillborn whale. . . ."

They all recoiled in horror. For his own part, the young man could only stare. Clad in a fishnet and draped in kelp, her body—what could be seen of it—bore roughly the shape of a scabrous old woman. Her hair was a mass of matted seaweed, full of starfish and crabs. Of her scaly face, only her large and unexpectedly lovely sea-green eyes could be easily seen. The rest was obscured from view by a veil of seaweed—or was it actually hair? A string of shark's teeth rattled about her half-hidden neck. Sand fleas scampered across her crusty skin. Instead of legs, she had a long, silvery eel's tail inlaid with barnacles. Remoras dangled from her sagging flesh, and there rose from her a stench like rotting fish.

"Heaven help me!" the young man stammered. "Are you my rescuer?"

The sea-hag nodded from the waves below. "Aye." And when she spoke, despite her repulsive appearance, her voice was as beautiful as before. "Hoist me aboard."

Most of the crew balked, but as their captain said not a word to the contrary, his first, second, and third mates tossed a line over the rail and heaved with all their might. No sooner had the stinking, seaweed-swathed form of the sea-hag flopped onto the deck than she scooted over to where the captain stood. The pirate lord cleared his throat and, for the first time in the two years the young man had known him, looked somewhat discomfited.

"Well met, good hag," he began. "How does the day find you?"

"As well as that day when last we met," she replied in her beguilingly sweet voice, "though considerably more lonely. Have you come to keep the bargain the two of us struck so many years ago?"

"Uh," the pirate captain uneasily began, "let's not be hasty."

"Twenty years is far from haste, good captain," the sea-hag demurely replied. "That is the length of time you have had the use of this ship which bears my name and all the good fortune that goes with it. I pulled you from the sea half dead, as I recall, and nursed you back to health. Have you come to make good your promise to me, in return for my generosity?"

The pirate captain blushed to the roots of his beard. It was a wondrous thing to behold. "I can't quite remember what promise that might be."

"Why," the kelp-covered monstress replied, "to return in a year and a day to make me a bride."

She batted her long eyelashes at him. Mercifully, the rest of her face remained hidden. The pirate captain choked back a gag.

"I was young and foolish when I made that promise," he gargled nervously.

The sea-hag sighed. "And so was I. Yet I have kept my end of the bargain. Yours is long overdue."

She reached to take his hand.

"I'm a bit past my prime," he protested, snatching his endangered limb away.

"Really?" said the sea-hag. "I don't mind."

"Would you consider a substitute?" the captain asked, stepping hastily out of reach. "One sounder of limb than I, with both eyes in his head and all his teeth? Younger and better looking, too."

He could be quite charming when cornered. Much to

the young man's surprise, he clapped an arm in comradely fashion about his erstwhile navigator's shoulders. Still talking to the sea-hag, the captain continued jovially.

"He's a good lad, smart as a whip. Been like a son to me. If you'd like him instead, I won't stand in your way."

"Hm," the sea-hag answered noncommittally. Her eyes flicked to the young man. The seaweed rustled.

"Now hold a moment," the object of her deftly redirected consideration started, striving mightily to pull free, but his captain's grip was an iron vise.

"Done then," the older man cried heartily, slapping one thigh as though all parties were suddenly in merry agreement. "I'll wed the pair of you forthwith."

"Wait!" yelped the young man.

"Which'll it be, boy," the captain growled in his ear. His whiskers tickled. "The sea-hag or the plank?"

That brought his prisoner up short. The young man cast desperately about—but being no fool, and quite unable to swim, he took the only course left open to him. "The sea-hag," he answered, "God help me."

"Good man," his master crowed. "I'll accept that in lieu of your answering my riddle. Your debt to me is paid and your liberty restored. Take away the plank!"

This the three mates promptly did, for they were as fond of the young man as the rest of the crew. They and the young man's other shipmates cheered their fellow's reprieve and clapped him on the back. Grog was fetched and passed around, for pirates, as you likely know, will use any excuse to avoid work and carouse instead. The captain himself was in such high good humor that he danced a hornpipe very ably despite his peg leg.

But in the midst of all this heartfelt celebration, the young man himself stood heartsick and morose. While thankful for his freedom and his life, he did not relish the notion of wedding—much less bedding—the sea-hag, even with his eyes closed and his nose pinched shut. The loathsome old wreck really did stink to high heaven. To make matters worse, the dripping horror had slewed up beside him now and taken hold of his sleeve in her coral-encrusted fingers.

"Young man," she said in her disconcertingly beautiful voice, "I have saved your life this day. Can you not do me the honor of appearing grateful?"

"Forgive me, good sea-hag," the young man had the minimal grace to stammer. "I'm badly surprised is all. I thought you meant to ransom me from my captain's justice by supplying me with the answer to the riddle."

"Ah, but I never told you I'd do that, did I?" she asked him sweetly.

"Well, no . . ."

She tut-tutted in motherly fashion. "You just assumed."

The young man squirmed. "Actually . . . yes."

"You need to be more careful about such things," the kelp-covered sea-hag admonished.

"I wish I had been," he answered earnestly.

"Even if I *had* given you the answer to the riddle," she

continued kindly, "did you imagine I'd just hand it over out of the goodness of my heart, asking nothing in return?"

"Well . . ." The young man's head swam. The other's stench was overpowering.

"Silly boy," she chided. "I have to look after my own best interests, the same as you."

The unfortunate navigator felt himself turning several shades of deeper green. "Captain," he called feebly. "I'm having second thoughts. . . ."

At this, the pirate lord interrupted his hornpipe just long enough to unsheathe his cutlass.

"Never let it be said that any aboard my ship does not keep his word," he thundered, rather insincerely, the young man thought, since the captain had, over the last two years, proved himself a shameless liar many times over. However, as the old blackguard was now pointing his blade squarely at the navigator's heart, the younger man chose not to argue the point. "Marry her, my lad, or I will spit you like a fish and grill you."

So truly, there was no appeal. The pirate master had decided his pupil's course. And though the young man's shipmates shouted drunkenly, "No! Never—throw the old hag overboard—" their captain threatened them all to sullen silence with his keen and flashing blade.

"Take heart, my dear," the sea-hag urged her intended, caressing his fine, strong hand between her crusty, cracked ones. "Life with me will not be so terrible. . . ." But if she had more to say, the young man did not hear it, for he suddenly became so seasick, he had to lean over the rail.

Afterward, the pirate captain would brook no delays. He married the unlikely pair on the spot. The young man's shipmates spent the afternoon trying to console their miserable companion—while the sea-hag sat off on one corner of the deck, downwind, drying out, friendless and alone. At dusk, she slithered into the cabin that had been set aside for their wedding night, and, cutlass in hand, the pirate captain goaded the reluctant bridegroom to follow, then locked the door behind him.

A single lamp burned dimly in the room, scarcely illuminating more than the writing desk beside the door. This the young man noted with relief as he entered: at least he need not look too closely upon his repulsive bride. For her part, the sea-hag sat in a heap on the shadowy berth, her desiccated seaweed mere strings and shrivels now, and its fishy reek considerably diminished therefore.

"More blessings for which to offer thanks," the young man grumbled beneath his breath, seating himself at the writing desk, as far from his lately acquired better half as he could get.

"Husband, come to bed," the gentle voice of the sea-hag called through the gloom.

"Soon, wife," he muttered, searching frantically for any means to put off retiring for the night. He seized upon a nautical chart, unrolling it. "I've a bit of work to finish first." But at last, once he had consulted every chart and plotted every course and practiced every pirate's knot he knew, the inevitable could be postponed no longer.

"Why do you delay?" came the beautiful voice from the tattered heap. "Am I so hideous?"

To his horror, the net-draped thing began inching toward him across the berth.

"Um," her panicked husband answered, groping for a compass among the instruments on the table with the vague notion of defending himself. "It's just that I thought you'd been betrothed to the captain all these years. It hardly seems right, your marrying me instead."

"Hm," the sea-hag answered, in that wistful way of hers. "True enough, yet try as I may, I can feel no remorse. He was quite right about being past his prime, you know." She sighed sadly. "He's not nearly so winsome as he was two decades ago."

In her momentary dolor, the young man perceived a ray of hope—immediately dashed.

"You, on the other hand," the sea-hag continued brightly, "are another matter entirely. I think the pair of us much better suited—don't you agree? Now come along to bed."

She had come rather too close for his comfort, almost within arm's reach. In his attempts to pry apart the two tines of the compass, the young man only succeeded in jabbing himself in the hand. He dropped the instrument with a whimper.

"It's the moral aspect of our situation which troubles me, wife," he said manfully.

"Oh? Is it?" she inquired. "Well, in that case, all is not

lost. There *is* a way I might be induced to release you from this marriage."

"There is?" the young man exclaimed in a passion of hopeful anticipation. He put down the wickedly pointed wick trimmer he had been toying with. "What might that be?"

"Why," his shadowy wife replied, "you have only to answer the riddle of what all men want. That is the same option I gave your captain so many years ago, that if he might find me an answer to that riddle, I would not hold him to his promise of marriage. I daresay he's been seeking it all this time and never found it, the poor ninny. Perhaps you can do better?"

"But," the young man protested, "I don't know the answer either. If I'd known, I wouldn't have needed your help."

The unseen creature gave a little snort that might have been a laugh.

"I'll give you a hint," she said beneficently. "Just tell me what it is *you* want. Are you not a man? Above all things in this world, what do *you* want?"

The young man stopped short. He opened his mouth and then shut it again, drew breath as if to speak, then let it out again. At last, he merely gazed about the darkened cabin, struck dumb with surprise. It had never occurred to him to go about solving the riddle in this way. After a few moments, he answered without a second thought.

"To chart my own course. To captain my own ship. To sail wherever I will with no man to say me nay."

"Exactly," the sea-hag said proudly. "Every living soul on

earth feels exactly as you do. It's really rather obvious. Now tell me truthfully, do you still wish to annul our marriage?"

So saying, she snapped her fingers, and instantly the lamp above the table flared as bright as fifty candles. Half-blinded, the young man squinted through the glare. As his eyes adjusted, he was barely able to make out the sea-hag taking hold of the seaweed-tangled fishnet that veiled her and pulling it off over her head. It slipped up and away, all of a piece, to reveal underneath not the horrid sea-hag of his conjecture, but the loveliest creature he had ever seen.

The figure seated before him on the berth had the graceful body of a fair young woman with long, flowing green hair and a silvery eel's tail. A necklace of shark's teeth lay atop her firm, high breasts. She was busily plucking the remoras free, the starfish, the sand fleas, the crabs, and stuffing them all into the bundle of fishnet and seaweed. Next, she dusted off the bits of coral and barnacles that had been clinging to her fingers and tail.

Within moments, no trace of the sea-hag remained, only a beautiful sea-maid, who was in every way the image of the ship's own figurehead. She smelled of sand and sea and clean salt air. Glancing over at the bedazzled young man, she smiled at him prettily and snapped her fingers once more to reduce the illumination in the room to a more bearable level. The young man sat blinking.

"How did you do that?" he stuttered.

"Enchantment," she said gently, "the same as gives such fair good luck to all who man this—"

"But you're so beautiful," he interjected, astonished. "That net, matted with seaweed . . . "

"My wedding gown?" she inquired. "Pay it no further mind. It has served its purpose."

Opening the porthole, she shoved the wriggling, stinking, filthy bundle out. The young man heard a faint splash as it hit the water below. The rancid stench in the cabin immediately vanished, replaced by the clean, salt scent of seafoam. The sea-maid smiled coyly.

"Why don't you get undressed, too?"

The young man rushed to comply.

"But who are you?" he panted, tossing shirt, britches, stockings, and shoes to the four winds. They collided with the walls of the little cabin and slid to the floor.

"Your wife," she answered pointedly. "Whom do I look like?"

"A . . . a sea-maid," he answered, reaching eagerly to embrace her. "Like the figurehead on this vessel."

"I own this vessel," the sea-maid replied, holding him at arm's length. She was surprisingly strong. "My former fiancé has had the use of it these many years, but in truth it belongs to me. I wonder if he realized that in relinquishing my hand, he has relinquished the captaincy of my ship as well?"

"On whom will you bestow the vessel now?" the other asked, trying hard to plant a kiss upon her apple-blossom cheek. Her great ruffled tail batted him effortlessly aside.

"Why, I had thought to bestow it upon you," she said.

"Did you not tell me you most wanted to captain your own ship?"

The young man paused a moment. "Why, yes," he told her. "Yes, I do. More than anything. Well, almost anything . . ."

Yet when he reached once more to take her in his arms, the mermaid turned suddenly away from him and began loudly to sob. Her astonished husband gazed at his lovely bride, weeping as though her heart would break.

"Wife," he cried, "what is the matter? Why do you weep?"

"Am I?" she asked him. "Am I your wife in truth? I thought you wanted an annulment."

"What? No! Of course not," he protested earnestly. "My moral dilemma is entirely resolved. I am determined to be a proper husband to you, from this day forward to . . . um . . . to the end of my days!"

The moment the words were out of his mouth, the mermaid's tears vanished. She turned back to embrace him, laughing.

"Well, then, you had best start considering how to instigate a mutiny," she advised him, "if you would seize the captaincy of your ship. You didn't think that rogue would surrender it to you of his own accord?"

"What? Oh. Yes, of course," the young man answered, somewhat preoccupied. "What is it exactly you would have me do?"

"Let me show you," she answered fondly, now returning

his kisses with an ardor that mirrored his own.

Thus, the young pirate and his enchanted bride spent together the happiest of wedding nights imaginable. The next morning, when he strode out on deck holding the beautiful mermaid in his arms, every member of the crew stood riveted in wonder. The young man had only to set down his bride, seize the former captain's cutlass, and speak a word to the crew. His fellows energetically threw in their lot with him and mutinied without delay.

They set their cursing, sputtering, ill-tempered former captain ashore on a balmy but deserted island and sailed away without a backward glance. Their new captain charted his ship's course with skill and ease, having learned not only when to trust his own wits, but when to bow to the wisdom of others in matters wherein their judgment outweighed his own.

One of his very first orders was to rename their worthy vessel *The Sea-Maid*. At their next port of call, he engaged a barrel maker to install a large swimming vat amidships and another, smaller basin in the captain's cabin, that his beguiling bride might remain comfortably afloat whenever she came aboard. She, for her part, gave the whole crew swimming lessons, which did wonders to ensure their loyalty. Thus it was that the new-made captain of *The Sea-Maid*, his lovely wife, and their jolly crew plundered the seven seas together in perfect felicity forever thereafter.

The Frogskin Slippers

I'VE ALWAYS been fascinated how changes in perspective can alter our view of the world. The slightest adjustment can sometimes cause us to see in a whole new light things with which we had thought ourselves eminently familiar. Microscopes reveal hidden ecosystems flourishing beneath our notice. Night-vision goggles unveil a nocturnal world ablaze with illumination and teeming with activity.

The way water bends light is another, subtler example. Underwater objects appear slightly foreshortened and displaced. A certain kind of lens can distort whatever is observed through it into a fish-eye view—but who's to say, really, which perspective is the more valid or real, the fish's or our own?

The Frogskin Slippers

DEAREST ROSE,

This must be my final letter to you. The physician says my condition now surpasses even his powers to heal. I weaken by the hour. How deeply I regret to be leaving you so young. Ten years is too tender far to suffer a father's loss.

I implore you, in the coming years, to attend to your tutors and be a help to your mother. She means well. Above all, rely on the advice and counsel of your godmother. She is wiser in the way of all things than any of us. Write to her faithfully once a week as you have done me, and do not marry without her consent. I trust her judgment absolutely.

Farewell, my sweetest Rose. Little did I suspect when I left Elverston Hall on the king's business two months ago, it would be never to return. I only wish I might see you again. Express to your mother my undying affection.

I depart this life your loving,
Father

Rose refolded the parchment, the last words her father had written to her before his death in the far-off capital, where he had been serving as interim dean of the Royal Academy. She had not been allowed to attend him, for fear of contagion. Now, years after, she still lived in the high-walled keep in which she had been born. She had never set foot past the strong-barred gate.

Her mother, the baroness, said the forest beyond was full of tigers. Evenings she took her carriage into town for a night of balls and gambling. Rose was always left behind. Her hours at Elverston Hall were drudgery. Her tutors had all been dismissed within a year of her father's death. Since her mother could no longer afford many servants, Rose saw to much of the housework herself. But the baroness was never satisfied.

"Useless thing," she muttered. "Your brothers all married rich merchantwomen, but do they ever send a penny of it home? Your godmother, the grand duchess, arranged such lucrative marriages for them. Pity no one seems to want you. Scrub! The servants are stealing us blind."

Rose bore it all without complaint. What else could she do? Fleeing into the forest would have meant being devoured by tigers. Every week, she wrote her godmother—who was also her great aunt—just as, before his death, she had promised her father she would do. She hoped wistfully that the grand duchess might one day send a carriage to spirit her away to the capital, where life held more than drudgery. The servants all gossiped of the masked balls that were hosted there every night.

So far, however, the duchess never had. Her posted

replies always counseled: *Patience, goddaughter. There will be balls for you in time.* So Rose scrubbed the floors of Elverston and sighed. Her only respite lay in the castle garden where, for an hour each twilight, she wandered alone. Her mother had given the gardener his leave years ago for having seen elves and fairies there. The baroness was very much afraid of sprites. She kept a cat to kill their kind.

Rose was not permitted any books of fairy lore—or indeed, any books at all now. When she had been very young, her favorite volume had been a gift to her from the grand duchess Sophie, a story about a little brown toad who changed into a maiden when kissed, and married a prince's son. After Rose's father had died, his widow the baroness had taken all such nonsense and frippery away. Rose's books, and most everything else, had been sold to raise capital. The country-bred servants were told to keep their tale spinning to themselves.

Rose, of course, listened to the servants whenever she could. They were country-born and so knew all about the wee folk of Faerie. Rose secretly hoped one day to stumble upon a tiny magical person, a slim little mannikin dressed entirely in green, perhaps, or a dew sprite perched on a may-apple or concealed in a flower. She wondered idly what it would be like to be granted a wish in exchange for a kiss. But to her sorrow, she had never seen any elfin folk, in the castle garden or anywhere else.

Since the gardener had been away, the rose hedges had all grown wild. The interior of the garden stood wholly private and quiet and still. A rectangular reflecting pool, very much neglected, lay at the very heart. Straight stone sides trooped in shallow steps down to the silty bottom of the pool, stocked with filmy goldfish, gray-green crayfish, water lilies, and snails. At dusk, little roseate frogs perched chirping along the rectangular pool's edges, making a sound like glass rattles filled with silver beads.

"Kisses," chimed the frogs. "Wishes. Mysteries."

One morning, Rose woke to find her mother's frost-gray tabby rampling the bedclothes, pale paws all over black mud from the garden. A tiny frog struggled in her jaws, deep rose in color, with great golden spots. Releasing him, the cat batted him across the hills and valleys of the white coverlet.

"No, Tab!" cried Rose, catching up the frog. His smooth, moist skin felt soft as a caterpillar. He smelled of watercress.

The cat hissed, yammering as Rose tipped the little frog gently into her silver-gilt jewel box. The filigree was open enough to let air pass through, but close enough to keep him from getting out.

"Don't fear," she whispered to him. "You'll be safe here till I can return you to the garden." She had not time just at the moment. To do so now would have made her late for her morning chores.

She set her pink coral brooch beside him, to keep him company. Carved in the shape of a rose, it had been a christening gift from her great-aunt Sophie, the only jewel she had left. Her mother said the servants had stolen the rest, but Rose suspected the baroness had taken them herself to sell for ball gowns and gaming debts. The cat prowled across Rose's lap and legs, mucking the bedclothes and staring at the jewel box with hot blue eyes. Rose kissed her finger and touched it to the frog.

"Till dusk," she told him, then latched the lid and shooed the cat out, making haste to dress. Her mother was expecting an important visitor tomorrow and would scold unmercifully if Rose did not complete all her duties today. Drawing the chamber door shut behind her and starting down the stair, Rose heard from within her room a faint trilling beginning to sound.

"Kisses," sang the frog. "Wishes. Mysteries."

All day long, Rose daydreamed about her frog. He was quite the handsomest, most elegant creature she had ever seen: sleek and slender, all sinew and bone, with luminous lime-green eyes. Even her mother's constant, fretful chiding could not burden her today. Dusk seemed to come in only a moment, and when the last of her tasks was finished, Rose fairly flew up the steps to her tower chamber. But her jewel box sat silent—still shut, but with the latch now lifted up. Inside, her coral brooch lay overturned—and missing its golden pin. Her little rose-colored frog was gone.

Staring into the empty box, Rose felt suddenly the oddest thought wash over her: that this morning, Tab had captured not a frog, but a fairy man, who had pried loose her brooch pin and stuck it through the keyhole to raise the latch, then levered open the lid and braced it while he slipped through, snatching the pin free after him as the lid banged shut. She pictured him shimmying down the bed-clothes with the pin thrust through his belt and then wriggling out under the door.

Rose burst into tears. Her head swam. She felt flushed and feverish. Her mother must have come looking for something to pawn, found only her daughter's living, chiming prize inside the jewel box, and ground him under heel in a fit of pique. That, or the cat had somehow gotten back into the room and made off with him again. Surely he had been nothing more than a little frog, and now, certainly, he must be dead.

Rose did not go down to the garden that dusk. She went early to bed and took no supper. Her mother did not bother to send anyone up to inquire after her daughter's loss of appetite, being still much occupied with preparations for the arrival of tomorrow's guest. Night poured like cold well water into Rose's chamber. She had forgotten to close the shutter. Beyond the high castle wall, a fallow moon peered over the rim of the woods. Someone, very softly, whispered her name.

"Wake, Rose. Wake," he said. "It's time for the ball."

Rose sat up blinking and peered at the slim figure standing across the room. She needed no candle, for the cool golden moonlight illuminated him: a tall young man, very slender, all sinew and bone. He wore a rose velvet jacket with

great golden buttons. At one hip, a slim golden rapier glint-
ed. He was quite the handsomest, most elegant person Rose
had ever seen. His large, clear eyes were pale, pale green.

"Who are you?" she asked, not the least bit frightened.
"How do you know me?"

"I've often seen you in the garden," he answered, bowing.
"My name is Rane."

Rose frowned. "Are you my mother's guest?"

He shook his head. "No, Rose, though I have been yours
and would like you to be mine. A dance is to be held in my
father's hall tonight. Will you come?"

"Where is your father's hall?" asked Rose. Elverston's
nearest neighbor lay miles and miles away through the wood,
so her mother had always said. She had never heard of any
gentleman called Rane.

"Come. I'll show you," he answered, taking her hand.

Rose hesitated. "I don't know how to dance."

He smiled. "Never mind. The frogskin slippers will see
to that."

Pulling a pair of filmy pantofles from his sleeve, he
handed them to Rose. Thin as gloves, they were the softest
things she had ever held, more supple than doeskin, so
smooth they felt velvety, and yet they gleamed, napless as
satin. As soon as she touched them, she wanted to wear
them. They were deep rose in color, with golden spots. Rose
gasped in dismay.

"How many frogs did you skin for these slippers?"

"Tender-hearted Rose!" Laughing, Rane shook his head.

"Not a one," he added gently. "Frogs that dwell in my father's kingdom shed their skins yearly, every spring. It's these we use to make our guests' dancing slippers."

He glanced at the window, then back to Rose.

"But see? The moon's already free of the wood. If we don't make haste, we'll be late."

As Rose slipped her feet into the weightless frogskin slippers, she felt a strange tingling to the marrow of her bones. The air smelled suddenly of watercress. She found herself no longer clad in her plain, muslin nightdress, but sheathed in a sumptuous ball gown of rose watered silk. Her hair was splendidly coifed and pinned. She felt giddy, light. Her bed seemed all at once much higher above the floor. Hopping down, Rose felt as though she were half falling, half hovering through space.

Rane caught her deftly and set her on her feet, then, taking her hand, swept her from the room without opening the door. They seemed to pass under it. The tower stairs loomed hugely before them, but Rane bounded down in lithe, graceful leaps. Rose followed as if floating. Another passage, another door. Elverston Hall fell away behind them. They began traversing a tangled, thorny wood.

An enormous tigress padded from the trees: frost-pale with charcoal stripes, muddy paws and eyes of burning blue. She snarled at them. Rose gasped and froze, but Rane drew his rapier. Darting forward, he stabbed the great cat in the nose. She retreated, hissing and spitting, into the shadows.

"Don't fear," Rose's escort told her. "You've already saved me from the tigress once. Now your thorn defends us both."

Rose had no time to puzzle out what he meant, for he had taken her hand again and was leading her rapidly on through the last of the trees. Faintly at first, then more and more distinctly, she heard ahead of them a skirling of fiddles and a droning of krumhorns, a banging of tambours and the groaning of viols, the nimble rippling notes of the lute and a wild, sweet piping that sounded almost like bells. It stirred her blood like nothing she had ever known.

Beyond the trees lay a great open ballroom, rectangular in shape and sunken into the earth. Wide, shallow stone steps trooped down to its glitter-strewn floor on all four sides. Rose saw no candles, no fire of any kind. Yet, full of the sweep and the motion of dancers, the hall was ablaze with golden light. Rose halted on the top step, staring down.

"What place is this?" she exclaimed. "I've never heard of it. Is it far from my mother's keep?"

Rane shook his head. "Not at all. Not far. Nearer than you know."

Descending toward the dancers, hand in hand with Rane, Rose felt a sensation like water pouring against her skin. The air felt deliciously cool and dense, redolent of reeds and pond lilies. Her silk gown clung, trailing, swirling languidly, like coral-colored smoke. All her limbs felt marvelously light.

"Come," her escort said, smiling as they reached the ball-room floor. "You must meet the other guests."

He introduced her first to the sisters Cyprinidae, two stout, round-eyed noblewomen in filmy ball gowns of flaming reddish-gold. Rose curtsied.

"Charmed," they murmured shyly, drifting on.

"Have you seen your aunt lately, my lad?" called Colonel Crayfish from across the room. He looked to be a crusty old bewhiskered military officer in a stiff, gray-green jacket. "When is she coming home?"

"Look. Rane's brought a guest this evening. How lovely she is!" cried the Widow Turtle, dancing by on the arm of Deacon Waterbeetle.

Rane confided all their names and titles to her. Rose's senses swam.

Flushed with excitement, she forgot the odd monikers the moment she heard them. It hardly seemed to matter. Everyone was most convivial. No one called her a useless thing. Rose liked them all very well—though more than one seemed a trifle uncanny somehow.

"Welcome, my dear," said Dame Salamander with a gracious curtsy. Beside her, her companion bowed gravely. Rane introduced him as Doctor Eel. He was a long, slim gentleman with a ruffle down the back of his ash-brown coat.

Rose blinked, realizing at last what it was about Rane's guests that had struck her as peculiar. They were all in costume and accordingly named. Each held a little visor on a stick—except that it seemed to Rose that the faces on the sticks were the human ones, and those that peered curiously from behind the masks were the visages of goldfish and mud puppies, water striders and newts.

"This is a masked ball," she whispered in delight.

Rane nodded, smiling. "Yes, Rose. Tonight we've donned our most glamorous guises just for you."

The music paused, and the dancers drifted to the edges of the floor like brightly colored ornamental carp.

"Are you hungry, Rose?" her escort asked.

More than hungry, she realized she was famished. Rane led her to a long table laden with delicacies, many of which she did not recognize: great, white bulbs and jewel-green stalks, dark leafy cresses, huge black fish roe, freshwater oysters as big as platters, and a vast, silvery smoked fish.

"What is it?" she asked, savoring its wild, gamey taste.

"Minnow," Rane answered, so that Rose burst out laughing. What minnow ever grew so large?

The musicians struck up another air. Couples hurried once more to the center of the room. Pearly stardust on the floor swirled upward, sparkling, as people began to dance, gliding and turning among slender green columns that lofted upward toward a canopy stretching overhead, smooth and reflective as liquid silver. Rose saw herself and the other dancers mirrored there.

"Dance with us! Will you dance with us, Rose?" the unattached gentlemen began to clamor. Rose felt shy suddenly and pressed closer to Rane. He squeezed her hand.

"Dance with me, Rose," he whispered. "Only with me."

Gratefully, she nodded and went with him out onto the floor. From somewhere beyond the rippling canopy above, a great, golden lamp shone down. First a minuet, then a pavane, then a jig and a reel eddied the dancers. Rose felt herself borne along as by a gentle, irresistible current. Rane proved the nimblest, and most light-footed of partners— and as he had promised, while wearing the frogskin slippers, her feet knew every step.

The pins of Rose's coif worked themselves free and floated to the floor. Her hair swirled. Her dress wafted and belled. She felt no fatigue in the cool, streaming, oddly buoyant air. Gradually, the golden lamp burning beyond the silver canopy overhead drifted westward until it disappeared. The light in the hall grew dimmer then, more gray. One by one, the strains of the musicians began to fade.

"Moonset already?" sighed Rane. "And nearly dawn. Before we go, Rose, I must present our hosts, who have held this ball in your honor tonight."

Astonished, Rose followed him to the edge of the floor. A regal pair stood at the foot of the stair. Rane bowed deeply to each, then turned to Rose.

"My parents," he told her, "King Catesbeian and Queen Palustris."

Rose dropped them each a startled curtsy.

"Dear girl," boomed the king in a hearty bass voice. "We are most grateful for all that you have done."

The queen added in her sweet, trilling one, "We hope that you will consent to come again."

Rose stammered her assent as gracefully as she could. Rane then bade their hosts good night and she and Rane took their leave.

"You didn't tell me you were a prince!" she exclaimed as they started back up the wide, shallow steps. He turned to her.

"Does that make a difference to you, Rose?" he asked softly. "Does it matter what I am?"

Breathless, she shook her head. "Not a bit. If you were a frog out of the pond, I'd love you just the same."

She had meant to say "like," but it had come out "love." Blushing, she whispered, "What I mean is, I love your dancing. I'd love to come again to dance with you."

Prince Rane threw back his head and laughed with relief. "Wonderful," he cried. "I'd love that, too."

"What did your parents mean," she asked as they neared the top of the steps, "'all that you have done'?"

"Why, that you saved my life this morning," he answered, startled. "Don't you recall?"

Rose shook her head. She had no idea what he meant. The silvery canopy grew transparent at their approach, then suddenly vanished. Rose felt a shock of cold, thin air. Looking back toward the ballroom below, she no longer saw the dancers clearly anymore. Their distant forms seemed to shimmer and bend. They all looked like goldfish to her now, or turtles, or eels.

"May I bring you here again tonight?" the prince asked her. "Twelve nights and one, the Great Ball lasts, until May Eve."

Smiling, Rose nodded with all her heart. She had fallen in love with Prince Rane in the space of a night. Wearing the frogskin slippers, she only wanted to dance and dance.

"Till dusk, then," he told her, bending to kiss her hand. "Guard the frogskin slippers well."

Rose stared at him in sudden panic, clinging to his hand. "What—do you mean to leave me here, in the middle of the woods?"

Prince Rane looked up. "It's dawn, Rose. I must."

"But, the woods are full of tigers!" she cried, glancing frantically back at the dark and thorny trees. "I'll never find my way home—"

Gently, Prince Rane took both her hands in his. "Don't you know, Rose? Haven't you guessed? You *are* home."

Rose blinked, not understanding. "How can that be?"

First the one and then the other, Rane brought her hands to his lips. "Kisses," he told her. "Wishes. Mysteries."

A rushing filled Rose's ears. The world seemed briefly to spin and then to right itself. When Rose opened her eyes, she found herself standing barefoot beside the square-sided reflecting pool in Elverston Hall's garden. She felt weak and unsteady on her feet. Her hair and her plain white nightdress were sopping wet. From behind a rose briar, her mother's gray tabby peered. One of the thorns must have scratched its nose, Rose thought confusedly, for she saw a spot of dried blood there. She glanced around, but saw no sign of Rane. Already her memory of the ballroom was growing indistinct.

"Was it all a dream?" she cried, dismayed. "Have I been wandering in my sleep?"

The song of the night fiddlers was just dying away. A droning of cicadas filled the garden. A last nightjar called. Rose began to shiver in the cold morning air. Her teeth chattered. Her hands and feet felt numb. But she was clutching something to her breast, she realized, something deep rose in color with golden trim. As insubstantial as a pair of crumpled handkerchiefs, the frogskin slippers dripped, *spit, spat,* onto the stone rimming the pool's edge. Hot tears spilled down Rose's cheeks as relief flooded through her, warm as mulled wine.

"It *was* real," she whispered fiercely. "Somehow, it was. And Prince Rane will come again tonight."

Someone was angrily calling her name. Rose looked up from the frogskin slippers with a start. Quickly, she tucked the soft, tissuelike pantofles into her bodice. They were parchment-thin, supple as glove leather and easy to conceal. A moment later, her mother's chambermaid rushed into the garden.

"Mistress Rose," the woman exclaimed in annoyance. "Come back to your chamber at once. Your mother has sent for you."

None too gently, the maidservant hurried her along through the forest of rose briars toward the keep. If she did not do the baroness's bidding and promptly, Rose knew, her mother would dock her pay or dismiss her entirely.

"Why has my mother sent for me?" asked Rose, doing her best to move quickly, but her knees shook from the long night's dancing.

"Why, to present you to her guest, of course," the other tutted, exasperated. "And look at you, just drenched with dew!"

In her chamber, Rose managed to hide the damp, wadded slippers in her silver-gilt jewel box before the maid stripped and toweled her. Spread on a chair before the fire, losing its wrinkles, lay her finest dress. Pale apricot satin, it smelled of attic must. Only the day before, Rose would have thought it gorgeous, enviable. Today, the heavy fabric burdened and confined her. The servingwoman hastily pinned up Rose's hair and laced the bodice so tight she could scarcely breathe.

"There you are," her mother said as Rose curtsied to her from the sitting room door. The baroness, richly attired in her own best gown of yellow velvet trimmed in claret, sat opposite a bearded man in the brocaded finery of a city merchant. His nose was small and flat, and he smelled of too much myrrh. His hard blue eyes, restless as a tiger's, slid over Rose, up and down, pausing here and there. Rose felt her skin draw. Involuntarily, she shrank away.

"Very well, madam," the stranger mused, smiling. Returning his gaze to the baroness, he added, "Make up your guest list. She will do."

Her mother dismissed Rose with a nod. Rose curtsied and left, puzzled. Was that all? She had not even learned the stranger's name. Back in her chamber, gasping from the climb, Rose unlaced the bodice of the ornate, oppressive gown. Pulling it off with a sigh of relief, she donned her own plain, accustomed clothes. Now she could breathe again, but her head still rang from the pins her mother's maid had jammed into her hair. With trembling fingers, she freed her coif and swept it up again, using only a few tortoiseshell combs to hold it in place.

That done, she made her way down to the scullery to begin the day's chores—but the scullions sent her off, saying she was to do no more scrubbing. So she tried the kitchen. But the cook would not have her either, or the laundress, or the sweep. Her mother had left new instructions: Rose's hands and knees were to grow silky smooth. Her complexion must become pale and fashionable.

She was to remain indoors, out of the sun. She was not to be allowed to work. No one would tell her why. More baffled than before, Rose climbed exhausted and unfed to her chamber. There, weary from the long night's revelry and the baffling morning that had followed, she curled up in bed and within moments had fallen deeply asleep.

Her mother played dice and cards with her guest in the afternoon, and the man rode away before nightfall. Yet for days after his visit, Rose had never seen such a flurry of cooking and cleaning and airing out of rooms. The baroness bought new clothes and new furniture. Old, country-bred servants were sent away, and new ones hired from town. Rose had no idea where the money came from.

"Perhaps your mother has secured a loan from her merchant visitor," suggested Rane one evening as they danced.

Dusk after dusk, the prince came to her chamber. Twilight after twilight, Rose donned the gossamer frogskin slippers and followed him through the thorny woods. Sometimes they met the tigress, but Rane had only to brandish his golden rapier now, and she fled. Night after night, the masked balls continued. Rose told Rane of her life in high-walled Elverston Hall, and Rane spoke of his own in the mysterious ballroom. Gradually, the prince's kind and gentle courtiers ceased to seem so odd to Rose. She looked forward to their nightly company so, she almost stopped wondering what was happening within her own keep.

"Or perhaps your mother is planning a celebration for May Eve," continued Rane.

Rose shook her head. She did not know. No one in her own household told her anything, and now that she was forbidden to work, she did not even have the opportunity to overhear the new servants' gossip. They were all strangers to her. Sometimes, bored to tears, she wandered the castle, keeping out of the way. Her father's books were long gone, the library newly converted into a gaming salon. She was not allowed out into the garden anymore, for fear of the sun. She slept most of the day now, eating hardly anything at home, taking her meals almost entirely in the evenings, at the prince's table.

Each morning at daybreak, when Rane kissed her hands, Rose found herself alone by the garden's reflecting pool and sped back to her chamber to hide the frogskin slippers. She had given up trying to fathom if her nights with Rane were magic or a dream. They seemed more real to her now than waking life. On the seventh dawn, as he stood with her at the top of the ballroom steps, Prince Rane turned to her suddenly.

"Stay with me, Rose," he said. "Don't go home. You're not happy there. Remain with me here, in my father's domain. Marry me, Rose."

Rose's heart opened like a flower. Nothing would have brought her greater joy than to remain forever in Rane's company, dancing in the mysterious ballroom. For a long moment, she considered, tempted—but at last, very reluctantly, she shook her head.

"I cannot marry without my godmother's blessing. I promised my father before his death. . . ."

"What do you mean?" laughed Rane. "You are a baroness. You need no one's leave."

Puzzled, Rose looked up. "My mother is the baroness."

"The dowager. Your father, the baron, is dead."

Rose halted, frowning. No one had ever seen fit to discuss her father's estate with her.

"If not my mother, then my brothers . . ." she began.

"Half brothers. Those are your mother's sons from her first marriage," snorted Rane. "They're not your late father's heirs. *You* are the mistress of this keep, Rose. Has no one ever told you that?"

Rose shook her head, mute with astonishment.

Smiling, Rane kissed her hands. "Ask your great-aunt's blessing if you must," he said. "But write soon. I must know your answer by May Eve, for I cannot come into your realm again for another year after the Great Ball ends."

Dear Great-Aunt Sophie,

I hope this letter finds you well. So much has happened since last I wrote! Mother has been her usual self, which is to say, perfectly beastly, and has dismissed all the old servants and hired many more new ones who don't know where anything is. She is renovating Elverston in a frenzy (with what funds, I don't know) and Rane thinks—

Oh, but I must tell you the most exciting news. I have met a perfectly magical young man. He has taught me how to dance! His father is King Catesbeian, so he himself is a prince. Prince Rane. He thinks I saved his life and says that I and not my mother am the baroness of Elverston Hall.

Is that true? If so, I would like to marry him and am asking your blessing. Even if it is not so, I would still like to marry him. He asked me last night. He is very handsome and brave and witty and kind and reminds me ever so slightly of Father. I am in love with him.

*May I have your permission to marry Rane? Please answer
without delay, for I must know by May Eve at the very latest.
After that, he will not be able to return to Elverston for a whole
year, and I think that in that time, I would die of loneliness. You,
of course, are most cordially invited to our wedding. (But I don't
think that I shall be inviting Mother. She has been so thoroughly
disagreeable of late.) Do write soon.*

 Your devoted grandniece and goddaughter,

 Rose

Rose posted her letter to the grand duchess that very morning. Each morning upon returning to Elverston Hall after
the night's festivities, she waited impatiently for the post
rider's arrival at noon. Days passed, but no answer came.
Rose began to chafe and fret. Her face became drawn. The
blush of her complexion paled. She seemed to be growing
thinner, for her clothing hung upon her—although the
frogskin slippers and the magnificent ballgown of rose
watered silk still fit her perfectly.

"Patience," counseled Rane. "Surely your godmother
will answer soon."

But no response from the grand duchess came. As the
twelfth morning dawned and Rose hurried sopping from the
garden toward her chamber, she glimpsed a great number of
guests arriving at the castle gate. She could not think what
they all could have come for and dared not pause to inquire,
so great was her hurry to conceal herself and the frogskin
slippers. When, later that morning, she asked the strange

servant who brought up the breakfast tray, the city girl would only say that the baroness had left instructions for Rose to remain all day in her chamber.

All morning, Rose waited in a passion of anticipation for the post. She could not eat and left her breakfast on the sill for the birds. Noon passed, and no rider came. Finally, she told herself that if she did not hear from the duchess before the final ball tonight, she would marry Rane anyway. She could not bear to be parted from him for a whole year until the Great Ball began again next spring.

"Rane says I am the true baroness," she told herself. "So I need no one's leave."

Exhausted, she lay down on the bed and slept late into the afternoon. When she awoke at last, it was to feel her mother roughly shaking her shoulder.

"Wake up," the dowager baroness said. "Wake up and put this on."

Standing alongside, her mother's new maid held a snowy white garment, all lace and stays and crinoline. Rose thought it must be a petticoat until she got it on and realized it was a gown, much too tight. Stiff strips of whalebone sewn into the bodice cut Rose's ribs unmercifully.

"This gown is so white," she gasped. "Is there to be a ball?"

"Of course it's white," her mother snapped. "And yes, there's to be a ball afterward. Hold still."

Impatiently, her mother and the new maidservant cinched the laces and fastened the gown's thousand little hooks and eyes.

"You've turned into such a skinny thing," her mother muttered. "All sinew and bone. And your eyes are growing such a pale, pale green. You're wasting away here. I daresay marriage will do you good."

Rose stared at the dowager baroness, as her mother's maid combed and twisted Rose's hair up so tight it hurt. Only the sash remained to be tied. How could her mother know of Prince Rane's proposal? Rose certainly had not told her. She knew without a doubt that neither Rane nor any of his folk would ever speak to her mother behind her back. A sudden chill swept over Rose as she realized: her mother could not mean she was to marry Rane. Her mother intended her to marry someone else.

"What do you mean?" she stammered, breathless. The ruthless corset made it impossible for her to breathe. "Whom am I to marry?"

"Your betrothed, you ninny," the dowager baroness exclaimed. "You met him a fortnight ago."

Rose's head spun. She remembered her mother's guest, the bearded merchant with the tiger's eyes. "He looked at me," she gasped. "I didn't meet him."

"Impertinent girl," her mother scoffed. "Don't quibble. Hurry up."

Rose felt herself flush suddenly. She was not a servant to be spoken to so. "I'm neither impertinent nor a girl," she answered hotly, with more certainty than she knew she possessed. "I am mistress of this keep."

Her mother stopped short. Her skin blanched sallow. "Who told you that?"

"Let us ask my godmother, the grand duchess Sophie," countered Rose.

The pale blue eyes of the dowager baroness flared. "By the time that old toad learns of this," she hissed, "there will be nothing she can do."

Seizing Rose by the arm, her mother pulled her toward the door. Rose resisted fiercely, though she was scarcely able to draw a breath in the smothering gown.

"I'll not," she panted. "I'll not marry him!"

Her mother gave her a furious shake. "Be still, you wretch. You'll marry, or I'll put you out the gate and let the tigers have you."

"Let them," choked Rose, wrapping her arms around the bedpost. "I'm not afraid of tigers anymore."

"Enough!" snarled the dowager baroness, letting her go. Circling, she came up behind Rose and yanked the white sash of the dress so hard Rose nearly swooned. "Vexation," her mother muttered a moment later. "I nearly forgot. The brooch. It's your only jewel, so you must wear it." To the maid, she ordered, "Fetch her jewel box."

The maid stopped trying to pry Rose's fingers from the bedpost and hurried to the dresser.

"No . . ." Rose tried to gasp, but the gown was now so tight, had she uttered a word she would have fainted.

The room reeled. Spots of black obscured Rose's vision.

Walking toward her across the slanted floor, the maid brought her mistress the silver-gilt case. Rose's mother lifted the latch.

"Put it on," she commanded, thrusting the carved coral into Rose's hand.

Dimly, Rose realized she was no longer holding the post. She swayed, unable to get any air. Her fingers clutched numbly at nothingness. Her mother thrust the brooch into her hand. Rose stood holding it. She could not have donned it had she tried. Its golden pin was gone. Her mother took no notice, distracted.

"What's this?" the baroness shrieked all at once, staring down into the jewel box and snatching out the frogskin slippers.

The servant, puzzled, curtsied.

"I'm sure I don't know, madam . . ." she began in her pinched, city accent, but the dowager baroness was not even looking at her.

"Elfskin," she hissed, her fingers tightening, the knuckles white. "That wretched cat has failed me."

With a strangled cry, Rose staggered toward her, trying to wrest the pantofles away, but her mother thrust her aside and held them out of reach.

"Little deceiver," the dowager baroness growled. Her fingers, sharp-nailed as claws, dug into the rose-colored dancing slippers. "Pale and wan and won't eat a bite? Slugabed! How have you been spending your nights?" She bent down close to Rose, her teeth long and white and keen. "You'll accept the hand I've chosen for you," she grated, "and dance at no more fairy balls."

Turning, she threw the frogskin slippers into the fire. Rose writhed, struggled, fought to reach them, desperate to pluck the delicate stuff from the flames before it caught. But her mother nodded to the maid, and the two of them hauled Rose back from the flames. With a scent like burning grass and cinnamon, the frogskin slippers blackened, curled, and were consumed.

Rose stared, fists clenched to her mouth in horror. Without the magical pantofles, she could not return with Prince Rane to his kingdom tonight. After this evening's final ball, an entire year must pass before the Great Ball would be held again. What had her mother called it—a fairy ball? Were Rane and his people all fairy folk, the mysterious ballroom nothing but elfin glamour?

She did not care! She did not care a bit! A sob welled in Rose's throat. Her eyes burned. Her ribs heaved, but she could get no breath. Rose felt a swoon enveloping her. The dowager baroness and her new maid still had hold of Rose's nerveless arms. Between the two of them, they half supported, half carried her, stumbling, out of the tower room.

"Haste," she heard her mother saying, above the rush of darkness that had engulfed her. "It's nearly dusk. The guests are waiting. We'll be late."

The great hall of Elverston Castle had been scrubbed and hung with garlands. It was crowded with people, all strangers to Rose. They stared at her with hard, inquisitive eyes, like the eyes of rats and weasels and stoats. The hall smelled rank of musk and civet. As the dowager baroness pulled her daughter half senseless through the press, Rose heard them all mewling and chattering behind their fans.

"Skinny little thing, isn't she?"

"A bit wan for my taste."

"Is there to be gambling afterward?"

"Old baron's daughter . . ."

"What's her name?"

The crowd parted as they neared the little chapel at the far end of the hall. There the bearded merchant waited, nose wrinkled, arms crossed, toe tapping in irritation. As her mother shoved Rose into place beside him, he smirked. A withered little wisp of a churchman opened a great gilt book and began to chitter.

Imprisoned in the stifling gown, Rose stared at them all, gasping for air like a stranded fish, unable to utter a word. Lifting her free hand, the merchant pushed a golden ring onto one of her fingers. It, too, was much too tight, making her whole hand ache and throb. Her other hand, she realized dimly, still held the pinless coral brooch.

"Health, long life, and happiness!" her mother was shouting.

All the guests applauded and threw hard little grains of barleycorn and rice. Hired musicians struck up a tune, a clumsy braying like the wheezing of mules, the bleating of lambs, and the peeping of sparrows. Rose's feet felt clumsy, heavy as lead. Her blood beat sluggishly. Yapping and tittering with delight, her mother's guests faced one another, forming couples for the dance. The bearded merchant grasped Rose's arm.

"Come, wife," he purred. "We'll dance a turn before I pluck you away to town. Have a last look at this dowdy old place. You'll not set foot here again."

Rose tried to fend him off, straining against the sash and the whalebone stays to protest, to speak. If she allowed the merchant to steal her away in his carriage, in a year's time, Prince Rane would never find her. Paying no heed to her feeble struggles, the great beast of a man prowled out of the chapel and into the center of the floor, dragging Rose along with him. Dusk had fallen. Servants who all dressed like city folk hurried about with tapers, lighting the chandeliers.

"I won't—" she made to gasp. No sound emerged. Vainly, she tried again. "I'll never . . ."

But the cruel stays stole the words from her. The only sound that came from her throat was a smothered sigh. Screeching music drowned it out. The bearded merchant turned Rose deftly to him and seized her hand.

"Stop," she barely managed to whisper. "Unhand me . . .!"

She dug her fingernails into his knuckles. The other lost his grip with a startled cry. The music died. The dancers turned. The merchantman stood staring at Rose. Eyes narrowing, he seized her hand again. Deliberately, his fingers tightened on hers, cutting the ring into her flesh. The coral brooch squirmed in her other palm.

Behind her, she heard her mother clapping officiously, ordering the musicians to play on, loudly exhorting the guests to dance. The strident strains began again. The rush of dancers started once more around them. Rose tried in vain to scream as the merchant pressed her to him, whirling her. Her feet could not find the ground.

"You penniless fool," he growled softly, conversationally, bending close. "Your mother owes me a great sum in gambling debts. I've graciously agreed to take you instead and extend her an allowance besides, that she might keep up appearances. Behave yourself, pauper, or—"

He would have murmured more, but just at that moment, a furious caterwauling sounded from outside the hall. The musicians broke off their cacophonous sawing. Dancers parted from one another in confusion. Rose saw her mother's gray tabby streak in through the garden door. One paw, bleeding from a wicked scratch, she held to her chest as she dashed through the forest of dancer's legs.

Behind her, a tall, young man stood framed in the doorway. Guests scattered from him, exclaiming in alarm. The left shoulder and sleeve of his rose velvet jacket had been clawed to ribbons, scoring one lean and muscular arm. In his other hand, he held a blood-stained rapier of gleaming gold. Full of sadness and reproach, his large pale green eyes looked at Rose.

"How could you?" he said to her. "How could you, Rose? You swore you'd never dance with anyone but me."

"Who are you? How dare you?" Rose's mother demanded. "I never invited you."

"Madam," Prince Rane replied, approaching, "it is for Rose to make such demands of me, should she so choose— for it is she, not you, who is mistress of Elverston Hall."

"Hardly," the bearded merchant sneered. His ferocious grip tightened on Rose's arm. "The girl's mine now, and so's the hall."

Gritting her teeth, Rose raked the coral brooch across her captor's bare wrist and tore herself free of him. Slicing furiously at the sash with the sharp edge of the brooch, she rent it from the rigid, strangling gown and could breathe then, just a little.

"Begone from my house," the young baroness panted. "I never agreed to marry you." Still fighting for breath, she could scarcely stand. Rane held out his hand to her, and she clutched it desperately. "It's you I love," she whispered, turning to the prince. "You must know that."

Gently, Rane squeezed her hand. "Of course I do, Rose," he answered with a smile. "Why did you think I came?"

Rose threw her arms about his neck. One armed, Rane caught her to him. With a growl, the merchantman started forward—but the prince leveled his golden rapier at the man. He and the other guests fell hastily back.

"Seducer! Abductor——" Rose's mother had begun to sputter.

No one paid her the slightest heed, for all at once, at the far end of the hall, the great doors burst open with a hollow bang. The dowager baroness's protests abruptly ceased. No human hand had touched the doors. A faint swirl of glimmering powder rose from them as they thudded against the great hall's inner wall. As the echoes died away, the soft boom of a cane striking the flagstone floor began rhythmically to sound as a grand dame swept into the room.

She was attired all in brown and olive green, the color of the forest floor. Her beautiful gray hair was upswept into an elaborate coif set with freshwater pearls the size of raspberries. The lace at her throat and cuffs was as delicate as spiderwebs. She wore a mantle so cleverly stitched and sewn as to give the impression of being made of all manner of foliage. The startled guests parted before her like a flock of sheep.

"What is the meaning of this?" she demanded indignantly. "A wedding to which I have not been invited? Surely, my lady dowager, you remember promising your husband on his deathbed that *I* should be the one to arrange Rose's marriage?"

"Great-Aunt Sophie!" Rose exclaimed, though her words came out more of a whisper than a cry. She stood struggling to unknot the laces of the stifling gown.

"Gracious, child," inquired the duchess, "what is that

contraption into which your mother has squashed you? Dispense with it at once."

She waved one hand encouragingly at Rane, then turned to gaze critically about Elverston Hall.

"I received your letter only a few days past, my dear," she continued over one shoulder—for all its briskness, her voice was very kind—"and came in haste to make all the arrangements—for I see the young man I have had in mind for you has already made bold to gain your acquaintance. How dashing. How are you, Rane?"

"Well enough, Aunt, I daresay," the prince replied, a bit preoccupied, "in spite of tigers."

He was using his rapier to nick apart the bodice strings of Rose's gown. In less than a trice, it was done. He helped her to unfasten all the thousand little hooks and eyes. At last, she could breathe again. Rose filled her lungs. It seemed heavenly, just to be able to sob, to sigh. Rose felt her color returning. Her limbs steadied. Her head cleared. Laughing, she and Rane embraced.

"How is it my great-aunt Sophie is your aunt as well?" Rose asked.

"Mine by blood. Yours by marriage," Rane answered. "She is my father's sister, born in my world—but she shed her skin many years ago by choice to marry a great lord of your realm."

Rose's mother had gone sallow and shrunk back against the bearded merchant at the grand duchess's entrance, but now she circled hissing and spitting like a cornered cat.

"Too late, you interfering old hag. Rose is already wed."

Rose stiffened. With a cry, she bit and tugged at the merchant's golden band, but it would not come off her finger.

"Poppycock!" the grand duchess snorted. "Laced up so, how could the poor girl ever have said, 'I do'?"

The merchant rumbled a protest. The elf dame gave him a withering glance before returning her gaze to the dowager baroness.

"You've made a mess of things as usual, Maude," the grand duchess Sophie snapped. "Marry him yourself, if you're so fond of him. Rose has no use for the brute."

Smiling at her grandniece, the fairy dame struck her staff three times upon the flagstone floor. "High time my goddaughter saw you all as you truly are."

A shimmer of dust rose from the duchess's cane, spreading throughout the hall. A ripple passed through the ranks of the guests. Their faces began to change, growing furrier, their eyes rounder, their white teeth sharper. In another moment, their visages scarcely resembled those of human beings anymore, but muskrats and shrews and voles. Shuddering, Rose shrank against Rane, who held her tight. The beastly guests drew back from one another, gaping and grimacing.

"Elf! Fairy elf!" Rose heard her mother mewling.

Her words rose into the nasal whine of a cat. Whiskers appeared on her pale, brindled face, hirsute now, and upon the face of the bearded merchant beside her.

"The nixie's thrown her glamour on us!" he yowled.

Ignoring them both, the grand duchess turned to Rose.

"Have you about you my christening gift, child?"

Rose opened her right hand to show her aunt the pink coral brooch. The grand duchess smiled.

"Cast it away."

Rose did so without stopping to question, and where her brooch struck the paving stones halfway across the hall, a red rose tree sprang up, gleaming with fairy dust.

"Do the same with your rapier, Rane," his aunt commanded.

As the prince obeyed, Rose realized for the first time how closely it resembled a great golden brooch pin: long and sharp, with a tightly coiled double loop, like a hinge, forming the basket protecting the grip at the unpointed end. Where the rapier struck the floor, a golden thornbush began to grow, shimmering. Quick as thought, the rose tree and the thorn entwined, reaching out, trailing swiftly over the floor and clambering along the walls, threading across the ceiling and curling out the windows.

Shouting in terror, her mother's transformed guests scurried about, beating the fairy dust off of their clothes and calling for their carriages—though by now their voices sounded more like the squeaking of mice and the nattering of squirrels. Though some retained their human limbs and torsos, animal paws now sprouted from their lacy cuffs, like costumed guests at a magnificent masked ball. The forms of the merchantman and the dowager baroness had shifted into those of tigers that gnashed and tore at one another.

"This is your fault!" the merchant roared furiously. "You promised me the girl was docile—"

"It isn't," the dowager snarled, cuffing him back, her own claws bared. "I said, marry her before May Eve. But no— you didn't believe in fairies!"

Their clothes fell away in shreds. Striped pelts bristled underneath. Arching and spitting, the baroness's gray tabby sprinted away from the battling pair and disappeared out the garden door. The grand duchess nodded to Rose and Rane.

"Run along, now, children," she told them. "Health, long life, and happiness."

One arm still about Rose, Rane held out his hand to the grand duchess.

"Won't you come with us, Aunt?" he asked. "Not a night passes that Colonel Crayfish does not inquire of your return."

The grand duchess sighed and smiled. "Crayfish was always such a fine old soul. With my dear earthly husband now so many years dead, I admit, I have missed my old beau."

With a nod, she swept by them toward the garden door. Rane caught and kissed her hand as she passed. She patted his chin and continued on. Rose stared as the grand duchess began to shrink, her skin growing pebbled and shading into the mottled olive and brown of her gown. Her gait took on a hopping motion. Still dwindling, she grew squatter and more wedgelike with each passing instant. In another moment, her mantle fell away entirely, leaving only a woodland toad, small as a child's hand, hopping determinedly toward the garden. Rose blinked, and the little toad was lost from view among her mother's still frantically fleeing guests.

"The frogskin slippers," Rose gasped suddenly, turning to Rane. The knowledge stabbed her. "I cannot go with you! My mother burned them—"

Rane laughed. "It doesn't matter anymore. They were nearly worn through as it is. It's May Eve, Rose. Twelve nights have you dined and danced in my father's hall. You've nearly lost your taste for human food and drink by now, haven't you? And human music scarcely stirs your soul at all anymore, I'll be bound. For the fairy music is in your blood, and your feet have learned the steps now for themselves. You've no more need of the frogskin slippers to teach you the way to Faerie."

Rose touched his cheek. Bending down, Rane gently put his lips to hers. The world spun. Rose felt herself falling through layer upon layer of crisp white cloud. The merchant's tight golden band upon her finger loosened, slipped heavily away. The hairpins clenching her hair into place fell like a rain of arrows all around. Her head felt instantly weightless, her hair floating unbound and free.

Opening her eyes, Rose found herself once more in the light and airy elfin ball gown of rose watered silk. The whalebone wedding dress lay in a mountainous heap all around. The vast, thorn-covered hall soared enormous around them. The flagstones loomed huge. Rane took her hand, and together they ran from the briar-invaded hall, dodging the great, pounding feet of the beastly guests, some beast-faced, some beast-bodied, all yammering and howling. A great shining hoop, like a little wheel rim or a small barrel loop, trundled over the flagstones ahead of them.

Outside, the rose briars in the garden had joined the flowering rose tree and the golden thorn in covering the whole castle, obscuring the windows and doorways all the way to the black slate roofs of the towers. From the stable yard drifted the noise of guests hying their horses and stampeding their carriages to escape before the gate became too overgrown to pass.

Rose and Rane turned from the sound, deeper into the garden. A white tiger fled away from them into the trees, hissing in fear. Ahead, Rose heard the wild fairy music skirling. Her blood stirred in answer. Her feet felt suddenly, wondrously light. The mysterious ballroom opened before them, lying below them, at the garden's heart. The golden hoop bounded chiming down the steps toward the moonlit dance floor below.

Colonel Crayfish stood at the bottom of the stair, holding out his hand to the grand duchess Sophie who was descending toward him. Rose could not quite make up her mind if her godmother looked like a hopping toad still, or a regal gray-haired lady in a filmy olive ball gown trimmed in mottled brown, as light on her feet as any girl. It scarcely mattered.

Hand in hand, King Catesbeian and Queen Palustris nodded in welcome from the twin thrones upon which they sat surveying the hall. Banquet tables stood sumptuously arrayed with every delicacy Rose could have imagined. Fairy dust eddied like glimmering silt. The slim green columns of water lilies swayed. The round golden ring rolled and circled lazily among the dancers swirling serenely past. Rose and Rane joined their joyous ranks.

"Are you happy, Rose?" Rane asked. "Happy that you came?"

Laughing in his arms, Rose answered, "Kisses. Wishes. Mysteries."

Dearest Rose,

Though Crayfish and I have enjoyed our honeymoon in the human world immensely, out travels here are drawing to a close. We should be back in the realm of Faerie before the turning of the year.

We looked in on your estate a fortnight past, and though the last twelve months have not been kind to Elverston Hall, the troupe of roofers and other workmen we have hired should put all to rights in a few weeks' time. Likewise, we have hired house-keepers and engaged half a dozen gardeners to prune the shrubbery into some semblance of order. One must, after all, keep up appearances.

While in the capital, we put round in all the proper ears word of your continuing happiness in your fortuitous marriage to your foreign prince and the likelihood of your remaining away for some time yet to come. A delegation of students from the Royal Academy have petitioned to be allowed into the garden to study the unusual rose-colored frogs that dwell there, and we have taken the liberty of granting them permission on the condition that they take no specimens. Purely as a precaution, however, kindly see that all the children remain indoors on Monday next.

You will no doubt be pleased to learn that after an exhaustive investigation, scientists from the Academy have concluded that the bestial delusions suffered by a handful of the petty nobility—several of whom still believe themselves to be hedgehogs—were induced by consuming contaminated fruitcake at a card party they all attended on May Eve. Their keepers are being asked to restrict them to a diet of boiled milk and vinegar to see if that will bring them round. Poor things.

More felicitous news: The two large tigers that have played such havoc among the rural flocks for the last few months were last week dispatched by a shooting party of local countryfolk whom Crayfish organized and instructed in the finer points of firearms. Their enthusiasm was doubtless spurred by the generous bounty I made bold to offer in your name. The dairymaid to whom the two gave such a fright last month has entirely recovered. Crayfish is having the pair stuffed. We plan to donate them to the Academy.

How I do run on. I must close now, as the chivalrous newt who has so kindly agreed to deliver this missive to you has been waiting patiently this last quarter hour. Do give our love to Rane and little Beauregard. He should be quite the young gentleman by now, nearly old enough, I daresay, to have lost his tail. We will see you all soon.

I remain your great-aunt and fond godmother,
Sophie

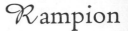
BRAINS AND determination count for a lot more in my book than mere physique. I've always been puzzled by stories that give female characters only one option to escape oppressive circumstances: impersonate a man. All very well if you're six feet tall, have the right build, fairly androgynous looks, and can pull it off. But what about the rest of us?

What happens if, like me, you happen to be shrimpy? Or have decidedly feminine features, hips the size of the Colosseum, the upper arm strength of a minnow, and can't see past the end of your own nose?

Are we to just sit around moping because we're not "manly" enough to overcome? Hardly. To my mind, the tasks of a heroine—any heroine, regardless of her size—should include figuring out exactly what she wants, making up her mind to achieve it no matter what, and exploiting any opportunities that come her way, cross-dressing included.

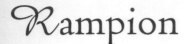

Rampion

WHAT I remember best about Castle Van is the women's garden. It was set in a little niche off the main courtyard, an open square of earth in the pavement, and it was planted with rampion. That was what we called it, anyway, after a similar herb that grew on the mainland. The herb that grew here in the garden was not native to our little island, or even to our world. It had been brought to the castle five years before my birth by Zara, the witch. The stranger. The madwoman. The woman who had come through the Portal.

Our little island was called Ulys, and we lay off the coast between Narby and Quint. On a clear, very fine day, you could sometimes just see the Downs of Upland Corl beyond the haze. Most days were not fair. We were a stormy place of rough tides and submerged rocks, a magnet for every squall. Few ships docked at our tiny port. We kept aloof.

My father, Halss, was the lord of Ulys. Originally, he had been a man of the Downs, the second son of a second son, who had left his clan and gone adventuring. He found his fortune here quite by accident, when the Saakish merchant vessel he was passenger on began taking on water and had to put in to the nearest land they could—even if it was a nothing-place like Ulys.

What a stir he must have caused among the fisherfolk: they had seen Saakmen before, but never a highborn man of Corl. He was certainly gorgeous to look at then. Even in later years, when I was old enough to take note of such things, I could see how glorious he must have been, with his fair, flushed skin and sandy-coppery hair—though by then age and wenching, drink and despair had thickened and coarsened him.

He had been taken in by the lord of Ulys at once and housed in the finest guest chamber, while the captain of the Saakish vessel and his men were left to find what lodging they could in town. The lord had only one child—my namesake, Alia—and she was of marriageable age. When the Saakish ship moved on, my father stayed to court the lord of Ulys's daughter.

Such a prize her dowry must have seemed! I have been told the weather was unusually fine that year, with hardly a storm. The winter, for once, was truly cold and dry, producing a fine crop of seafoxes, those small, thick-furred water dogs that visit our rocks. In winter, the keep men all go out with clubs and kill as many as they can. We sell the pelts to the Downsmen merchants of the mainland.

My father married the lord of Ulys's daughter in spring

and, and when the old lord died a year later, became regent for the lady Alia. But she died childless, of the coughing sickness, barely three years after. That left him in a fine mess.

He could have left us then, gone back to Upland Corl, but he did not. Shame or pride, I don't know which motivated him. Perhaps it was only inertia. Or greed. The seafoxes brought in a good income. His family had cut him off penniless when they had heard of his marriage outside the Downs.

The dowager lord Halss spent the next four years improving the island. He formed a small militia of castle guards and took charge of the fishing fleet. He repaired the boats of the fisherfolk and rebuilt the castle's crumbling outer walls. He even had a sea chain stretched across the narrow harbor as a defense against pirates. Poor as our island was, raiders had been known to land—but only at the harbor. Reefs protected the rest of our shore.

These were the prosperous years for Ulys. It was during this time that the outland woman Zara came. I remember her a little, dimly. She was very tall, with dark red hair and dusky skin. She was not Saakish, and she was not of the Downs. She would not say where she was from. Some called her mad or sorcellous. My father, it seems, was fascinated with her.

But he married Benis in the end, who had been the lady Alia's cousin. Once more he could rightly be called the lord of Ulys. It was not a love match. I was a born a year later and named Alia, though called Alys. But it was sons my father had been hoping for. Lady Benis managed the castle contentedly enough, stitched tapestry in the evenings, and ordered the servants about by day. But she bore no sons who lived.

My father, with only the one daughter and no heirs, was not a seafaring man either by birth or inclination, so there was no escape for him from this little prison he had entered into by marriage. How he hated the rampion! I remember it growing in squat clumps of jagged, fleshy leaves. In spring, clusters of cone-shaped flowers appeared on top, smelling pungent, like leeks. My father complained that they reeked, but to me the scent was rich and wonderful.

My lord wanted to dig up the garden, throw out the rampion, and plant something useful. He had no need of women's herbs. But my mother said no, to his face, quite definitely. It was the only time I remember her standing up to him openly and winning.

"I won't have you undoing the garden. I don't care where it came from—it is the only herb on the island that helps me. Once a month, I send the girl to pull the leaves and make a salad for me."

She didn't mean me. She meant her maidservant, Imma. I hadn't known that about the rampion. All I had known was that sometimes when my mother was ill, she shut her door and would not see me. Her women moved quickly and quietly then, and told me to go away.

I tried eating the rampion once, when toothache was making me flushed and feverish. The taste was sharp and peppery, almost bitter. It made my eyes weep, but it didn't do any good. I learned later that this was not the sort of illness it relieved. I was not old enough to have that sickness yet.

My earliest clear memory is of confronting my sister in the women's garden. It was summer, but the sky was cloudy, the air hot and damp. My mother was ill and had sent Imma for the herbs. I had following secretly and stayed behind, and now stood among the miserable little clumps of rampion in violet and bluish bloom, each stalk blossoming like a mace among the glossy, dark green leaves. I was glaring at my sister—of course, I hadn't known then that she was my sister. I must have been about four years old.

To me, she was only Sif, mad Zara's child. My eyes were not good, and I recognized people more by shape and coloring than by details of feature. Sif was a lanky girl, with straight hair, long and yellowish, never combed. Her face was always smudged with grime, as were her patched, ill-mended clothes. I could see just well enough to note she had a long, strong jaw with a definite cleft to the chin and eyes that might have been any shade between blue-gray and sea-green. The day was dark, with storms coming. The light was bad. I had never been this close to her before.

"What are you doing?" I cried, stamping my slippered foot and bunching the gores of my gown at the hips. "Stop that at once."

Not a moment before, I had seen her empty a bag of kitchen scraps over the garden plants.

"Throwing rubbish on my mother's rampion," I shrilled. "Stop! Pick it up."

Sif looked up with a start, then squared her shoulders, obviously caught by surprise but unwilling to run. She was wearing trousers like a peasant or a boy. She didn't say anything. I was a cheeky brat, much spoiled, and seeing my advantage, came forward.

"Pick it up," I said in the tone my mother used with wash maids, but Sif only looked at me. I flew at her in a fury of fists, shrieking, "I'll tell! I'll tell! My mother will send for the boatman, and he'll box your ears!"

Sif didn't fight me as I kicked and buffeted her, but she did catch hold of my wrist and whispered fiercely, "Very well, then, *do*, you little sut. See if I care. He can't do worse than he already does."

I stopped hitting and looked up. I was close enough to see her face almost clearly now, and I realized that what I had thought was a smudge on her one cheek was a bruise. She had another on the same side, just at the jawline near the chin. Her fingers twisting my wrist hurt. I jerked away and fell back a step. We stared at each other for a few moments, panting.

"It's not your mother's garden anyway," Sif said after a moment, still angry, but not so fierce. "It's *my* mother's. She started it."

I squinted, trying to see her better. "Your mother's *dead*," I said, doing my best to sound contemptuous. The truth was, the bruise on Sif's face had shaken me.

She answered without nodding. "Yes."

"She died on the rocks," I added in a moment.

"Yes."

Six months before, mad Zara had stolen a boat and tried for Clevven. It had been a foolish thing to do. Women were no use in boats. She had broken up on the reef and washed back, drowned. Her body and some of the wreckage had been found on the beach two days later.

I had heard my mother talking to her maids about it, little edges of disdain and horror and triumph in her voice. When Zara's body was found, my father had bolted himself in his chamber for two days and refused to come out. I was too young to understand these things. Old Sul, the boatman, kept Sif now.

I stared at her across the rampion. I could not see her well enough in the murky light to tell if her face had any expression. It seemed expressionless to me, a chalky blur.

"And it isn't rubbish," she said, toeing at something among the fleshy plants. Her voice was low for a girl's, like a sounding horn. "See for yourself. It's fish bones."

I knelt down and peered at the little white skeletons. They stank. "Why did you dump them here?" I demanded, looking up, feeling righteous. I wrinkled my nose. "Throw them on the midden like everyone else."

Sif was kneeling across from me. "I didn't dump them," she answered, calmer now. "I put them there on purpose. For the rampion. They're good for it. Can't you see the plants are dying?"

I squinted at the flowering clumps. They looked well enough to me.

"They need bones," Sif was saying. "Something in the bones nourishes them. And oyster shells. I put down crushed oyster shells when I can get them."

I rubbed my wrist and looked at her. My gown was already muddied. There was nothing I could do about it now—perhaps my mother was so sick the maids would not notice, or, if they did, would not make a fuss. I knew I should be getting back, but strangely, I wanted to stay with Sif.

"Why?" I asked her. "Who told you this?"

"I *told* you," she answered. "My mother started the garden when she came to Ulys, ten years ago. She told me."

I had been born in the Year of the Cockatrice, Sif some three years before. That would make her nearly eight. If she spoke true, her mother had come to Ulys three years before Sif's birth. Before the lady Alia died—I had not known that.

And Zara had lived at the castle once. I knew that somehow, had heard it somewhere, whispered. My mother could hardly abide hearing her name mentioned. Sif's mother had been brought here by Saakmen, who had found her in the sea, and since she had no money, only a watertight bag of healer's herbs and cuttings, they had put her ashore at their first landfall. She could not get off the island after that. My father would not let her go.

But she had left the castle when he married Benis, gone down to the beach and built a little hut. She had lived by scavenging, beachcombing, and as a sort of healwoman, practicing the herb craft. Some called her a witch, but the fisherfolk and even some of the keep folk went to her. My mother would not have allowed her to set foot in the keep— if ever she had presented herself at our gate. But she never did. And she went mad in the end. Ulys drives many of us mad. Sif's mother never wed.

I wanted to ask Sif about her mother then, where she had come from and why she had stolen the boat. Why she had wanted to go to Upland Corl, or Clevven, or wherever she had been headed, and had she truly been a witch, like those white-robed women in their strongholds across the sea?

I had no inkling then that she had not been of our world at all, but from another place, beyond our world and time, beyond the Portal—but I heard my nurse calling me, and, since I didn't want her to come looking and find me with dirty Sif, I ran away.

After that, we were not such enemies. I slipped away from my nurse to meet with her. I had never had a friend before. Sif took me down to the wide, deserted ribbon of sand below Castle Van. All the sea wrack washed up there—nothing valuable, only bits of driftwood and shell. Once we found the blade of a Saakish oar, broken off from the handle and partially burned, and once a harpoon head made of bone. Sif liked that. She put a string through it and wore it around her neck.

Sif showed me how to find shellfish under the sand, and

how to skip a flat stone over the waves—I could never see well enough to watch it go, but my wrist soon gained the feel of the flick. I showed her my secret place at the top of the tower. It had been built long ago as a lookout for warships and pirate raiders, but Upland Corl had long been at peace with us, and since my father had devised the harbor chain, pirates no longer troubled us. No one used the tower anymore.

Save Sif and me. We stayed in the tower often, crouched on the highest landing, three flights up, whenever Sif could get away from the boatman, Sul. He gave her all the hard work to do, she said, scraping the hulls for barnacles and hauling the catch from the hold to the gutting tables. My mother and her maids taught me mending and needlework.

Sif told me tales, tales her mother had told her of the land beyond the Portal. Impossible tales, mad tales that grew more marvelous with each telling, of a land where people lived ageless till the day they died. Everyone there was a sorceller with a house the size of Castle Van. Hundreds of castles built side by side made up vast cities of shimmering stone. People rode ships that sailed the air. Carts pulled themselves. Sometimes, I think, she was making it up.

"If your mother lived in such a wonderful place," I said once, scoffing—I must have been seven or eight by then, and Sif eleven or so—"why ever did she come here?"

We stood on the rocky slope above the beach under a dark autumn sky. Arms spread like seagulls for balance, we picked our way forward, hopping from stone to stone, looking for heggitt's eggs. Sif took my arm and heaved me over a wide gap. I was still much smaller than she, and wearing a keep woman's voluminous gown that beat about me like wings in the wind.

"She said her world was very old, very crowded," answered Sif, bending to pluck from a crevice a blue egg twice the size of my thumb. She put it in a little bag with the others. "The sorcellers had all had too many children who lived. And some people were tired of the sorcel, the palaces, and the carts. They wanted to come to a new place, and try to live without them."

She straightened. I stared at her, astonished. "They wanted to come here, to Ulys?"

Sif laughed and shook her head. "Not *here*. In the north somewhere. Where the Portal is. Her people have been coming through, she said, in little groups, for years."

Still staring, I lost my balance and caught Sif's arm to steady myself. We had legends of the Portal, even here, even in Ulys—brought in snippets and fragments from the mainland. It was a place in Clevven, a terrible place, where monsters came from and men disappeared. It was guarded by unspeakable horrors. It did not exist. It existed, but there were more than one. It moved about. It was impossible to find except by accident.

"Why did your mother come to Ulys, then?" I persisted.

Sif gave an exasperated sigh. "She didn't mean to. She'd been on her way to Upland Corl when a storm caught her. She'd been in the sea three days when the Saakmen found her."

"Why?" I asked. We were picking our way carefully now.

"Just to see it!" cried Sif. "She said her people had stayed in one place for four generations without exploring. My mother decided to see what the world was like. She was a great traveler. She told me she had already been across the sea to the stronghold of the witches when her boat went down."

I scoffed again, clutching Sif's arm once more against the wind. Sif was strong. "Women don't travel," I said. "Except to marry." Sometimes girls on Ulys contracted to marry on the mainland. It was a rare and wonderful thing. Then their mothers gave them semroot to make them sleepy and bundled them onto brideboats to be ferried across. "Women don't travel," I said again.

"My mother did," said Sif. There were no bruises on her face today. Old Sul had not been in his cups the night before.

"They're useless in boats," I said, coming after.

"My mother wasn't," answered Sif, leaping the gap.

Your mother died on the rocks, I thought, but didn't say. I jumped, and the tall girl caught me.

"And neither am I!"

"What do you mean?"

Sif just grinned, looking more like a boy than ever, thrusting out her long jaw with its cleft chin—not ducking shyly as a woman should. Her teeth were long and even, and her brows, which were darker than her yellow hair, met above the bridge of her long, straight nose. I poked her.

"What do you mean?"

She helped me down off the rocks. We had come to the strand. "Old Sul is teaching me the handling of boats," she whispered, and then squeezed my hand.

"He isn't!" I cried. "He can't. Women can't. It's . . . *bad*." Women in boats brought sickness and storm. Everybody knew that.

Sif set off down the beach with her long legs striding and pulled me after. "He is. He has to!" Her voice was rushed with excitement. "He gashed his hand with a bait hook a half a year gone, and it's been numb in three fingers since. He needs someone to help, and all he has is me. He treats me like a boy, anyway. It doesn't matter."

I stopped then, simply staring at her. The heggitts and the robber gulls wheeled overhead. Sif reached out for one. It veered away. She watched it, and laughed.

ᘒᕯ II ᘒᕯ
WOMEN'S PLIGHT

Sif and I spent what time we could tending the rampion. She still brought fish bones and oyster shells. I saved bones and brought the shells of eggs when I could get them away from the table. The rampion struggled on in our loose, sandy soil. It was stubborn—but Ulys kills all things in time.

One day Sif brought a rampion leaf up to our landing at the top of the tower. We were still young, too young to know the true use of it yet. We had the vague feeling that it would make us women. Sif drew the long, jagged leaf from her sleeve and brushed the dirt from it. We stared at the dark green thing, and then Sif, very carefully, folded it along the vein and broke it in half. The juice was clear and colorless.

Silently, we ate—as I had eaten once before, before I knew Sif—grinding the leathery skin between our teeth to reach the wet within. The taste was strong and green, the smell like onions. Our eyes watered. We waited for a month after that: proud, expectant, secretly terrified. But nothing happened. We were too young.

Once, in the tower, Sif told me more of her mother, red-haired Zara, who had worn her hair cropped short and trousers like a man.

"Was she really a sorcelress?" I asked.

Sif chafed her arms and shrugged. It was full night, the window in the wall above where she sat full of darkness. I crouched on the stairs. The candles guttered in the cool evening wind. Sif tore at the heel of bread I'd brought her. It was summer. She would not freeze in the tower that night. Old Sul had left a red weal across her shoulder that would last for days. She had shown it to me. She would spend a night or two in the tower, then go back to Sul, and things would go quietly for a while.

"I don't know," she said at last, and it took me a moment to realize she was replying to my question. She was silent a few moments. She was always silent after Sul had raised his hand to her. Then she said, quietly, "But I know the place my mother came from. It's north of here—I know that much. If I had a boat, I could find it."

She glanced at me.

"I made my mother tell me the way we were to go."

"Go?" I said. The tongue of flame on the candlewick made the stone walls seem to leap and shudder. "She left you behind when she tried for Clevven."

Sif shook her head and gnawed at the bread, moving her shoulder as she did so and wincing. "It wasn't Clevven she was heading for. And she took me with her."

The candle guttered.

"Down to the shore to say good-bye," I said, not believing what she was telling me.

Sif shook her head. "Into the boat. She put me in and shoved us off from the shore. The water splashed about her legs, then up to her hips. It was early morn, the clouds obscuring Upland Corl, gray as dragons' breath."

She spoke calmly, as was her way. Sif rarely let passion overrule her—as I did invariably. I came up the last two steps and stood by the window, gazing out at the far, black, moonless sea. The starlight shone on it, a moving white blur to my eyes. But I could hear the sound of it, the crash and wash of distant waves, and I could smell it.

"It was a light boat, no draft at all," Sif went on, "the shallowest she could find. She hoped it would ride high enough to pass over the reefs. I didn't know anything about boats then. I must have been about seven. She waded out, shoving the boat, with me in it, before her until the water was up to her waist; then she hauled herself aboard. I wanted to help, but she bade me stay where I was or we'd overbalance. Then she took the oars and rowed."

Sif nibbled at the bread.

"I'd never seen a woman row: long, even strokes. I thought it was wonderful. I thought my mother must be the strongest woman in the world. We drew near the reef. The sun was coming up, a white glare behind the shadow of Ulys in a gray-streaked sky. The tide was high, but going out. There was a gap in the reef she was making for, a little gap."

I saw Sif's hand tighten where it gripped her knees.

"But she had misjudged the depth, or our draft, or the time and tide. She could have made it, I think, in a smaller skiff, built only for one, or even in that boat if I had not been there, weighing it down."

Her voice was very quiet now, bitter and deep.

"Our hull caught on a jagged rock. My mother tried to use the oar to lever us free. I started to stand, but she told me to sit and cling tight to the gunwale. The bottom scraped and grated. Mother leaned against the oar. A swell lifted us. We seemed to float free for a moment. Then a cross-wave struck the boat, spinning it, and we broke against the reef."

Sif stared into the candle flame. I could not think of anything to say.

"My mother was thrown beyond the rocks, I think, or onto them. I did not see her again. I was pitched shoreward. The currents are strange around the reef, with a fierce undertow going out with the tide. But I was so light, and rode so high in the water, that the waves carried me along parallel to the land for a while, then closer to shore. Old Sul was coming along the beach. He fished me out."

Even in the bad light, I could see Sif had grown pale. I touched her arm, which was cold. "I didn't know that," I said softly, able to speak now. "That she took you in the boat with her."

Sif shrugged into the sailor's blanket we kept in the tower to use against the wind. "No one does," she answered, "except maybe Sul. He guesses, I think."

She had finished the bread and now sat looking about as if there might, somehow, be more. There wasn't. Cook had been in a foul mood that evening, and half a loaf had been all I could beg.

"Your mother washed up on the beach two days later," I added, not asking.

She nodded, tucking the blanket more closely about her. "Yes."

Some years passed. Sif grew taller, while I gained barely an inch. She told me tales she heard the fishermen tell, of people and kingdoms under the sea. Sif was better at tale spinning than I. I told her what the fishwives in the market said, and the gossip from the kitchen and my mother's maids. My needlework improved. My father's hair got silver in it. My mother bore my father another short-lived son.

Then I found Sif doubled over in the tower one afternoon, not up on the landing, but below, near the bottom, on the steps. She was on her knees, bent forward, her forehead pressed to the wood.

"Sif, Sif," I cried, dropping the napkin of bannock I had brought for our supper. I ran to her and knelt.

When she lifted her face, I could see she was very pale. Dark circles lay under her eyes, which had a wild and hopeless look. She was panting and shaking, and I could see where she had been biting her lip. She was twelve now. I was nine.

"What is it—has Sul hit you?" I asked. I could see no bruises.

She looked at me blankly, then turned and put her head down. "No. No, it isn't that."

I bent closer. "Are you ill? Is it fever?" I touched her arm, but the flesh felt cold, not hot and damp. Sif twitched.

"I . . . no—don't touch me," she panted. "I can't stand to be touched." Her teeth were clenched. I felt baffled, helpless.

"Something you ate?" I tried. We were seafaring folk, and every one of us knew to eat fish fresh or not at all. But Sul was a lazy sloven these days, Sif said, and who knew what he might have given her?

She shook her head. "No, no." Her hands resting on the wood of the steps were fists. Silence a moment, then, softly, "Go away."

I sat back, startled, staring at her. She had never said such a thing to me before. I frowned hard, tracing the grain of the wood on the step, thinking. I had no intention of going. That was out of the question. Sif needed help, and I must think what to do. I gazed at her doubled figure, listening to her shallow breath, and then, suddenly, I knew.

"It's woman's plight, isn't it?" I asked her. Sif panted and said nothing. "Has old Sul told you what to do?"

Sif made a strangled sound. I couldn't tell if she was weeping or not. "He doesn't know anything—old fool—and wouldn't tell me if he did."

I chewed on that for a moment, feeling strange. For the first time, I knew more about something—something important—than Sif. A pale spider ran across the step beside my hand, jumped, and floated down on a thread of silk.

"Do you have any things?"

"No!" gasped Sif. Her teeth were clenched. "I hate this," she whispered. She was weeping. "I wish I were a boy."

I rose. "Stay here," I said idiotically. Sif wasn't going anywhere. I unpinned my cloak and put it over her. She didn't move or turn to look at me. I put the napkin of food on the step near her hand before I left.

I went back to my mother's apartments and stole some of her bloodlinens. No one was about. She and her maids must have been down in the kitchen or the spinning room, or out of the keep altogether at the market in the village. It didn't matter. I went down to the women's garden and tore up a handful of fat, dark green leaves. Clutching them and the bag of linens to my breast, I went back to the tower and Sif.

She hadn't moved or touched the food. My cape was

slipping down from her shoulders, and she hadn't bothered to pull it back up.

"Sif," I said, kneeling. "It's me, Alys. Eat this."

Sif looked up, her face pasty. "I can't eat," she whispered. "I feel boatsick."

"It's rampion," I said. "My mother uses it. Eat. I promise, it helps."

She stared at the leaf I held out, dully, as though she had never seen such a thing before, as though she had no idea what it was. Slowly, she moved her hand toward it, then stopped. "My fingers are numb."

Her voice was a ghost. I fed the leaf to her, bit by bit. Her lips were cracked and dry. I made her eat two more. Then we waited. The tower smelled of dust and seashells. The summer air was warm. I played with the ants that were carrying bits of chaff down the tower wall. The wind murmured. An hour later, Sif slowly straightened. She still looked pinched and weak, but her breathing had quieted, and some of the color had come back into her cheeks.

"I feel better now," she said quietly. "It still hurts, but it's bearable."

I gave her the last of the rampion, which she ate without complaint. Then I handed her the bloodlinens. She stared at them.

"They're my mother's," I told her. "Put one on."

Sif kept staring, and then looked at me. "How?" she said finally, so blankly I laughed. I showed her. We fumbled, but managed. I was too young yet to be wearing bloodlinens, but I had seen my mother's maids putting on theirs.

"How long . . . ?" I started.

Sif blushed to the bone. "It began last night. I felt ill this morning and couldn't haul the nets. Sul tried to box my ears, so I ran." She shrugged. Now that the pain was past, she seemed more her old self. "But running made it worse."

I sighed and mouthed a phrase I had heard my mother use. "We're born to suffering."

Sif gave a snort and picked at the crumbs of bannock in the napkin I'd brought. "My mother never said that." She shrugged again and gave me back my cloak. "I'll wager it isn't like that, beyond the Portal."

The winter I turned ten, my mother put a woman's gown on me, one that dragged the ground, though I was young yet to be called a woman. The garb was so heavy it slowed my steps, like a gown of lead. She kept me inside with the women then, saying I must learn to spin and weave and wait on my lord at table if I were to marry well. I found it all absurd. Who would marry the ten-year-old daughter of a tiny island lord? I wanted to know.

"Whoever'd have the fur trade hereabouts," my father laughed, stamping the snow from his boots and holding his hands over the great hall's fire. My mother cleaned the blood from his fingers with a warm, wet cloth.

It had been a good clubbing that year, the foxpelts thick and soft. We would do well in spring when the fur traders came from the mainland. My father laughed again.

"Goddess knows, that's why I wed. And truth, no one'd have you for your looks."

I could not tell if he were joking or not. He boxed me across the backside as I passed, hard enough so I nearly dropped the pitcher I was carrying. He smelled of ale and the blood of seafoxes. My mother said nothing. She never crossed my father in public—or in private, either, for that matter.

I missed the outdoors and my freedom, the wind and wave smell, and the running on the beach with Sif. I hardly saw her anymore. Old Sul kept her working breakback at the nets and boats. He hardly lifted a hand himself anymore, and Sif had to do it all.

On rare occasions, we met in the tower. She looked brown as a boy, her shoulders straining the seams of the narrow shirt she wore. I made her a new shirt. She had never had much breast—unlike me, whom my mother wrapped tight lest I look older than my years. Sif didn't show beneath the baggy front of her blouse. When she rolled up the sleeves, her arms were corded and hard. She spoke like the fisherfolk. I scarcely recognized her anymore. More often than our meeting, she left me presents in the rampion: a bright shell, a seastar, the speckled claw of something crablike and huge.

Then came the night when I was nearly eleven; Sif must have been about fourteen. It was the very end of winter, near full moon feast, but already warm enough for spring. I had seen the strand of kelp draped over the seaward gate: our signal to meet in the tower. It was nearly dusk, and I would be due in the supper hall soon. My mother always scolded when I was late; sometimes she pinched. But Sif had hung the seaweed, so I went.

I found her on the landing, pacing—not sitting at her ease as was her wont. Her shirt was torn at one shoulder, and she held it up, striding, striding the narrow space. She was two palm widths taller than I was—I realized that with a start. For the last year, when we had met, it was always crouching in secret, not running and walking the beach as we had used to do.

The look in her eye stopped me short on the last step: it was fierce and burning, half wild. I had never seen her so. Her face was flushed and bruised.

"Sif," I started.

She cut me off. "I'm going. I've got a boat."

I just stood, speechless. The candle in my hand, flaring and guttering, made the tower walls jump and dance. I shook my head, not understanding. My heart was pounding from climbing the steps.

"I got it out of the castle shed last autumn," Sif was saying. "Sul let me take it. He said it was hopeless. But I've patched it. It'll hold—long enough to get me to Narby, anyway."

"What are you talking about?" I started to say, but she wouldn't let me speak. Her free hand clenched, the knuckles white.

"Sul was in his cups again—had been since noon. This

morning he found a keg of the red washed up on the sand unbreached, unspoiled. Never a word to my lord, mind you. Kept it all to himself, and not a drop to me, either."

Her words fizzed, popping like the candle flame.

"And then a couple of hours back, he says what a pretty thing I am and how he's always liked them tall and fair. He told me I reminded him of a lass he once knew—save for being so skinny—and didn't I like his hand on me? I'd come under his roof so long ago, he could hardly remember if I were a lass or a boy, and he'd see for himself if I wouldn't show him."

She fingered the rip where her shirt's shoulder seam had parted. She was shaking with fury.

"I hit him with the gaffing hook. It drew blood. He fell—maybe I killed him. I didn't stay to find out." She chafed her arm a moment. A trickle of ice bled through me.

"He can't be dead, Sif," I whispered. "You wouldn't hit him that hard."

"Could and would," she muttered, then pierced me suddenly with her eyes: sea-green, green-gray. "Even if he's not dead, I can't stay here. I must get off Ulys, or I'll go mad."

The trickle of ice in me had become a torrent. I started to shake. "No, don't go," I said. "I'll tell my father. He'll punish Sul—make him leave you alone. I'll get Cook to give you a place in the kitchen. . . ."

The words trailed off. Sif had stopped pacing. She leaned back against the stone wall beside the window, looking at me. Then she laughed once, a short, incredulous sound. "Do you think your father cares one tat what happens to me?" she asked. "If he'd any honor, he'd have taken me in himself when Zara died."

"I don't understand," I stammered. "My father is a just and noble—"

"Oh, don't talk to me of your 'just and noble' lord," spat Sif, suddenly furious again. She straightened and stood away from the wall. "It's his noble justice left me in Sul's care all these years." She was close to shouting now. "Your fine lord father would have *married* my mother if I'd been born a boy!"

I found the wall behind me with a hand and leaned against it. I needed that support. I stared at Sif. She did not approach.

"I don't know what you mean," I whispered at last.

"By Lithana," choked Sif. "Who did you think my father was?"

I did not answer, could not. I felt myself growing very pale. I had never, not once, ever imagined such a thing. I suppose if I had bothered to think of it at all, I would have guessed Sul.

"He promised to see she got safe to Upland Corl," Sif was saying, "with money enough to buy her passage north—he promised to take her north himself, but later, once his position as lord of the island was more secure." Sif leaned her head back. "She grew to love him. He was kind to her. She told me that. But she didn't bear him an heir—only me. So he wed *your* mother and left mine to find her own way home."

"That isn't true," I whispered. My voice was shaking. I was close to tears. "My father would never . . ."

"Be so dishonorable?" she finished for me, then gave a sigh like one very weary. She spoke softly now, but the words were fierce. "Be glad he was, chit—for your sake. Else it'd have been me trussed up in those fine mucky skirts of yours and you'd *never have been born.*"

We were silent for a while, looking at each other. The spring night air was cold. Her eyes implored me at last.

"I'll need food, Alys. I've already got the boat."

I did weep then. I couldn't help myself. She couldn't mean it. Not Sif. She couldn't truly mean to be leaving me.

"Where will you go?" I managed at last.

Sif turned away, started pacing again. "I don't know. To Upland Corl, first. I'll sign as a seaman. They'll think I'm a boy."

"They won't," I said. "They'll find you out."

"I'll move on before they do," growled Sif. "I'll go north. I'll find my mother's Portal."

It was all absurd, as if she could really go.

"They'll never let you out," I said. "Even if Sul isn't dead, they'll never drop the harbor chain to let you pass. . . ."

"I'm not going by the harbor," my sister snapped.

Panic seized me. "You'll drown like your mother— you'll die on the rocks!"

She stopped pacing and came back to me, stood above me on the landing. I stood on the steps. She reached out and touched my shoulder.

"It's midmonth, Alys," she whispered, and eyed me, wondering. "The full moon's in two days' time: spring tide. The water's deep. Don't you know that?"

I shook my head. I had lived on this little island all my life and never once sat in a boat. I knew nothing of tides. Sif's hand tightened.

"You have to help me," she said. "Sul kept no stores, and I've had no time to lay any in. I'd wanted to wait a year. But it must be now, tonight. I can't get into the kitchen, but you can."

I could indeed, but I didn't want to. I didn't want to help her leave me. Yet at the same time, I knew that Sif would do what Sif would do, as she had always done, with or without my help. Then I realized she needn't have told me at all. She didn't really need me; she wouldn't starve between here and Upland Corl. She had come to say good-bye.

For a wild moment, I wanted to go with her, wanted to beg her to take me along—anything to keep her from leaving me. But I remembered her tale of her mother's boat catching the reef because of too much weight. I would only burden her. I was just a girl. Women in boats were bad fortune. Everyone knew that. I was just a girl, and Sif . . . was Sif.

That was part of it, part of the reason I didn't beg her, simply stood there with her hand on my shoulder and held my tongue. The other part of it was that suddenly I knew, with a certainty beyond all doubts and shadows, that full moon or no, high tide or no, spring tide or no, she would never succeed. Sif would die on the rocks.

I brought her everything she asked of me and more—though I had to wait till after supper. All through the meal, I waited on my father's table. I stared at him as he ate his fill, laughed with his men, and played games of chance, till my mother pinched me and asked what made me so walleyed. Both of them looked like strangers to me. I didn't know them.

When I was dismissed, I lingered in the kitchen until Cook and her maids were at their own fare in the adjoining room, before seizing everything I could lay hold of and wrapping it up in an oiled cloth for Sif: roast fowl and hard-cake, seagranates, and two pouches of wine.

I brought them to her in the tower, along with a little bag of sewing floss. I mended her shirt by candlelight and helped her carry her journey fare down to the seaward gate. No one saw us. My father's guards were slack and full of their own importance and never kept good watch. The reef and the harbor chain were all the watch our island needed.

I gave her my good green cloak, which was closewoven of seahair to keep out the damp, and the gold brooch my mother had given me the year before, when she had first put a woman's gown on me. The month after Sif left, when I told her I had lost it, she gave me a slap that bloodied my nose.

Standing there by the seagate in the darkness under the

high, near-full moon, Sif bent down and kissed my cheek, a thing she had never done before, and passed the bone harpoon head that she wore on a string around her neck into my hand. I got my last good look at her face. She was smiling.

"You're not afraid, are you?" I asked.

She shook her head. "I know the way as far as Narby—I've made sailors at the inn tell me as much. It should not be too hard from there."

I hugged her very tight, holding the bone harpoon head till it cut my hand. I never wanted to let her go. But I did at last, when I heard her sighing, impatient to be gone. I released her and stepped back.

She bent and gathered the things I'd given her and was off—striding down the steep, narrow, moonlit path toward the sea below. She had eyes like a cat in the dark, and I had the eyes of a mole. I didn't stay to watch her go. I would not have been able to see her long anyway. I shut the seagate and turned away, back to Castle Van. I knew that I would never see her again.

೦୭ III ೦୭
SEASINGER

It's strange sometimes how the scent of someone lingers, like smoke in a still room after the candle's out. Sif's presence lingered with me for months. I kept expecting to see her, striding along the beach below Castle Van, or ducking into the tower, or to see a strand of kelp draped over the sea-gate—but I never did.

They never found her body. Sometimes the sea does not give up her dead. Old Sul turned out not to be dead after all, and I could not help feeling bitter that he was not. It meant my sister had died for nothing. She could have stayed.

That spring when Sif disappeared was the start of Ulys's long misfortune. All the luck seemed to wash away. The weather turned bad—a constant, dismal, murky damp; wind so cold that it cut the bone; and no snow drying the air. Fishing fell off, and the red deadmen's hands got into the shellfish beds, prying open the shells with their little suckered fingers and devouring the sweet meat within. Shore fever took many of the fisherfolk—but not old Sul. He lived another three years before expiring of an apoplexy. Inwardly, I rejoiced.

But worst of all, the seafoxes dwindled. Perhaps they found another place to winter. I hoped so. Every year my father's men came back from the clubbing with fewer pelts; almost no white or speckled or silver anymore—only the black and the brown, and those thin and small. Second-rate fur—the Downsmen paid little for it.

Castle Van went into debt to the Corlish merchants from whom we bought many of our goods. Certain valuable heirlooms about the palace quietly disappeared, sold on the mainland, I think. My father made the crossing more than once to secure us loans, always smaller than he had hoped and at exorbitant rates. He lost a good deal of that money gambling and, probably, wenching.

My mother, in a white rage, whispered—but not to him—that he ought to ask his Downsmen kin for help. He was too proud for that. They had disinherited him years ago. At last, there were no more loans to be had. My father, resourceless, prowled the confines of our small, gray keep and our small, gray isle, and began to go mad.

My mother, with a kind of desperate determination, refused to despair. All would be put right, she vowed, when I married. She and her maids got me by the hair then and took charge of my rearing—a task she said they had grossly neglected before.

Got me by the hair quite literally. I was no longer allowed to trim it off below the level of my shoulders, but must let it grow and grow, a waterfall of reddish-gold that was heavy and, in summer, hot. Why couldn't I cut it, I wanted to know? Why must it be so long?

Because that was what a woman's hair was for, my mother said, parting the strands along the center of my scalp with a comb—to be a beauty to her husband's eye. But I didn't have a husband, I protested. *Yet*, she countered, brushing, brushing. It would be sooner than I thought—didn't I want one? No, I didn't want one, I answered, but only to myself, silently. I wanted my childhood back. I wanted Sif.

When I was thirteen years old, my father betrothed me to a minor lord of a minor clan of Upland Corl, one Olsan. A brilliant stroke, he called it. Not for sixty years had the daughter of a lord of Ulys actually lived upon the mainland as a lady of the Downs. My mother made me embroider six handkerchiefs to send to him.

I was to remain on Ulys until I was fifteen, then go to join my lord. He wrote me letters I could not read. My mother read them (or pretended to) and summarized. I had the impression he must be older than my father. No one would say, but he already had children, sons. His first wife was dead.

When I was told that the arrangements for my betrothal were being made, the envoys with the ceremonial marriage ax already on their way, I went down to the beach and looked out at the rocks. I wondered what it would be like to drown, to be torn apart by the gray and heaving sea, to die on jagged stone. I wondered whether I was brave enough to follow Sif, to wade to my death rather than marry an old man whose household would probably laugh at me.

I was not brave enough. I was a coward at heart—or perhaps I was only practical. I knew that freedom was impossible for me. It was only a question of death or life. And I wanted life, even as the plain, untutored, provincial young wife of a stranger. I turned away from the rocks, from the storm-gray sea, and went back to the castle to face the ax.

After my betrothal, I was taught how to pin my hair, how to walk, how to speak, how to wear my clothes. My mother sent to the mainland to learn how the Downswomen's gowns were cut. I was made to recite poetry. They gave up on singing—I had no voice. I could dance a little. My mother was passionate to impress on me all the arts and graces she fancied a matron of Upland Corl would know.

My husband even sent a Wise One, one of the religious women of the Downs who live without men in sacred houses and worship Lithana. This woman was to instruct me in my husband's religion. My father's clan had followed other gods. My needlework impressed her, but that was about all. I could make little of what she told me of gods and duty and sacrifice, but was able to rattle off the phrases quickly enough by rote.

I think Wise Elyt sensed my reluctance. She did not stay long: two months. The unrelenting gray of our weather grated on her. She gave me a pat on the cheek and told my mother she would instruct me further when my lord sent for me. Then she went down to the harbor and took passage on the next boat to the mainland. My mother was furious, saying I had driven her off with my stupidity.

The rampion died. Without Sif, I had not the heart to tend it. I came to womanhood not long after my betrothal and suffered without relief the woman's plight of which my mother had always complained. Nothing grew in the garden anymore. At regular intervals thereafter, whenever the moon turned dark, it was the same. I thought of Sif, and dreamed of the dark leaves' green and bitter taste.

My betrothed, Lord Olsan of Upland Corl, died when I was fourteen years old; some border dispute among the Downsmen, and he was killed. We had mourning. For three months, my mother tied black ribbons in my hair. I was told to look sad. Secretly, though, I did not mourn.

Then I learned that my father had not even waited for the days of mourning to elapse before offering me to any of Olsan's sons who would have me. He was soundly rebuffed. They were all but one married themselves, to good Downswomen. I had been but a toy for their father in his age, but they had heirs to get and needed no beggars from Ulys on which to do it.

So my father demanded that the part of my dowry that had been sent ahead be returned—and was laughed at. The sons of Olsan knew we of Ulys had no friends or armies to insist on justice. My mother raged. My father suffered fierce headaches and fits of temper. I crept about dejectedly, like a whipped dog, until it occurred to me that what had passed between the Downsmen and my father really had nothing to do with me.

When the castle's debts fell due, he offered me at large in Upland Corl. Few lords even bothered to reply. Some of their scorn was for me, I think, as a pauper's daughter—but mostly for him: the madman who would sell his kin so openly. There were delicacies to be observed in the barter of daughters, and he had not observed them. Ulys became a laughingstock, and some of the fisherfolk began to say it was a curse that had driven the lord of the castle mad and chased the seafoxes away.

My father, who had always enjoyed our meager island vintages, began to be too much in his winecup then, and to gamble in the evenings with his men. When castle stores ran low, he sent men-at-arms to seize the fisherfolk's catch. He ordered the people to gather oysters and search for pearls, though our shellfish are not the kind that bear many pearls. His headaches grew worse. The gates of the castle began to be barred in the evenings, a thing that had never been done in the history of Ulys.

Eventually he began to revile my mother. I remember once we sat in the hearth room just off the kitchen after supper; my father, my mother, me, and a few of their men and maids, there together for the warmth. It was winter, and we were short of fuel. My lord and lady had been arguing about something, some little thing, over supper, but had been silent since, when suddenly my father looked up from his cup and growled.

"What is wrong with you, woman, that you never gave me sons? Sons to bring commerce to this little spit of rock, sons to sail and find where the cursed seafoxes have gone?" He looked at the wine dark in the bowl of his cup and muttered, "All you could give me was a chit."

My mother, tight-lipped and hemming a handlinen beside the hearth, could take much from my father and had done so over the years, but his saying that she had not done what women were made to do—that is, give their lords sons and heirs—was too much. Before I could even blink, my mother was on her feet, crying.

"I gave you four sons, live out of the womb." All this from the time I was two till I was nine. "They were your seed, my lord, but they died." She had pricked herself with her needle, and the cloth held a bright red stain. "Do not complain to me that you have no sons."

At which, my father cast his cup away with a shout and gave her such a blow it put her on the ground. He was seized with one of his headaches then and was not fit company for days. He was clearly mad.

My mother grew to loathe the sight of me, and my father did as well. I came to move between the pair of them furtively, like a shadow. My weak eyes did not help. I could not always tell what expression sat their faces. I stayed out of reach. I thought of Sif dodging old Sul, and looked back on her plight with new understanding.

There was no one on Ulys high enough or rich enough to marry me, and no one in Upland Corl would have me. My mother spoke once—only once—of sending me to dwell with the Wise Ones in Farstead, but my father shouted that by the Crowned Man, he'd not send even a worthless girl to serve the superstitions of the thrice-cursed Downsmen and their Goddess-Crone.

It was not, I think, that he had forgotten he had been a Downsman once himself, but rather that he remembered and at the same time knew beyond all shadows, to his bitter rue, that he could never be one again. Ulys had got him by the hair, too. He could never go back.

I was seventeen, unmarried and unspoken for, when the seasinger came. The girls on Ulys wed at thirteen and fourteen. I was an anomaly, a quirk. A jinx, some said. No man would have me. I had learned not to go down to the market anymore, even with my mother's maids. The looks some of the fishwives gave me made my blood run cold.

Perhaps they thought I was the reason the catch and the seafoxes were all so scarce. Or perhaps it was just that I was my father's daughter. He took their labor and their goods, calling such his due, and shared none of the castle stores with them, even when they were starving. They had begun to hate us, I think.

But the seasinger changed all that. He arrived on a ship of Corlish merchantmen come to look at our meager crop of furs. It was spring. He was not a merchant himself, that much seemed plain. He spoke more like a Downsman than not, but the cut of his hair was different: bangs across the brow in the front and long down the neck behind. It was fair hair, dark gold, though his beard was reddish. A fine, thick beard—no boy's—so he must have been in his twenties, surely. His face, they said, was neither lined nor weathered, though well browned by the sun.

Not a common seafarer at all, perhaps? Higher born than that, perhaps? That was what some of the maids speculated. I got all my information from them. They invented excuses to go to the market to see him, to gather news of him.

He played in taverns down by the wharves, songs of Upland Corl, and other songs such as none of us had ever heard—though he knew the Ulish fishing songs as well. His accent was good. He picked up the way of our speech very quickly.

All my mother's maids were wild for him. He paid them polite attention and nothing more. They mooned and sighed over him shamelessly, I am sure, while he—never cold, never aloof—yet never seemed to favor one over another, or return a sidelong longing glance, or answer an urgently whispered plea to meet behind the tavern or in the cowshed or on the strand.

When the furriers went back to Upland Corl at week's end, he stayed. That sparked great interest among the fisher-folk—among my mother's maids as well. Another four days passed, but none seemed to know what the stranger's business in Ulys might be. He would not say.

One of my mother's maidservants came to me when the seasinger had been on our island a week. It was Danna, a saucy girl with dark brown curls. She was younger than I by a year, unmarried, but spoken for. That did not stop her flirting. I sat by the open window making tapestry, a task I was good at, bending close and peering so I could make out the threads. Danna was a good enough sort. I did not dislike her.

"He asked about you today," she said, her voice pitched low, conspiratorially.

I sighed. "Did he send you to fetch me?" I asked, grown used to my father's whims, but unwilling to go before him without some accompaniment to help ensure my safety. "Where's my mother?"

Danna laughed and slapped her hip. "Your mother's below, with Madam Cook, else I would not be telling you this. And it's not your father I mean who asked for you. I mean the stranger, down by the tavern. The singer—*he* asked."

I frowned and looked up. "What do you mean?"

Danna was not close enough for me to see her face well. I could not tell if she were teasing me. As it turned out, she was, but by telling the truth, not otherwise.

"I was at the market," she said, "buying the fleckfish your lady and Madam Cook are now discussing. And I saw him leaning against the inn wall and looking out over the square, eating a fat carnelian fruit in slices with his dagger. So I called out to him, bold as heggitts. I said, 'Ho, singer, why are you not singing in tavern, as that's what you do?' "

She gave a nervous titter at the thought of having been so brash.

"And he said, tossing me a slice of fruit, 'Not all the time, my lass. A man must eat.' "

I sat looking at her. She had covered her mouth with her hands and was blushing—I could see that well—but her tone told me she was more delighted than ashamed.

"And then he said," whispered Danna, "then he said, 'You're Danna, aren't you—Uldinna's daughter?' Truly, hearing him say that, I nearly jumped out of my hair, and I didn't eat his fruit. I came to myself. I said, 'And how do you know that?' And he said, shoving away from where he was leaning. He was smiling—oh, he does have a foxy smile: all his teeth straight and none missing. But truth, I was a little ware of him by then.

"But he said, soft and courtly as a lord, 'Oh, I've learned many things, Danna, in the little time I've been here—about you and about this place. For example, I know you work in the lord of Ulys's keep.'

"'I do,' I said. 'I am maid-waiting to the lady Benis.'

"'Ah,' he said, 'and I hear the lady Benis has a daughter, a famous daughter, one of whom all Corl speaks. . . .'

"And I said, forgetting myself, I said, 'Hold right there, you. It wasn't the lady Alia's fault, her Downsman lord dying and my lord all in debt. She's a fine, *good* girl, and all this talk of a curse is nothing. . . .'

"But he laughed! 'No, no. You mistake me. That is not what I have heard at all,' he said. 'Word is, where I am from, that she is a handsome lass, fair as morning light, with all the virtues a highborn maid should have. But she is proud as her father is rich, and spurned the lord to whom she was betrothed, till he died of grief. Then she spurned all the other desperate suitors that clamored for her hand.' He smiled at me. 'At least, so they sing the tale where I am from.'

"'Where are you from, sir?' I asked him, but he only laughed, again.

"'Ah, that I cannot tell you just yet, my lass.' He sounded so like a Downsman then. But not like a merchant—more like your father speaks, like a lord. I'm sure he cannot but be some highborn noble of Upland Corl, and the way he speaks to sing us songs in tavern all pretense."

Danna was gazing at me earnestly now. I did not know what to make of her words, nor whether she might be gaming with me. Flustered, I tried to turn back to my tapestry, but the threads kept tangling. My mother's maidservant went on.

"'But how is it,' the seasinger now says, 'in all the days I've been here, and all the ladies of Lord Halss's keep'—imagine him calling maids such as I *ladies*—'all those that have come down from the keep to hear my singing, that I have never so much as glimpsed this celebrated girl?'

"'Well, she never comes out of the keep,' I said.

"'What, never?' the young man asked. He seemed truly surprised. 'Does she not walk along the beach of a morning, or come down to the village on market day?'

"'No, sir, she does not—my lord and lady keeping such a close watch on her as they do, not wanting her to fall in with mere common sorts.'

"I said that, looking hard at him, for suddenly I couldn't tell anymore whether he seemed a common seasinger or a highborn Downsman lord—and the moment before, I'd been so *sure*. But he never so much as blinked."

I gazed out the window then, at the blur of emptiness beyond that was the sky. Danna's words ran against my ears like water for a little space, meaning nothing. Close watch indeed! I was a prisoner of my father's keep and my mother's isle, withering and dying by inches, like the rampion. I felt frozen, and old.

"He seemed to think on that a little while," Danna was saying as I began listening again. "And then he said, 'Might this young lady be in need of music lessons? Every fair daughter of a high lord surely must. . . .'

"'Oh, sir, she's hopeless,' I cried. 'The lady Benis tried and tried. . . .'"

I glanced at Danna, and the dark-haired girl had the grace to stumble to a halt and blush. I sighed again and turned back to my weaving, satisfied that I knew this seasinger now for what he was, a fortune seeker, and one who clearly thought my father richer than he was. We had no gold to spare on fripperies like music. But even my glare had not silenced Danna.

"Well, then, all he said was, 'Commend me to the young lady Alia and tell her I stand ready at her service,' and I said I wouldn't, he had a fair tongue, and that I had it in mind to tell the lord Halss himself that an impertinent tale singer had been asking after his daughter.

"But—and here's the odd part, my lady—he only just smiled at me. He didn't seem angry or frightened at all; any common man would have been. And his voice grew all Corlish and noble again suddenly. He just smiled and said I'd do no such thing—didn't I want to eat my slice of fruit that was dripping all over my hand?

"And then, truth, I just didn't want to tell my lord, or anyone, save you, and I was ravenous for that bit of fruit. So I ate it quick, and when I did, it was the sweetest thing."

A strange sensation ran through me, hearing that last which Danna said. I began to wonder if there might be more to this mysterious seasinger than just fortune seeking. My mother's maids continued their silly speculations that he must be some prince of the mainland traveling disguised, adventuring, or—here they sighed—even bride seeking.

But the more I pondered Danna's tale—of his causing her, with no more than a word and a smile, to relinquish her intention to report to my lord and savor a fruit she did not want—the more the strange fear grew in me that he must be some conjurer, about what game I could not tell. I resolved to stay wide of him; even if there were no need, with him soundly barred from keep and me securely prisoned within.

To my surprise, I did have need of my resolve, and soon. The very next afternoon, the seasinger presented himself at the castle gate. My father was ill with headache and could receive no one, and so my mother was sent for. She was suitably indignant at this mere entertainer's cheek and kept him waiting an hour before donning a fine, fox-trimmed robe and going down to the audience hall, a crowd of maids and ladies revolving around her like satellites.

I was instructed to remain out of the way and on no account to show my face in the audience hall. This I gladly did, having no desire to don a formal gown too small in the bodice to breathe in and too voluminous to walk in with ease. I dawdled in the kitchen, helping Cook make tarts. I had no wish to see the seasinger. I hoped my mother would send him away.

But she did not. She entertained him for two hours in

the hall, listening rapt to his songs and stories. Twice she sent to the kitchen for refreshments, first for cakes and candied eels, and shortly after for the good yellow wine—not the common cellar stock, either, but my lord's private store.

Cook was astonished. I went back to my mother's chambers to await her return with a sharp sense of misgiving. She returned at last, she and her maids all in a flutter, their faces flushed from the strong yellow wine.

"Oh," my mother said, clinging to Imma for balance while another maid helped her off with her slippers. "Oh, he is an impressive young man."

A third assisted her with her outer robe. They were all a little unsteady on their feet.

"Such wit, such courtesy. Surely Ulys has never seen the like—saving only my lord husband, of course." She hiccuped and sat down suddenly. Her maids, some of them hiccuping themselves, giggled. My mother joined them.

"And wasn't it clever," she added, "wasn't it clever of me to call for the wine? It put him in a garrulous mood, did it not?"

"A fine mood, m'lady," Imma echoed her. I could see Danna just beyond them on a footstool, dozing where she sat.

"The thing or two he let slip after the second cup!" my mother laughed, worrying the pins holding her hair. Imma stumbled to help her.

"The way he talked, m'lady, I wouldn't be surprised if he were a prince disguised, a prince of Upland Corl come adventuring."

My skin prickled and drew up; he had them all believing

it now, and even saying so in front of my mother. I glanced quickly at Danna, but she never so much as stirred in her sleep. My mother nodded.

"I am sure he is of the Haryl clan," she answered. "He mentioned their Down."

I blushed. The scent of yellow wine was strong in the room, like spilled cider. Imma and her fellows buzzed around like bees. Clearly they had all had several more after the second cup—and probably done no better than make fools of themselves before this common conjurer. My mother laughed again.

"Surely he is rich."

I looked up sharply. What could she mean—a seasinger, rich? My mother seemed to catch sight of me for the first time.

"Look, Alia; look," she exclaimed. "See what the young man has presented to me."

She beckoned her other maid, Rolla, forward. The girl held an oblong something covered with coarse brown sacking. She laid it on the bed. My mother awkwardly pulled the sacking off, and I saw a bolt of cloth—but such cloth as I had never seen.

The threads were very fine and slick, the weave tight, not the least bit sheer. I ran my hand over it; it was soft, yet strangely crisp. It made many tiny wrinkles but did not keep them, springing back from the touch. I sensed water would bead on this stuff. It rustled. It whispered. But the oddest thing about it was its color, appearing from some angles pearly blue-gray or silver, and from others, pink.

I stared at it. The cloth had sorcellous feel to my hand. All the fine hairs along my arm were standing up. My mother held a length of it up to her, fingering it.

"Oh, we must make him welcome, that we must," she crowed. "One who knows where they make this cloth—he could make us rich! Alia, have you ever seen the like? How much would even a yard of this bring in Upland Corl? Wealth!"

The hairs on my head felt charged and alive, the way they did before a storm. I felt strange, troubled. I could not think of anything to say. My mother dropped the cloth suddenly and frowned a trace. "What a pity he declined my invitation to stay at keep."

She glanced at me.

"Well, no matter," she said. "Alia, my dear"—she spoke very distinctly now, against the slurring of the wine—"we must make you ready. I have invited this young man to full-moon feast two days from now. Your father will be over his headache by then, and we must be certain you are looking your best."

I drew back, my heart dropping like a stone. My throat was suddenly tight. The cloth on the bed snapped and sparkled where my mother stroked it. I began to fear more than wine and flattery had had a hand in my mother's change of heart: inviting strangers to table and calling them lords. Conjurer—sorceller, more like! I wanted nothing to do with him.

"Must—must I, Mother?" I stammered. "The time of the moon is wrong. I shall be ill that night, I know it." It was a lie. My time was always at moondark, not fullmoon feast—but it was all I could think of. My mother's lips compressed.

"Well or ill," she snapped, "you'll make yourself ready and be glad on it. The young gentleman—who is calling himself Gyrec at present—has expressed a particular wish to see you." She glanced away, her eyes a little unfocused. "Imma, my patterns. We must see my daughter has a new gown."

I shuddered then and could have wept. So they were offering me up to seasingers now. Who would it be next—Saakmen? Sea captains? I had begun to think myself safe from this bargaining at last; my father too ill and indebted, my mother too resourceless to try again. I had been a fool to hope. I thought of Sif, tossed and dying on the rocks, and envied her.

∽ IV ∽
FULLMOON FEAST

I was made ready for fullmoon feast: bathed and scented and bundled into a many-gored, fur-trimmed gown of russet and olive. I had never had a fur-trimmed gown before. My mother had meant to make me a gown of the seasinger's silk, but my father had seized the stuff as soon as he had learned of it and, above my mother's protests, sent the bolt to the mainland to be sold.

It brought a staggering sum, enough to pay half a year's debt and more. He was in a fine expansive mood by the time of the feast, chucking my mother's cheeks and telling her what a clever thing she was, arranging for this excellent young Downsman to come sit at our table—they'd have me married yet.

What a banquet it was that they held. We must have gone through stores to last a month in that one meal: sweetgrain and date sugar, honey and nutmeal for cakes and cozies. Broiled fish and baked bird, eels fried and spitted and dressed seven ways. Shellfish in bloodsauce and succulent pincushion fish, sea currants and ocean plums, apples stuck with spice pricks and steamed in cider. New butter brought over from the mainland in tubs. Cook was a madwoman and beat the kitchen boys for pilfering.

At last the board was laid and the guests in place. My father sat in a high-backed chair at the center of the table, bedecked in all the finery of Upland Corl that he had left. The garb was old, a little shabby, and tight across the belly even where the seams had been let out.

But he wore it with such an air of unfeigned pride that for a moment, approaching him, I caught a glimpse of what he must have been like when he was young. My mother sat on his left. She had never been a beautiful lady—her hair was graying, her eyes surrounded by tiny lines—but that night she was a regal one.

The stranger sat on my father's right—of middle height for a man, so far as I could tell, well proportioned, with long legs. He was dressed in a tabard and breeks of blue and dark red, gold-chased, finer far than anything anyone else in the hall had on, thereby reinforcing the rumor that he was some disguised lord of Upland Corl, as I was sure was his intent.

His hair was indeed dark gold, as I had heard tell, with bangs across the brow and the ends curling under at the shoulder, much longer than the hair of a man of Ulys. And, unlike a man of Ulys, he was bearded. A thick fringe of curly reddish hair ran along his jaw and upper lip and chin, but left the cheeks for the most part bare. The effect was strange to my eye, both enticing and oddly menacing at once.

I dropped my eyes as I approached—as my mother had instructed me to do—curious as I was. I did not have a seat at the table, of course, being only an unmarried girl. My task was to serve the wine and other victuals. I was not to speak unless directly addressed, and then to answer softly with a bob—any other response being a breach of maidenly modesty.

I filled my father's cup, and then my mother's, but as I bent near to fill the stranger's, I became uncomfortably aware that he was watching me. I knew that I must not look up, but his gaze on me was so fixed, so intent, it made my skin prick.

I did look up then, and found him staring. His eyes were gray, dark-looking by candlelight. The hall was ablaze with torches and candles that night—another store we were using recklessly in ostentatious display. The seasinger's eyes, like a steady-burning flame, never wavered. He said nothing.

I backed away from him and dropped my gaze, and, my first serving duty done, retreated in confusion to the kitchen. He had been looking at me as though wishing to see into my very soul, or impart some urgent message. Surely it had been those eyes, conjurer's eyes, that had made Danna eat the fruit.

I began to be afraid then, and cowered in the kitchen until the guestcup was drunk and the next course ready to be served. Every time I went into the serving hall, I felt those eyes on me. My lord and lady did nothing to discourage it. I sat trembling in the kitchen between times and could not eat.

Soon enough my parents began openly to encourage him by discussing the merits of their lovely daughter, a mere child, trained for the life of a lady in Upland Corl—until the unfortunate demise of her intended lord. They spoke as though it had been only months, not years ago, as though I must be heartbroken. The young man Gyrec replied to them wittily, absently, and stared at me.

He had a fine voice, a bit light, but he used it well. He did not quite have the accent of the isles, but his way of speech was close, very close. There was about it, too, a hint of something I had heard before—Saakish speech? I could not say. It troubled me, making me want at once to listen more closely and to run away.

My father and mother began to praise my virtues one by one. Lord Halss went on about my youth, beauty, modesty, obedience, and sweet nature. He might have been describing a stranger. Then my mother held forth about my skill in all the womanly arts: how well I sewed and cooked and could mend a legging. She told him I recited the pious offices of the Goddess and sang like an idyllbird in spring.

At that the stranger suddenly laughed, a surprisingly deep-throated, likable sound. He covered this breach with some pleasantry to my mother that if her daughter's voice were half so sweet as her own, I must be a jewel indeed. My parents nearly killed themselves for smiling then, but I knew with certainty that the singer was well aware I had no voice. Danna had told him so in the market square. And he did not care.

When I brought in the next course, the candied fruit between the soup and the meat, the singer's fingers brushed my hand. I shied away and made myself gone as quick as I could, but when I brought in the meat and was taking the soup plates away, he actually caught hold of my wrist, quite unobtrusively and not hard, but I was so startled I jerked away and nearly dropped the dish.

He did not seem angry, only perturbed, and when I next entered the room, he ignored me. My parents were not amused, however, and my mother caught me aside to hiss, "Do not be so standoffish, you silly chit. Smile and be receptive to the young man's attentions. Speak to him if he should speak to you."

Fear bit into me to hear her say that. Desperation made me bold. "I won't!" I whispered. He was no Corlish lord, I *knew* it. "He's some conjurer—"

"He's none, and you will," my mother snapped, pinching me hard enough to make my eyes sting.

"I can't," I gasped, half weeping now. A sidelong glance showed me my father and the long-haired sorceller deep in some convivial talk. "I don't like him!"

"That's nothing," my mother said fiercely under her breath. She gave me a shake. "Do as you're told."

A strange, sudden calm that was nearer numbness descended on me, and I stopped weeping. I realized then that I would not marry, ever, any man at my parents' behest. I would live in Castle Van all my life a withering maid if I must, but I would not anymore do as I was told. I would fling myself from the tower first. I'd die on the rocks.

But how to survive this evening was my first concern. Once more I retreated to the kitchen. Once more I emerged to serve a dish. This time when I approached the table, I found my father and his guest at a game of chancesticks. My mother sat watching, seemingly rapt.

She did not know how to play, chancesticks not being considered a suitable game for ladies, but I did. Sif had taught me. My father was a fair enough player, but the seasinger was better. Nevertheless, twice during the next few rounds, I glimpsed our guest surreptitiously discarding a counter to give himself a losing score.

"So," my father said, rubbing the pieces between his palms for luck, "tell me where you found this marvelous cloth with which you gifted my lady. Somewhere north of here—Clevven, perhaps?"

He cast the sticks. The stranger laughed.

"Ah, my lord, were a man to divulge such a thing, he'd

not long keep his monopoly." He shook the counters between cupped hands. "No, my lord, I am not looking for a confidant. I am looking for a port—preferably an island off the coast of Upland Corl. I've already surveyed your neighbors to north and south.

He threw, but the score was low. My father won the round.

"What good's an island port to you?" my father asked, marking the tally and gathering up the sticks.

"As a place to display my wares to the lords of the Downs," the seasinger replied.

My father threw. "Why not take your goods directly to their ports?"

The seasinger smiled and collected his sticks. "Because they would tax me, my lord."

He breathed upon the sticks. My father took a cup of wine, eyeing the other meditatively. Most men were uneasy in my father's presence, if he chose to make them so. But the seasinger showed not a trace of unease. His hand was steady, his air relaxed. My father fingered the stem of his cup.

"And would I not?"

The stranger threw. "Think, my lord," he murmured, watching the counters fall. "Think of the fat Corlish ships coming into your port—Saakmen, too. Tax *them*, my lord, when they come to buy my cloth."

My father roared with laughter, and set down his empty cup. The round was his again. My mother ran her linen napkin through her fingers, watching, watching. The gold the bearded man counted out to my father was new minted in Upland Corl. *Ting, teng,* it rang. My father's eyes glittered.

But I caught a glimpse the seasinger stole at him while handing over the gold: unsmiling, narrow-eyed, calculating. Suddenly I had the uncanny feeling that he disliked my father—no, more than disliked: *hated* my father for some reason I could not even guess. My parents, I was certain, sensed nothing of this, and the seasinger's look was gone in a moment, as if it had never been.

I had been lingering, watching and listening to what the two players said. I had drawn closer to the seasinger without realizing it. This time he caught not my wrist but my sleeve. My lord and lady conveniently studied the board.

"Ho, gentle maid," the stranger murmured—and again, his eyes were on mine with an alarming urgency. "Stand beside me and bring me luck."

Surreptitiously he pressed something small and crumpled into my hand and made to draw me nearer, but I passed on quickly, alarmed, blushing to the bone, determined not to stand long enough to let him get hold of me again.

"Leave me alone," I muttered, just low enough that my parents might not hear.

Safe in the kitchen, I looked at what he had pressed on me: a little slip of brown parchment covered with tiny scratchings and signs. They meant nothing to me—surely none sorcel. I threw it in the kitchen fire and scrubbed my hand with salt.

I didn't want to go back into the banquet hall then, but

Cook made me. It was the last course. After that, I could flee. The full moon shone down through the open window of the hall. The evening was wearing late.

Even as I entered the dining hall, I dropped my eyes. I would not look at him. Conjurer, sorceller—doubtless eager to see if his scribbled spell had made me pliable. I squared my shoulders defiantly. I was bearing a basket of spotless goldenfruit, so sweet and ripe that it bruised if so much as breathed upon. Eyes still downcast, I began serving my father. He caught me about the waist with seeming affection.

"Not so fast, not so fast," he laughed—there was an edge to it, though. I had grown adept at hearing such undertones. "Bide a while, my duck. Do not hurry off. From your haste, one would think you eager for this night to end."

A smile, another laugh, a less-than-gentle squeeze. He was very angry with me and would seize an opportunity within the next few days to box my ears, I could be sure. I didn't care. I served my mother then, and she looked daggers at me. She did not speak, but I could fairly hear what she was thinking: *Chin up, now, girl. You've got his eye. Toss your hair and swirl your skirts a bit. Show your meager gifts off to the buyer at their best.*

I tucked my chin and held my neck perfectly rigid, glowering fiercely, but the stranger would not stop looking at me. My father rose, cup in hand, and began offering a toast, going on about it so as to give the singer some cover to talk to me. I fairly hated my father then. I think I had hated him all my life, for not once had he ever consulted me about my fate as he went about arranging it. At that moment, I would gladly have put a dagger in his heart if I could have done so and lived.

The stranger took my father's cue and bent near me as I passed, taking hold not of me nor of my sleeve this time, but of the basket's edge, as if to examine its contents. He pretended to, and I stood trembling in fury. Sorceller or no, I was tired of being afraid.

"You read the note?" he said, very softly, lifting a fruit from the basket and turning it to the light.

"I threw your ensorcelled scrap in the fire," I hissed.

He looked up, startled, nearly dropping the fruit. I saw the bright red bruises his fingers made in the smooth golden flesh.

"What—why?" he gasped, astonished. I felt a little surge of triumph.

"I wouldn't have read your spell even if I could," I said in a low voice. "I can't read."

"Can't . . . ?" he started. "But your mother—"

"She lied," I murmured, with relish. "I can't sing, either. You know that much from Danna in the market."

"Sweet Lithana . . ." He swallowed the rest of the curse. "There's no time. Meet me on the strand, tonight, before midnight, after the feast. I must—"

But I cut him off, wrestling him for the basket. "I won't. I'll not go anywhere with you, sorceller."

"Alys," he said then, and I gasped that he could have

discovered my secret name. Both my parents had been naming me Alia all night. Surely he was a sorceller if he could know such things.

I got the basket from him then and stumbled back, hard, into my father as he stood making his toast. Wine slipped from his cup as I jostled him, sopping his sleeve, and the goldenfruit spilled, to roll bruised and ruined among the platters on the white tablecloth.

"Stupid . . . !" my father burst out, and raised his arm as if he meant to backhand me there before all the hall—it would not have been the first time. But the stranger leapt up suddenly and got between us under the pretext of steadying my lord's cup. He was as tall as my father, nearly, though lighter built.

"My lord," he cried, his voice hearty, not a trace of alarm or anger to it. He never so much as glanced at me. "My lord, you have offered me a worthy welcome this night, and for that, my thanks. My resources are, at the moment, meager, but allow me to repay your hospitality as best I can."

He kept my lord's eyes square on himself, and I seized the opportunity to retreat a few paces, out of my father's reach. I dared go no farther. My father's stance, as he eyed the young man, was angry still. If I had not known better, I might have thought the seasinger were protecting me. *No!* This was all part of his game somehow.

"The time has come to breach the keg, my lord, with which I presented you earlier this even, when first I arrived."

His voice had a fine ring to it. It carried well, commanding the attention of everyone in the hall. My father began to look a little mollified. Already the seasinger had him under his spell. Already he had begun to forget about me. Slowly, my father smiled.

"Indeed," he cried at last, and motioned to two of his men standing across the hall. "Bring it up."

My father's soldiers knelt and lifted something that had rested between them, and came forward with it. As they set it down before the table, I realized it was a wine cask. One of the guardsmen knocked a bung into it. The stranger spoke.

"My lord, lady, good company of the hall, I am a seasinger. I have been far over the ocean wide, seen many places, and drunk many fair wines—but none is finer than the stuff they call seamilk, which is made in a place far north of here, where I have lately done some trading."

He motioned to my father's men. They hefted the cask and came forward again. The singer held out his own cup, which was empty, and let the liquid splash into it. It was amber gold, with a strong, aromatic scent. I was standing close enough to note all this—but under the gold there seemed to be a darkness to it, a blueness like smoke or shadow in the depths, for all that the surface sparkled and shone like fire.

"A sup, now, a single sup for every person in the hall— for luck," the stranger continued, and I noted a quickening in his tone, not fear, but an eagerness that had not been there before. Holding out my father's cup, he let the soldiers splash in a measure to mingle with the wine already in the bowl.

My father stood, seemingly a little perplexed, as though not sure how he liked the singer's presumption now that he thought upon it. The guardsmen moved down the table and poured a little in my mother's cup. She stood holding it, looking at my father uncertainly. He ignored her, but when the men-at-arms paused, he gave them a nod to go on around the hall.

"Drink, drink up, my lady, lord," the seasinger urged, his tone commanding yet convivial. Smiling, he raised his cup as in salute. My father brought his own cup to his lips and sipped. I saw his eyebrows lift in surprise, and then his whole face eased.

"By the Crowned Man, that's good," he exclaimed, and downed the strange wine in a draught. "Give me another. Let the whole hall have it!"

The stranger gave my lord his own cup, untouched. I saw my mother sipping now, and the same reaction of surprise and pleasure on her face.

"What d'you call that stuff again?" my father asked, taking the full chalice from the seasinger eagerly. My mother eyed the bottom of her cup in disappointment.

"Seamilk, my lord."

"From the north—where in the north?"

"The same spot the silkcloth comes from—but you'd have to offer me a fine bargain indeed to make me tell you that." The stranger laughed. This time I saw him glance at me, and my father, following his gaze, laughed, uproariously, with him.

"Got any more with you?"

"Not this trip. Drink! Drink up, the hall!" cried the seasinger. The soldiers had made their way a quarter of the way around now, and I could hear the sighs and soft exclamations as people tasted each a splash. I saw servers and kitchen boys scrambling—for cups, I guessed. No one was to be denied a sip, not even servants.

And the hall was full, packed to overflowing. I realized that in some astonishment. I had taken no note of it before. All come to see the seasinger, I guessed, or to steal a bite of that magnificent feast. Probably there was not a stable lad or chambermaid in the keep who had not come. Now they all held out their cups as the men-at-arms made their round with the smoky seamilk, and still the singer talked. "But my lord, my lord—your health and the lady's. The seamilk is only the first part of my gift. Here is the second."

∽ V ∽
WEREFOX

Reaching down, the seasinger caught up a little harp hardly bigger than my hand—I could not see where he had been keeping it. It almost seemed he plucked it from the air. Then in one swift, striding sweep, the seasinger was around the table's end and standing in the middle of the hall, in the open space between the other tables. He faced about.

"Let me tell you a tale of the seafoxes, my lord—a song they sing in the spring in that lonely northern place whence

I have lately come. You will find this tale of interest, my lord, for I gather you know something of seafoxes here."

Again my father laughed, and half the hall with him, though I thought the stranger's jest—if jest it were—a feeble one. The soldiers had made half the circuit now, and it seemed to me that that half of the hall was very merry. The singer put his hand to the strings, and the little harp, for all its tiny size and shortness of string, had a surprisingly full, rich sound. The soldiers continued their task, and the aroma of seamilk pervaded the room.

"Once was there a prince of the seafoxes, good people, on a tiny isle far north of here. A man he was upon the land, a silver fox upon the sea. . . ."

He told the tale of that seafox prince, and his beautiful sister who swam south one year and disappeared. She had been captured by a cruel lord who kept her prisoner in his keep until she lost the power to become a seafox. When she tried to swim away from him, she drowned.

It was a haunting tale, skillfully sung. The singer had a fine, full-throated tenor voice that soared to the high notes with no trouble at all. The men-at-arms completed their circuit with still a little seamilk in the keg. No one offered me a cup, and I was strangely glad.

I glimpsed a kitchen maid bearing a full chalice through the kitchen door—for Cook and her minions, I supposed. I wished that I, too, might slip from the hall, but I could not have done so without attracting my father's eye. He was sitting down beside my mother, intent upon the singer, seemingly in a fine mood once again, but I could not be sure. The two men-at-arms stole quietly from the hall with the last of the keg—to share it with their fellows on watch, no doubt.

"That prince, he waited long years for his kinswoman to return," the seasinger sang. "But at last he said, 'I fear the worst. Some evil has befallen her. I will trade my human shape for a fox's skin and search for her.'"

The hall should have been very still by then, out of respect for the singer, but it was not. A constant ripple of low laughter ran through the crowd of banqueters; there was much grinning, a chuckle, even a guffaw now and again—though I could find nothing mirthful in the strange, sad tale. The seasinger, however, did not seem to mind. I could not make out his face well at this distance, but he seemed to be smiling.

"It was years; it was a very long time that that prince of the werefoxes searched, but at last he found the isle whither his kinswoman had come. He put on the shape of a man once again and entered the town as a seasinger. Thus he learned her fate."

It seemed half the hall was laughing now, a little madly, like men drunk at the sight of land after a long voyage or a storm. There was an odd sound to the hilarity, an eerie wildness—as though the listeners laughed less at what they heard than because they could not help themselves. Unease danced a feather down my spine.

"Then, after a week's time, the lord of the keep called him up to his hall," the seasinger sang. "'Come sing to my people; come sit at my board.' And the prince of the seafoxes sang them a song, and gave the lord of the castle two gifts: a cask of seamilk sweeter than honey on a lying tongue, and a bolt of silkcloth that glimmered like fishskin, or pearlstuff, or oil."

My hands and feet had grown very cold. I stood staring at the seasinger, unable to move. He had turned, gazing intently at my father now, no longer facing the hall, no longer making any pretense at a smile. The edge I had heard before in his voice returned.

"The lord offered him his daughter's hand, saying, 'Take her, good sir. You seem an enterprising young man. And I need an heir.'"

The hall had quieted a little now, but no one seemed in the least alarmed. The half of the hall that had drunk the seamilk last were laughing the loudest now. The first half were nodding and yawning, even the guards. I saw my mother bowed over her cup and my father resting his jaw on one hand and rubbing his eyes with the other.

"'I will take your daughter,' the seasinger replied, 'and your wealth, lord, and the good fortune of all these people here—for I have learned that not only my kinswoman perished here. Scores of my people have lost their lives upon this rock. In winter, you and your men go out hunting—bat the seafoxes' heads in and steal their skins. . . .'"

His voice had changed utterly now. He was not singing anymore. Abruptly, he stopped, turned, and surveyed the hall.

"But enough of songs," the stranger barked, returning his attention once more to my father.

He came forward and tossed his harp upon the table with a carelessness that frightened me. I shrank back against the wall. Once again those piercing eyes looked at me and pinned me where I stood. My father took no note of any of this, still rubbing his eyes.

"My lord, the seamilk and the song were but the first parts of my business here. There is a third part. Do you know what that might be?"

My father looked up bleary-eyed. He licked his lips. "Eh?"

I wanted to cry out some warning—or run—but the sorceller's eyes had paralyzed me.

"Do you know the third part of my business here this night, my lord?" the singer repeated, sharply. My mother snored over her cup. At the other's words, my father's head snapped up, but quickly sagged.

"Oh . . . my daughter," he muttered. "Benis says . . . must lose no time, contract you to marry her. Before you leave the isle."

I could not swallow. The seasinger laughed.

"Your daughter will be coming with me, never fear," he answered lightly, his tone all darkness underneath. "After this night, you will never see her more. But she will not depart here a bride, my lord."

My heart twitched in my breast. I leaned back against the wall. The stone was hard and cold. I hardly felt it.

"What?" my father cried, half rising, but his torso seemed somehow too heavy for his legs, and he had to rest one arm upon the tabletop. With the other hand, he clutched his chair. "The girl . . . the chit goes nowhere . . . till she's wed and bred me an heir." He squinted, peering at the bearded young man before him. "You're no Corlish lord. . . ."

"I never said I was," the other snapped. "Nor am I a common seasinger. Did you think it was only some singer's tale I told? It was a true account. *I* am the prince of the seafoxes of whom I sang. This is the isle where my kinswoman perished. You are the cruel lord that held her here."

Once more he turned and seemed to appraise the hall. It had grown far quieter at last. I saw people, some slumped where they sat, others still upon their feet, but like sleep-walkers, gazing vacantly. I saw a serving boy very calmly give a great yawn and lie down upon the floor. A soldier staggered and leaned against the wall. My father had slumped back into his seat and sat looking stupidly at the stranger as though he were speaking a foreign tongue.

"Kinswoman?" my father muttered. "Kinswoman?"

Again the stranger's cutting laugh. "Can you not recall her name, my lord—has it been so long? *Zara.*"

I saw two of my father's men try to rise from their seats, and fall. The seasinger's hand went momentarily to his sleeve as if to draw something concealed there. A weapon? A dagger? But he left the motion uncompleted as both my father's would-be defenders fell. He turned back to my lord.

"Yes, Zara." His voice was low, furious. "You kept her prisoner on this crag—ten years."

My father shook his head again, his speech thick and difficult. "No," he muttered. "No." Then, "Zara."

"You promised to take her to the mainland and buy her passage north," the seasinger answered, advancing on my father.

"How did you know that?" my father whispered. "Sorceller."

The seasinger smiled, leaning nearer. My father's eyes rolled. I had never seen him afraid.

"You broke your word," the other said, very softly.

"I told her . . . told her what I had to. . . ."

"Had to?"

"To keep her. To keep her by me!" My father's words were a moan. They frightened me still further. I had rarely known him to express any strong emotion but rage.

"She wanted nothing more to do with you," the seasinger half shouted.

For a moment, the grimace on my father's face vanished. His head fell back. He smiled, clumsily, remembering. "No, not after. But those first years—those first years, she loved me."

"Why didn't you marry her?" the seasinger demanded. He had regained his composure, spoke quietly now.

My father's teeth clenched. Again the look of pain. "Wanted to. If she'd given me a son . . . !"

"But she didn't. So you married Benis."

"Had to! They'd never have kept me lord here without an heir—my claim was by marriage. Oh, it was all Benis. Old lord's niece; she wanted it. She forced it—if she'd married someone else, *he'd* have been lord."

He seemed unable to stop talking, part of the seasinger's spell, I knew. My father rested his forehead on his hands. They curled into fists. His voice shook.

"If I'd had a son, a son by Zara, I might have resisted. With an heir, perhaps no one would have cared if I married Benis or no. I held out, hoping. . . ." His tone darkened, no longer shaking. His jaw tightened. "But all I got was that brat, a girlchild: Siva."

"Sif." The bearded man's voice dropped, low and dangerous. "Also my blood. Why didn't you let my kinswoman go?"

A moan. "I wanted . . . I thought she'd come back to me."

"With you wed to another?"

My father's head snapped up, his voice a wail. "I didn't think the cow'd live forever! Her cousin, Alia, the first one, died young." A moment's silence, then, softer, "I thought I could get a son on Benis, and Zara would take me back."

"Ten years," the seasinger hissed. "And what became of the brat, the girlchild, Sif?"

My father shook his head and swatted the air as if to slap away a relentless fly "Dead. Dead."

"You left her in the care of the old boatman, Sul. He'd have worked her to death if she'd let him—or worse. Nearly did."

My father gazed ahead of him, at nothing. "Trapped," he murmured, not making sense. "Prisoner."

"You could have raised her here in the keep," the seasinger persisted. "She was your daughter—would that have been so hard?"

My father shrugged, petulant. He was growing more sluggish. "Benis'd have killed her. Shoved her down steps or poisoned her in kitchen." He sighed, frowning, scratching his arm and looking about as though he had lost something. "If Benis could have had a son," he murmured, "she'd not have cared a whit about the girl. Or Zara."

"*You* didn't care what happened to her."

"I needed a *son*."

My father's last spark, gone in a moment. The seasinger was very quiet then, for a long breath fingering something in his sleeve. "Did you . . . ?" he started, then stopped a moment, as his voice caught. "Did you ever love her, lord?"

My father blinked, slowly, confused. "Alia? Married her for the keep."

"Not Alia," the seasinger said.

"Benis. Had to. Keep my hold on Ulys—all I'd got. And for sons."

"Sif?"

"Brat."

"Zara," the singer said finally, and my father murmured, "Zara."

I thought at first that was all he would say. But he drew breath in a moment, with difficulty. "Only one I ever did.

Love. Only one . . . never did a thing I wanted, unless it suited her. And I loved her . . . moment I saw her. And those first years . . . she loved me."

The words trailed off. My father's eyes were vacant, his head tilted slightly askew. The seasinger seemed to consider a moment more, turning over the course he was meditating on, but then he straightened and his expression, though fierce and determined still, eased ever so slightly. He left off fingering whatever it was in his sleeve.

"I'll not kill you, then, old man."

He looked away, raising one hand to his cheek, but his face was turned, and I could not tell what he was doing. All at once, he broke off, turning completely from my father's table and going to inspect the other guests.

I gazed, frozen where I stood, while he took their measure—mostly just by looking at them, but one or two by shaking and tapping lightly upon the cheek with the back of his hand. All stayed as they were, staring vacantly, except one girl, a kitchen maid, who moaned. The seasinger raised her cup to her lips and guided her to drink the rest. She did not resist or move again.

The guards he was especially wary of, shaking them roughly. One he slapped hard—but they did not stir. They must have drunk deep of the seasinger's draught. That would be like them. Only the stranger himself and I had drunk none of it. Like everyone else in the hall, the guards stood or leaned or slumped or lay—motionless. The seasinger took their swords and threw them in the fire.

I found myself thinking stupidly then that I was just standing there, waiting for whatever the sorceller might do. And I realized I must not, must not simply stand—as I had stood waiting all my life, waiting for others to do what they would with me. I wanted to scream, shout for help, but I dared not draw the sorceller's eye. Perhaps I had stood so still he had not realized I was not under the influence of his dram—it was a slender hope, but I seized it. Perhaps he had forgotten me.

I tried to think. What could I do? I had heard somewhere that a sorceller's spell is like a circle or a chain. If one link could be broken, one person roused, then the magic might weaken, the others become easier to free. I realized I must try to wake someone, rouse him from this sorcelrous sleep. Dropping to a crouch, I crept forward, trusting the table to hide me from view. Still crouching, I caught hold of my fathers sleeve and tugged at it.

"Father," I whispered, terrified of speaking too loud. "Father, wake."

He sat like a man stunned, his body holding its position and balance, but his eyes were empty, his jaw slack. I shook harder.

"Father," I hissed. "Throw off this spell. The seasinger has cast some sorcery on you. Wake!"

He never stirred. I let go his sleeve, and his hand slid from the chair's arm to dangle limply. I seized him again, by the shoulders this time, and shook him roughly, my breath short. I could see the seasinger across the room, his back to me. He was holding an empty plate onto which he was throwing food snatched from the banquet table. I stared at this, astonished. My father did not move.

"Rouse, my lord!"

The seasinger turned and cast about the hall. I ducked behind my father's chair, my heart in my throat, afraid that he had heard me, was looking for me. But he was not. He spotted a wine pitcher on another table and went to fetch it. Once more his back was to me; stealthily, I crept to my mother's chair.

"Mother," I whispered, desperation edging my voice. "Mother!" She remained as she was, head bowed over onto her arm resting crooked on the table before her. The breath snored and guttered in her throat. "Wake and help me rouse the others—help me!" I entreated, my voice turning to a squeak. I bit back the sound, shaking her vigorously till her head slid from her arm onto the table, and there it stayed. I was close to panic.

"Alys!"

The cry brought me sharp around and into a crouch again. I saw the seasinger, pitcher in one hand, his platter of food now full in the other, casting about the room. His call had not been loud.

"Alys, where are you?" His use of my name made my skin prickle. I stayed motionless. "Alys, I know you're here," he cried softly. "Don't hide from me."

He saw me then. I tried to duck, to get out of his line of

sight, but it was useless. His tense stance eased. He seemed relieved—I did not stop to wonder why. As he started toward me, I sprang up, shaking my father furiously, no longer bothering to whisper.

"Father, help! Hear me—please!"

The seasinger halted in seeming surprise. "Let him alone," he said. "Do you want him to wake? He sold you to me for a bolt of foxsilk and a cask."

I stared at him, terrified, and fell back as he approached. He was not really looking at me, though. His eyes were all for my father now. His expression clouded as once more he came before my lord.

"Know this, lord," he said quietly, but very clearly, as one who speaks to penetrate a dream. "I have much reason to hate you, but I will spare your life, and all the people of this isle—upon a condition. There is indeed a curse upon this place, because you are killing the seafoxes. You must kill them no more, never again."

He set the pitcher down.

"The seafoxes must be allowed to regain their former numbers, for it is they that eat the red deadmen's hands that are ruining your shellfish beds. When your shellfish come back, they will seine out the little toxins and bitternesses in the waters about this isle that drive the fish away."

He spoke calmly, but full of urgency. Then his tone eased. His face quieted. He leaned back a little, sure of his triumph, a man well satisfied.

"I will take only one thing from you, my lord, in payment for my kinswoman's life." He nodded toward me with hardly a glance. "Your daughter. One kinswoman for another. That is a fair exchange. You will have no heirs, and there will be an end to the lords of Ulys."

He tossed the plate of food down onto the table in front of me then, still not really looking at me. He spoke to me, but his eyes were on my father yet.

"Here, eat this. We've a long journey ahead of us, and you haven't touched a bite." He nodded over one shoulder. "That kitchen boy there looks about your size. Trade clothes with him. Then I'll cut your hair."

I couldn't move. The seasinger glanced at me with a snort of disgust.

"Alys," he said. "We haven't much time."

He reached across the table, for my hand, I think. Suddenly, my father's table dagger was in my grasp. I have no memory of snatching it up, only shrieking as I lunged with it. I had no intention of going anywhere. I felt the point just graze the seasinger's arm.

He fell back with a startled cry and brought the pitcher down on my hand with force enough to knock the knife from it. It skittered away across the floor. But I felt a momentary triumph. Sorceller or werefox he might be, but he was afraid of sharp metal like any other man and bled red blood. And I had gotten him away from me and off balance for a moment. I ran for the kitchen door.

∞ VI ∞
THE ROCKS

He was after me in less than a moment, vaulting the table instead of going around. I had not anticipated that. I scarcely ducked through the stone doorway and shoved the heavy wooden door shut before I felt his weight collide with it. I fumbled with the bar, swung it down shut as his hand found the latch. It rattled furiously.

"Alys," he cried, striking the door once, twice. His voice was muffled. "Alys, let me in! I must tell you, I'm not—perish and misbegotten!" A rain of blows. "There's no time for this. The dram doesn't last long. And we must be away while the moon's high. Within the hour!"

He said other things, but I clamped my hands over my ears, afraid he might be able to cast some spell on me by voice alone. I had heard of that. The door held. I felt another rush of triumph. Danna had told me once that sorcellers could pass through doors like mist. Well, this one couldn't. I leaned against the wood a moment, catching my breath, then turned around.

A strangled cry escaped my lips. I had not expected what I saw: Cook slumped against the great hearth and two kitchen maids beside her. Another stood across the room, the half-full chalice still cupped in her hand. I fled the kitchen, down the long back hall. There was no one about. I wanted to shout, but the sight behind me had stolen my voice.

I found the stairs and climbed them, breathless, to my chambers. I entered, staring and turning, expecting to find the sorceller awaiting me in every corner. My chambers were empty—were all the maids down at the feast? Of course they were. Everybody was. And anyone who could not get a place in the hall had more than likely gone down to the taverns in town.

Everything was very still. The little square room looked strange to me, frozen, a stranger's room. I had the overwhelming desire simply to stand and do nothing. A spider danced across the floor. I started, jarring a table, and my hairbrush fell to the tiles with a crack. A moment later, I found myself outside, descending the long, narrow steps, then hurrying down another hall.

All around me was only darkness and empty rooms. I found a door leading out into the open courtyard and tried it. Outside, the night was mild and still. The sky, for once, was clear. I could see the stars and the round moon, swollen and full of light, nearly overhead. I ran for the front gate. One of my father's guards stood sentry there.

I cried out, coming toward him, but he didn't move, didn't answer, gave no sign of having heard me. I drew near and halted dead, seeing the cup still held in his hand. I shook him, knowing it would do no good. The cup fell to the flagstones with a loud clang. I glanced back over my shoulder. Light was spilling into the far side of the courtyard from the open window of the feast.

I glimpsed no movement within, no sign of the seasinger.

That only frightened me further. I wanted to know where he was. I ducked around the dreaming sentry and tried the gate. It was barred, of course. It was always barred at sunset now. My father feared the townsfolk would steal castle stores. The bar was far too high and heavy for me to lift.

I thought of the seaward gate suddenly; it had only a bolt and no bar. Surely I could open that. Nothing lay beyond but open beach. It was a long way around to the village along that strand, but it was better than no escape at all. I started across the courtyard toward it—then reflex froze me.

The seasinger had emerged from a doorway not far from me. He had a torch. He must have got into the kitchen by another way and been searching for me there. He did not see me, but I could not reach the seagate now. I shrank back into the shadows, stood motionless. The seasinger gazed out across the courtyard, away from me.

"Where are you?" he cried. His call was urgent, but not loud.

I remembered what he had said about departing within the hour. If his spell only lasted a little while, perhaps I need only elude him for so long. I began to hope. He shifted his torch to the other hand with a sound of desperate frustration and started across the yard toward the seagate.

A torch throws light, but also blinds the bearer to all that lies beyond him in the shadows. I skulked along the bare, moonlit wall of the courtyard, well behind his sidelong vision. If he had turned, he would have seen me. The torch's flame hid the side of his face from me. In a moment, I reached my new goal and ducked through the open doorway into the tower.

I had not been inside it in years, not since Sif had gone. No one else ever went there either. It was in ramshackle disrepair, but I needed no light. I knew the way up the winding wooden steps. A rotten board cracked under my weight, and I fell, hard forward, barking my knee. I gathered my gown and scrambled up, hurrying on, panting up the steps.

I reached the landing. Moonlight streamed into the window and fell silver on the floor. Something lay there, small and drab—I could not tell what it was. I knelt and lifted it. It was my sewing sack. I had marked it missing the day after Sif went, six years ago, and had never thought to look for it here.

The fabric was weathered thin as cobwebs. It shredded in my hand. A little mat of faded floss fell out, and then my needles—a shower of splinters, blazing in the moon's light. They bounded on the floorboards with a brief sound like rain, then rolled, some of them falling through the cracks.

I was overwhelmed with a remembrance and a longing for Sif. She, at least, had lived her life at no one's behest. She had never done what Sul had told her unless she had felt like it, which was why he had so often beaten her. She had not been happy, nor had she been loved by anyone but me—but she had been free. Freer than I. And she was dead for it. But I realized now that I would rather have had that than this, to be trapped in a stone place at the mercy of lords and sorcellers.

I heard a rattle and a curse. With a start, I realized I had closed my eyes. Carefully, I peered out the window. In the yard below, the singer had found the seagate bolted—obviously I had not gone that way. I saw him glance up, but not at where I stood. His gaze was toward my chamber's window. The accuracy of his guess unnerved me—or did his sorcery somehow tell him where my apartments lay?

He looked at the moon, as if gauging the time, and ran across the courtyard toward the entrance that would take him to my room. I turned from the window and leaned back against the wall. My legs trembled. I sank down, hoping—hoping that his time would run out, that he would give up. Give up and go away! My breath was still coming hard, and I realized I was sobbing, dryly, without tears.

I must try for the seagate—I realized that suddenly—*now*, while he searched for me elsewhere. He had already checked that avenue of escape. With luck, he would not check again, or not immediately. My chamber overlooked the yard, but it was a risk I had to take. I had no idea how long I had sat there cowering.

I scrambled up, my breathing calmer now—and halted suddenly. There was someone below me in the tower. I heard footsteps on the hard-packed earth below. Trembling, peering over the handrail, I saw torchlight. The seasinger stood below, torch in hand. He looked up, up the well between the turns of the stair, and saw me. I ducked back into darkness—too late.

"There you are," he cried.

I heard him taking the steps two at a time. The torch-light bobbed nearer. I stood, heart pounding, then whirled and stared out the window at the courtyard far, far below. It took only a moment to make my decision. I caught hold of the gray, weathered shutter, which groaned horribly beneath my weight, and pulled myself up onto the stone sill. I crouched there, one hand upon the shutter, half turned and looking over my shoulder. The seasinger rounded the turn of the steps, and seeing me so, gave a cry of astonishment.

"Alys! Don't—" He lunged up the steps.

I didn't wait. I was completely calm. He was quicker than I expected, but I still had plenty of time. I had thought he would halt, possibly bargain or cajole, even threaten or command. And of course, he could have used sorcel if I had given him time. But he tried none of these, just came charging up the steps, calling my name.

I turned away, looking out over the stones below, the light of the silent banquet hall shining into the yard, the barred front gate and the motionless guard, and beyond the wall on the seaward side, the far waves running and foaming, high on the beach. I thought of Sif, dying on the rocks, and let myself fall.

The sky spun. The rush of air against my cheek was cool. I heard a shout that was almost a scream from the seasinger. It seemed to come from just behind me, far too close—and then I felt a tremendous jerk. My gown went tight across the bodice and under the arms. I couldn't breathe.

The seasinger had caught me by the gown. I cursed my

women's clothing then. My feet had not even left the sill. I tried to struggle, to let my feet slip, but I half leaned, half dangled at such an awkward angle that I was virtually helpless. With a sickening swing, the seasinger hauled me back into the tower.

He had dropped his torch. It lay on the step below the landing, the burning end swung out over empty space. The light around us was eerie, yellow and amber by turns. I struggled toward the window again, but he had me still by the back of the dress and was much stronger than I. It was no use.

He was panting, struggling to hold me and cursing under his breath. I saw him reaching for the torch with his other hand. He had to go down on one knee to get it, and he pulled me down with him. Catching hold of the burning brand, he straightened, leaning across me to set it into the wall niche by the window.

I scratched his face, as hard as I could. He ducked, biting off a cry and letting go of the torch, but not of me. The brand wobbled in its niche but did not fall. I got hold of something and pulled, then pulled again. His beard was coming off in my hands. I stared at the dark red curls I clutched. The ends were bloodless. They had no roots. They were sticky.

I shook my head, unable to make it out. Startled, staring, I reached to yank another clump from his jaw. The seasinger hissed in pain and got his free hand on my wrist. He forced it down, twisting till it hurt.

"By Lithana, you little idiot." His voice was an angry, grating hiss. "Alys, stop. Stop—don't you know me even yet? It's me. *Me*. Sif."

I did stop then, stopped flailing and struggling, stopped kicking—I hadn't realized I had been till I ceased. I nearly stopped breathing. My heart seemed to stop. The seasinger let go of me. I slumped back against the wall, staring, my hands making fists in the clumps of loose hair. The one before me reached to his face, yanked and scrubbed the red curls from it—and *was* Sif suddenly, even to my bad eyes; Sif with her forward-thrusting chin with the cleft in it. Her jaw and upper lip looked red and sore where the false beard had been.

"Crowned Man, how that itches," she gasped, clawing vigorously. "I had to put it on with fish glue."

I tried to swallow and could not. "Sif," I said, my voice a chirrup. "Sif."

She nodded, leaning back now and looking at me, her arms crossed. "It's me," she said. "No shapeshifter and no ghost." She had grown two inches since I'd last seen her. "Why'd you go out the window, little fool? That's a long drop. You could have broken your leg."

Or died. She didn't say that. I swallowed again, succeeding this time, and tried to get my breath to come back. Gingerly, she fingered the cheek where I'd scratched her.

"Didn't you know me—truly? I thought if any on this isle would guess, it would be you."

I scrambled up, feeling relieved and angry now. "How could I," I stammered, "with your face under all that hair? Why didn't you tell me . . . ?"

Sif rose, too. She looked at me a moment more, then put her head back and laughed. "Lithana! How I tried. I thought I might meet you in the market, or on the strand—but then I learned they were keeping you close guarded here at keep, and there was no one I could trust to get a message to you. I thought I might see you if I could get into the keep, but they'd let you see no man alone, so I learned. The banquet hall—it was the only way, and I was out of time. . . ."

I shrank against the wall, my blood grown cold again suddenly. "Are you a sorcelress?"

Again Sif laughed. "No!"

"But what you said in the banquet hall, that tale you told . . ."

She snorted. "It was just a tale. I made it up. I really am a seasinger."

I shuddered, unwilling to believe her. "That dram you gave my father and mother, and all the others in the hall—"

Sif shook her head. "It's only seamilk. I swear it."

I thought of Cook and Imma standing staring in the kitchen—about the others I didn't really care. "Will it hurt them?" I cried, coming toward Sif. My hands were fists still. "If you've hurt them—!"

Sif took me by the shoulders—gently. She towered over me. I'd barely grown at all since she had gone. "Not a bit," she answered quietly, and I let myself believe at last. "They'll stand dreaming an hour or two and then wake, I promise you."

Something dangled in her sleeve. I reached to touch it through the fabric. Not a dagger, more of a tube. I couldn't make out what it was. "You meant to kill my—our father, didn't you? There in the banquet hall."

Sif dropped her hands from me and looked away. Her color heightened. "Not at first. At first all I wanted was to get you away. But then . . . there I was. And there he was— I don't know," she ended shortly. "I don't know what I meant to do."

I was sure then. "Would you have done it," I asked, "if I hadn't been there?"

Sif blushed outright. "I wanted to," she whispered, "but I couldn't."

I stood still, feeling cold and stiff, remembering my own thoughts in the banquet hall. Who was I to admonish Sif? I shivered. "It doesn't matter. He'll be dead soon. There's a pain in his head."

Sif looked at me, her eyes wide. She hadn't known that, of course. Her face was uncertain. "Do you love him?"

I shook my head.

Sif looked off again. "I used to envy you," she murmured, "living here, in this keep, safe and warm, always enough to eat, no rags for clothes. And then I heard the songs they were singing about you in Upland Corl."

Surprising myself, I laughed. My limbs felt suddenly less

knotted. "I used to envy you." Carefully, I reached out my hand to hers. I knew beyond all shadows then that she was real. "You're not dead," I whispered. "You didn't die on the rocks."

"I got safe to Upland Corl," she replied, tossing the hair back out of her eyes. I could see her brows then, how they met. "Patched boat leaked all the way. I sold your brooch for food and clothes, then signed on as a cabin boy on a Saakish ship. I've been across the waves, Alys, and seen the eastern lands: Orland and Kynnston and Harizod."

My breath caught. "You haven't."

I had heard such names only in stories and song. They could not be real. Sif sat down again. We both sat down.

"Orland is ruled by a tribe of witchwomen. In the hills south of Orland live a race of mounted men who leave women alone except to visit them once a year. Kynnston and Harizod"—she shrugged—"are much as here."

She drew breath, not looking at me, frowning a little now.

"The Saaks are good people. They never treated me ill— but there is something stirring about the isle of Nuum near Saakish Keep, some treachery. War comes, I think. I did not like the way the wind smelled in Orland, so after two years with the Saaks, I came back to Upland Corl."

I watched her. Still looking down, she found one of my needles and lifted it, turning it over in her fingers. It gleamed. The torchlight played smoky-dusky across the side of her face.

"I had enough then to buy my own boat, a small thing, two masted. I coasted along the Corlish shore, trading, and when I couldn't keep myself with trade, I sang and told stories in taverns. My voice is good enough."

She glanced at me.

"That's where I heard those songs the Downsmen sing of you." She scratched the needle across the bone dry floorboards, raising dust. "I sang a few songs of my own about you then. If they did even a bit to change anybody's mind, I'm glad." She smiled, a brief smile. It quickly vanished. "Then I went north."

Setting aside my needle, she worked her shoulders to get the tightness out, chafed her arms.

"Did you find your mother's Portal?" I ventured, when she did not speak.

Sif gave a laugh that had no smile in it. "I found *a* Portal, in Clevven, long deserted and unused. Burned out— it leads nowhere. Not my mother's Portal."

She sighed bitterly.

"I almost came home then. It's a strange place, Clevven, and I was very tired. I spent some months high off the coast, pondering. And then a storm plucked me far away from land—farther to the north than even my charts showed. I nearly wrecked.

"But at last I made landfall, among a tiny group of islands the inhabitants call Vellas. They speak something near my mother's tongue, and they know nothing of any

Portal—but oh, Alys, such a place! In the great bay between the islands, the seafoxes summer. On the inner shores they bear their young."

She leaned forward now, very intent, gazing down at the gray, wave-grained floor as though it were the bay of those islands that lay between us.

"The people of Vellas, they do not kill the seafoxes, Alys, but gather the wool of their shedding coats. It washes in to the shore like silver upon the waves. And on spring nights, they go down to the strand and sing: *Ililiilé ilé ilé. Ulululé ulé ulé.* A long, strange, melodious piping that brings the seafoxes in to shore.

"Black and dappled and silver, they come, marl and burnt umber and frosty white. They come to the singers as tame as children, for they know those people will offer them no harm—only comb out the mats of dense winter hair and gather the shed up in long, trailing bags. It's that they spin into the foxsilk, Alys. They showed me how—the singing and the combing and the weaving, all of it. That bolt of cloth I gave your mother—I made that."

I sat quietly amazed. I had never before heard Sif speak with pride of any of the womanly arts.

"They do not divide the work there as they do here," she was saying. "The women go out in boats and fish. The men may mind the little ones, or sing to the seafoxes and spin their hair. The children learn what skills they like—it was a boy taught me the weaving of foxsilk. It is very strange there. It is so strange." She shivered, half shaking her head. "They know little of our southern ways and have no wish to know. I like it well."

"If it is such a place as that," I said softly, "why did you come away?"

She smiled just a little then, and glanced at me. "I came for you," she said. "I was there, happy, and I thought of you, here. And I knew that I must come back and tell you of it. And take you there."

She spoke, her eyes shining as they always used to do whenever she spoke of her mother's tales, of the fabulous country beyond the Portal. But this was no such land she spoke of now. It was here, in our world, a tiny clutch of islands far to the north. I sat, not quite certain what I should say or think; I had never thought of leaving Ulys, except to marry and go to a new prison in Upland Corl. Escape had never seemed possible before, so it would have done me no good to think on it. Now I must.

I said slowly, "How do you mean to get me away? You've no ship of your own here, and even if you did, the harbor is chained."

Sif smiled at me. "I don't mean to go out by the harbor, Alys." She must have seen my eyes go wide, for she took my hands. "I've a little boat hidden down on the beach. But we must go while the moon's high. Now, at once."

She rose, pulling on my hand, but I held back. "We'll never clear the rocks," I exclaimed.

"I did once."

"But not with me in the boat! Your mother tried that."

"It's a different sort of boat I have this time," she said, voice growing urgent. "A northern boat—a coracle." She leaned near me. "You *must* come, Alys. Come now. He'll marry you off to anyone he can to get heirs for this place."

"But . . . what will the people do?" I stammered, clutching at straws. It was all too fast. "When my father dies, they'll have no lord."

"And what good did the lords of Ulys ever do them?" snapped Sif. "Save take half their catch and one workday out of three. It's the lord of Ulys who's ruined their fishing—by clubbing the seafoxes. It's they that eat the red deadmen's hands. That part of what I said in the banquet hall is true."

She fixed me with her eyes.

"When the seafoxes come back, they will eat the deadmen's hands, and then the shellfish will come back. When the shellfish return, they will strain the waters so the fish will breed again. It will take years, but it will come."

I hardly knew whether to believe her or not. It sounded so fantastical, fabulous as the shimmering cities and the self-drawn carts in her mother's tales. Sif snorted.

"The people of Vellas have no lord, and they are glad of it."

She had pulled me to my feet and was trying to get me down the steps. I resisted still.

"But Sif," I cried. "What if you can't find this Vellas again? You said it is beyond your charts. . . ."

"We'll find it," she said, in a tone that brooked no argument.

"And if we don't?" I demanded. "What becomes of me? You are tall and sturdy-made, with a full voice and a fearless heart. You can pass for a man if you want. But what of me? No one would ever take me for anything but what I am. I could never be a seaman, or a seasinger, either. The only thing I know how to do is *sew*."

My voice grew more impassioned. It was my life she wanted me to risk, everything I had.

"I won't pretend to be a man," I cried. "I can't. I'm not like you, Sif. I can never be like you. I won't don men's breeches, and I won't cut my hair!"

Sif stopped, really looking at me for the first time in some while. She studied me, and I realized I had never been so frank, with her or anyone—not even Sif could tell me what to do. If I were to leave Ulys, I must do so not because Sif wanted it, but because *I* wanted it. Sif touched my cheek, and let go my wrist. She smiled, a wry smile that was also rueful.

"Then you'll just have to come as you are."

I looked at her, and felt the fear that had been holding me back dissolve. I could go. I needn't change me, becoming something other than myself, a task my parents had been hard at all my life. And I had let them. My freedom, I realized, was not to be a heggitt's egg, falling easily into my grasp, but the heggitt itself, a flying bird that must be chased and reached after, a long time, desperately, and even then might not be caught. But I had held such a heggitt once, and let her go. Now, years later, she had come back to me. If I let her go this time, she would never return.

"I'll come then," I told Sif.

She nodded, letting out her breath. Then she fetched something out of her sleeve and gripped it. My eyes widened; I stared. I had never seen such a thing before. It looked like a hollow tube.

"What is that?" I whispered.

"Elfstraw," she answered. "Throws tiny poisoned arrows on a puff of breath. I got it in Orland. In case any of the guards missed their dram."

She took my hand. I gripped it tight. She had said she was not a sorcelress, but she had learned such things since she had left as to seem very near one to me. I shivered, and then shoved all doubt away. None of it mattered. She was Sif. We hurried down the rotten steps and out of the tower, leaving the torch still burning in the window above.

We crossed the moonlit courtyard to the seagate. Sif slipped the bolt. There were no guards, or none who showed themselves. The stone steps down the steep, rocky slope were slippery with sand, the beach beyond flat and open and infinitely more light. We ran across the dry, silvery grit to the highwater mark. The tide was going out. I could hear the surf booming on the reef.

Sif put the elfstraw back into her sleeve and knelt beside a great heap of seaweed. She pulled it away, and underneath I saw a boat, but such a boat as I scarcely recognized. It was not made of planks, but of skins (or perhaps some fabric—I could not tell which) stretched tight over a wooden frame. I stared at it.

It looked far too light, too delicate, to be a real boat—more like a child's toy. Sif carried it under one arm out to the waves. It rode so high I was astonished; it had barely four fingers of draft. She held out her hand to put me aboard. I took it, but held back, looking over my shoulder at Castle Van, standing still and silent, a ghostkeep under the moon.

"The people," I said, "my father's guests in the banquet hall, and Cook and the guards—truly, you haven't hurt them?" I glanced at Sif. "They'll wake?"

She squeezed my hand. "Truly. They'll be waking very soon."

I turned away from the keep. "Will they remember?"

She smiled. "Only some muddled something—how a prince of the seafoxes came to claim the lord of Ulys's daughter. Come."

She took my arm. The waves lapped at my feet, soaking the hem of my gown. I lifted it.

"And you never found your mother's Portal."

Sif laughed. "Never—perhaps we'll find it yet."

I let her hand me into the boat. It pitched beneath me, and I clutched the sides. Sif waded out, knee deep, then waist deep in the waves. They were sucking away from shore. I could feel that in their motion. Sif pulled herself aboard, and the shallow craft bucked and yawed. Sif sat in the bow and unshipped the paddles—much shorter-handled and broader-bladed than the oars our people used. The little skiff leapt forward to her strong, even strokes.

I crouched and clung to the gunwale poles. The waves swelled and jostled beneath us hugely. I did not know how to swim. In my heavy gown, if we overturned or if I fell in, I'd drown. I tried not to think of that. I had heard others say that the motion of the sea made them sick, but I did not feel sick. I had eaten nothing at all that even. I felt very light. Ulys was slowly growing smaller, pulling away from me with every dip of my sister's oars.

I thought of Sif's mother, Zara, and her marvelous land beyond the Portal that I would never see, and of the islands called Vellas, which I might—if we cleared the reef. I heard Sif straining at the oars, biting her lip, her breathing hoarse. She sat half looking over one shoulder, her legs braced as she struggled to maneuver us—toward some gap, I supposed. I could not see it, but I sat still, trusting her. All around us, the heaving waves rose, fell, darkly brilliant under the moon, as wild and green as rampion.